HABITS OF THE HOUSE

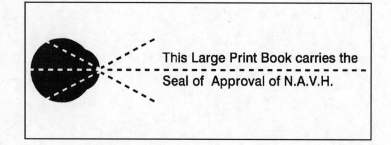

This Large Print Book carries the
Seal of Approval of N.A.V.H.

HABITS OF THE HOUSE

FAY WELDON

THORNDIKE PRESS
A part of Gale, Cengage Learning

GALE
CENGAGE Learning®

Detroit • New York • San Francisco • New Haven, Conn • Waterville, Maine • London

GALE
CENGAGE Learning·

LIBRARY OF CONGRESS CATALOGING-IN-PUBLICATION DATA

Weldon, Fay.
    Habits of the house / by Fay Weldon.
      pages ; cm. — (Thorndike Press large print historical fiction)
    ISBN-13: 978-1-4104-5593-2 (hardcover)
    ISBN-10: 1-4104-5593-9 (hardcover)
    1. Upper class—England—History—19th century—Fiction. 2. Household employees—England—History—19th century—Fiction. 3. England—Social life and customs—19th century—Fiction. 4. Large type books. I. Title.
PR6073.E374H33 2013b
823'.914—dc23   2012043988

Published in 2013 by arrangement with St. Martin's Press, Inc.

Printed in the United States of America
1 2 3 4 5 6 7 17 16 15 14 13

HABITS OF THE HOUSE

THE HOUSE AWAKES

6.58 a.m. Tuesday, 24th October 1899
In late October of the year 1899 a tall, thin, nervy young man ran up the broad stone steps that led to No. 17 Belgrave Square. He seemed agitated. He was without hat or cane, breathless, unattended by staff of any kind, wore office dress — other than that his waistcoat was bright yellow above smart striped stove-pipe trousers — and his moustache had lost its curl in the damp air of the early morning. He seemed both too well-dressed for the tradesman's entrance at the back of the house, yet not quite fit to mount the front steps, leave alone at a run, and especially at such an early hour.

The grand front doors of Belgrave Square belonged to ministers of the Crown, ambassadors of foreign countries, and a sprinkling of titled families. By seven in the morning the back doors would be busy enough with deliveries and the coming and going of kitchen and stable staff, but few approached the great front doors before ten, let alone on foot, informally and without appointment. The visitor pulled the bell handle too long and too hard, and worse, again and again.

The jangling of the bell disturbed the household, waking the gentry, startling such servants who were already up but still sleepy, and disconcerting the upper servants, who were not yet properly dressed for front door work.

Grace, her Ladyship's maid, peered out from her attic window to see what was going on. She used a mirror contraption rigged up for her by Reginald the footman, the better to keep an eye on comings and goings on the steps below. Seeing that it was only Eric Baum, his Lordship's new financial advisor and lawyer, Grace decided it was scarcely her business to answer the door. She saw to her Ladyship's comfort and no one else's. Baum was too young, too excitable and too foreign-looking to be worthy of much exertion, and her Ladyship had been none too pleased when her husband had moved their business affairs into new hands.

Grace continued dressing at her leisure: plain, serviceable, black twill dress — a heavy weave, but it was cold up here in the unheated attics — white newly laundered apron, and a pleated white cap under which she coiled her long fair hair. She liked this simple severity of appearance: she felt it suited her, just as the Countess of Dilberne's colourful silks and satins suited her. Her Ladyship would not need to be woken until nine. Meanwhile Grace would not waste time and energy running up and down stairs to open the front door to the likes of Mr Baum. A sensible man would have gone round to the servants' entrance.

'Bugger!' said Elsie the under housemaid, so startled by the unexpected noise that she spilled most of a pan of ash on to the polished marquetry floor. She was cleaning the grate in the upstairs breakfast room. Grey powder puffed everywhere, clouding a dozen mahogany surfaces. More dusting. She was short of time as it was. She had yet to set the coals, and the wind being from the north the fire would not draw well and likely as not smoke the room out.

This was the trouble with the new London houses — the Grosvenor estate architects, famous as they might be, seemed to have no idea as to where a chimney should best be placed. At Dilberne Court down in the Hampshire hills, built for the first Earl of

9

Dilberne in the reign of Henry VIII, the chimneys always drew. No. 17 Belgrave Square was a mere rental, albeit on a five-year lease. The servants felt this was not quite the thing; most of the best families liked to own and not rent. But the best families were also the landed families; and land was no longer necessarily the source of wealth that it had always been since the Norman Conquest.

Elsie, along with the majority of the domestic staff, lamented the annual migration to London for the Season, but could see its necessity. The Dilberne children needed to be married off; they were too troublesome single. The young Viscount, Arthur, needed a wife to grow him up, and to give him the children he needed for the succession to the Dilberne title and estates: he was nearing twenty-six, so at least had some time to spare. Rosina, at twenty-eight, most certainly did not. The urgency was greater since she was no beauty and had recently declared herself to be a New Woman and resolved never to marry. London was the place for them to be, but the Season ended in August and here they all still were in October. The change in routine unsettled everyone.

Everyone knew Lady Isobel much preferred giving balls and dinner parties in town to hosting weekends in the country. The rumour also was she hated hunting, being afraid of horses — though otherwise fearless — and was out of sympathy with the male passion for shooting birds. This year the shoots had been let out to neighbouring estates. And also his Lordship had found himself obliged to spend more time in the House of Lords since the trouble in South Africa had flared up. Apparently he had business interests in the area. Neither Mr Neville the butler, nor Reginald the footman had discovered quite what these were: short of steaming open letters when they arrived (which Reginald wanted to do but Mr Neville forbade, for in his view reading letters left around was legitimate, steaming was not) there was no way of finding out. Mr Baum the lawyer carried documents away with him, or his Lordship locked them safely in the safe. And Elsie had overheard his Lordship say to her Ladyship that he could not forever be travelling up and down from Hampshire to attend the House, so they would stay in London until the New Year.

Elsie, personally, thought the smart new gambling dens in Mayfair and the company of his new friend the Prince of Wales was probably a greater attraction for his Lordship than politics. Elsie had been with the family for some fifteen years and knew as well as any what went on.

'Three monkeys, three monkeys!' Mrs Neville would urge — 'hear no evil, speak no evil, see no evil' — in an attempt to tamp down the servants' hall gossip, though in fact she was as bad a culprit as anyone. And Grace, her ladyship's personal maid, would point out that since upstairs saw so little need to preserve their privacy in front of the servants, any more than they did in front of their dogs, they hardly deserved any. All wished Grace would not say this kind of thing; it smacked of disloyalty and the servant's hall, no matter how much it grumbled and complained, knew that by and large it was well off, and happy enough.

Elsie was not prepared to open the front door, no matter how hard and repeatedly the caller pulled the bell: there was smut on her face and she was not yet in her cap and apron. Anyway it was Smithers' job. Elsie would wait for a direct instruction from someone higher in the hierarchy. This overlong stay in London meant she missed her sweetheart. Alan was a gamekeeper on the Dilberne estate; they were saving to be married. The sooner that happened the better if she was ever to have children. On the yearly trips to London, as it was, Alan, back in Hampshire, consoled himself with drink and frittered the money away. By the New Year there would be precious little left. Elsie was not in a good temper these days, and she was tired of working in a cloud of ash.

There were few cabs about at this early hour, and since receiving the morning telegrams from Natal, Baum had taken a bus, but half-walked, half-run much of the way between Lincoln's Inn Fields where Courtney and Baum had their offices, and the Square. He did not grudge the effort, since on the whole he wished the Earl of Dilberne well, and had certainly lent him enough money in the past to want the debt repaid, and the sooner his Lordship's affairs were in order the sooner that would happen. But while Eric Baum pulled and pulled the bell and no one came, he began to feel aggrieved.

A Certain Slackness

7.10 a.m. Tuesday, 24th October 1899

Isobel, Countess of Dilberne, stirring in her cosy bed, was woken by the repeated jangling of the bell. One of the servants must have left ajar the green baize door which sealed the kitchen areas from the rest of the house, so the racket could be heard all over the house. It was too bad: they were getting slack: something must be done. London demoralized them; they were essentially country folk, accustomed to traditional ways: the city was awash with anarchists and revolutionaries, whose ideas could be infectious. At least her daughter Rosina, so far, confined her radicalism to the rights of women — and who could not be in sympathy? — but if you challenged one aspect of the established order you were all too likely to doubt them all. On the other hand, what decent and propertied young man from the shires would want to marry so headstrong

14

and emancipated a young woman as Rosina? She was more likely to meet her match in London. The oh-so-amusing tale of how the sheer force of Rosina's intellect had exasperated her choleric grandfather to death had got round rural society to the great detriment of her chances as a blushing bride. As for Arthur, he was certainly in more moral peril in London than in Hampshire, the city being awash with bright young women with new ideas and no background, but so far as she could see he was more interested in engines than in girls.

But Robert, irritated into action by the jangling of the bell, was now getting out of bed, letting cold October air in under the blankets, bringing the agreeable wandering of her thoughts to an abrupt end. She would rest more peacefully if Robert slept in his dressing room, but he said he liked the feel of his arms around her in the morning and as often as not spent the night in her bed. Now, as he gently covered her again with blankets, she decided that his continuing affection was more important to her well-being than the unbroken slumber and wandering thoughts of those who slept alone.

'It's not your place to answer the front door,' she said. 'The servants won't like it if you do.'

'It must be some emergency,' said Robert. 'Bad news comes by night.'

'It isn't night,' she said, 'it's dawn.'

'Too near the night for comfort,' he said, but she sat upright to urge him to be more like Sir Francis Drake and finish his game of bowls before setting off to defeat the Spanish Armada, or like the Duke of Wellington finish his dinner before engaging with Bonaparte at Waterloo: so he delayed to admire her breasts, and that done, to embrace her.

His Lordship had great faith in his wife's wisdom. The blood of a successful, if not aristocratic, man ran in her veins. For her father was Silas Batey, who had made his fortune in the sixties in the Newcastle coalfields. If Dilberne had married her to spite his brothers, who had married with more propriety into landed families, which at the time she had rather assumed was the case — he had come to love and value her most dearly.

She considered this good fortune as his shape rose and fell above her: decent women kept their eyes closed, but that, she imagined, was because they were lacking in passion. He was a tall broad-shouldered man with crinkly, still plentiful fair hair, and the

16

strong jaw and sharp nose which was reckoned to be a mark of venerable French and Viking, Norman descent. In truth his nobility arose a good six centuries later. The original Earl — Hugh Hedleigh, Master Draper and Alderman of the City of London — being a commoner who had risen in power and influence to be ennobled by Henry VIII as the first Earl of Dilberne. Isobel, as it happened, was far more of a Viking than he. She came from Newcastle in the north-east, where the early violent migrations had been from Norway: she also was fair and pale, with wide-apart blue eyes and silky hair: less wily than her husband but quicker to act, and perhaps more principled.

In the meanwhile, ignored, Mr Baum waited on the step. He began to feel it was no coincidence that he was made to wait. As so often in this heathen land of ignoramuses, his race and religion told against him. The wealthy looked down their short, sharp noses and were happy enough to take advice and borrow money — though always reluctant to repay it — while feeling free to despise him for not being one of them. Thank God he was not. He stopped manhandling the bell-pull and sat upon the step, although it was cold and wet upon his behind, and contemplated his wrongs.

A Certain Reluctance

Mrs Neville the housekeeper assumed Grace or Elsie would be on their way to the door. She herself could hardly be expected to attend to it; the wares of dairyman, fishmonger, butcher and baker all seemed to be arriving at once at the trade entrance for the big dinner that evening. Everything must go perfectly. The Nevilles, butler and housekeeper, with forty years in service behind them, including some ducal experience, also fretted at their employer's decision to stay on in London through the autumn. Life was more tranquil at Dilberne Court: they were in their fifties and had seen the job as semi-retirement. In the country the home farm provided most of the food, and the number of staff, mostly live-in and all loyal, was sufficient to make sure the household ran smoothly.

Here in Belgrave Square, accommodation

18

was more cramped than it ought to be: only a handful of regular staff could live in. Agency staff had to be taken on, and Londoners were known to be a light-fingered lot, so that Mr Neville must forever be checking for missing provisions, cutlery, linen, wine and what have you. This morning though he was nowhere to be seen. Mrs Neville had ordered that he was not to be roused — he had not got to bed until past two because of his Lordship's late arrival home the previous night, and this night's big dinner would go on until the early hours. Mr Neville suffered from pains in the chest and Mrs Neville worried for him.

'He's fifty-three,' she'd say. 'A man can expect to live to fifty and a woman to fifty-seven. Now if only it suited the Good Lord to take three years off my lifespan and add it to Mr Neville's, we could both go at fifty-four and be in paradise together without inconvenient delay.' Grace, who was good at figures, faulted Mrs Neville's arithmetic, but reckoned it all kept the older woman from brooding and grieving, so kept quiet.

In Mr Neville's absence Reginald was in charge. He was a Dilberne Court man, and acted there as head footman. Here in London his duties were more numerous. He also drove the family cabriolet as required.

Horse and carriage were kept in the mews at the back of Belgrave Square. Viscount Arthur liked to drive himself, and sometimes Miss Rosina would insist on taking the reins, though her mother felt it scarcely meet and right so to do. Reginald was a handsome, lively young man of quick, if sometimes rash decision. He was well-liked, frequently reprimanded and frequently forgiven. His unfortunate, rash, decision this morning was to ignore the caller at the front door. In his opinion Elsie was too dirty from the grates to be sent; Grace too grand to be asked. Cook was still in bed and Smithers the parlour maid in her absence already seeing to the staff breakfast. Reginald was hungry and did not want his morning meal delayed. He solved the problem at source by shoving a crust of bread between the bell and its electric wire to deaden the sound should it happen again.

'Some street urchin, who'd best be whipped,' said Reginald. 'Ignore it.'

'But it could be anyone,' said Smithers from the stove. 'Perhaps it's the Prince of Wales calling by for his Lordship,' she said now, 'with tales of what he was up to last night. Best answer it, or it will end in tears.' Smithers knew better than to joke about the Prince of Wales were Mr or Mrs Neville in the room, but she was alone with Reginald who had an agreeably ribald approach to the amorous lives of the nobs. Smithers, at thirty-six, a stout country lass with a double chin and bright small eyes, had long since given up any hope of marriage, but like so many of the female staff was happy enough to have the society of Reginald in their lives, as a source of shock, awe and adoration. Smithers was gathering ingredients together, leftovers from last night's upstairs table to cook up as good a staff breakfast as she could. She was more generous when it came to cooking food than Mrs Welsh, but took more time about it. She planned to use beef fat to fry up last night's bread rolls, chopped, with patties made from leftover chicken stuffing. The chicken itself was mostly gone. Arthur had a good appetite. The servants' breakfast was never separately catered for, but left to their devices to make an adequate meal, to be served whenever time allowed. At Dilberne Court the routine was more set: in London the unexpected happened, even if only a doorbell ringing out of turn.

It was for Reginald's sake that Smithers now added bacon to the fry-up. The flitch had been brought up from Dilberne Court where it had been cured in the Hampshire way, with sea salt. London bacon was cured with common salt, too little sugar, and too much saltpetre, thus hastening and cheapening the process, but souring the result. In more frugal households the staff would have been fed London bacon, mean yellow stuff which would have to have the sulphur scraped off it before broiling. But it was her Ladyship's policy, though others thought it most extravagant, to allow her staff the luxury of eating much the same food as the family, although not necessarily, as could be seen from today's breakfast, freshly cooked. Loyalty, as Lady Isobel was well aware in these troubled times of servant shortages, had to be earned, and could not just be expected. The smell tantalized Reginald, who had once told Smithers that when she was cooking bacon she looked almost attractive enough to marry. She had daydreamed sometimes since that this might possibly happen, but realized the folly of such hope. Reginald had a taste for bad girls, everyone knew, and Smithers simply did not have the looks.

'Dirty Bertie,' said Reginald, 'and don't let your betters hear you calling him that, has a wife to go back to whom they say he tells all, and quite enjoys the telling. He won't be knocking on our door.' Since the

Princess Alexandra was known to have struck up a friendship with one the of the Prince's mistresses, the rumour had arisen. 'Telling' was a misnomer since the poor woman was stone deaf. But that did not stop the rumour. 'If they're so desperate, whoever it is can come round the back.'

THE EARL OPENS THE DOOR

7.35 a.m. Tuesday, 24th October 1899

So it was his Lordship himself who eventually unlocked and opened the double doors of No. 17 to an ill-tempered Mr Baum; the bell had by now stopped ringing and Baum sat bad-tempered and cold-bottomed on the step. His Lordship found the doors surprisingly heavy and realized, startling himself, that he had never before actually answered his own front door. He wondered if paying others to do so made him less or more of a man. Less, in his own eyes, he supposed; more, in the eyes of the world. Less, because fate had landed him in this situation; it was not merit but circumstance of birth had led him to this pass; more because the world presumed his energy was so important it had to be reserved for more important things than opening doors. Worse, Reginald would make light work of the task, being a well set up young man, but even the maids seemed to have no trouble. He was growing old. It was alarming how the awareness struck him with increasing frequency. Mind you, bloody Gladstone had lived until ninety, working mischief and scribbling to the end. But on the other hand, Robert's fellow Tories felt confident that if the Liberals finally brought in a Pensions Bill for the impoverished and very old — those over the age of seventy — few would live to collect it.

He the Earl was not immortal. His son Arthur must get going, get married, provide an heir to the estate. Otherwise, on his death his own younger brother would collect the title — and the estate debts, of course, which were plentiful. These days vast estates meant vast debts rather than vast wealth — and poor Isobel, if she lived so long, would be ousted even from the dower house, which was in a shocking state of repair as it was, which would not suit her at all. A pity Arthur had so little interest in political affairs, and Rosina so much.

By the time the door was finally opened to Mr Baum his Lordship was so pre-occupied by his own thoughts that it was moments before he recognized the fellow sitting on the steps.

'Good God,' he said, seeing Baum. 'You!

Why?' It was scarcely a genial greeting, and Eric Baum thought he deserved better.

Baum stood up slowly, and winced from a stiffness in his legs. He had, he explained, some urgent news from South Africa which he thought should be imparted to his Lordship before he set off for the House.

'In my experience, news that is urgent is seldom of permanent interest,' said his Lordship with a detached smile and the polite charm of the old Etonian who is actually delivering an insult, but one that only his own kind will recognize. 'However, dear fellow, since you're here — you'd better come in and tell me all about it.'

Robert courteously stepped aside to allow Baum to enter. He noted that Baum was wearing a bright yellow waistcoat with a stiff high collar, in the current fashion amongst some young men, apparently aping that of those who lived in God's Own Country. Which was how the English sardonically enjoyed referring to the Americans and their vulgar, money-grubbing, noisy, self-affirming ways. His Lordship wondered quite how it was that he had ended up with a financial counsellor so attuned to the worst of contemporary taste. Once lawyers and professional men of all kinds had been predictably old, grey and cautious. No longer.

Baum repeated that, in his opinion, time was of the essence, and more that since his news affected the finances of the whole family, the Countess should perhaps be present at an immediate meeting, and the children too — they both being well into their majority and having so much of their wealth now invested in Natal. His eyes seemed to dart about uneasily, as a man's might when he has something to hide.

His Lordship was mildly disturbed by his lawyer's presumption, but since he was currently in debt to the fellow to the tune of some thirty thousand pounds, merely pointed out that her Ladyship normally breakfasted in bed and since neither of the children was a trustee of their trust funds, and he was, there was no necessity at all for their presence. And surely it was seemly that business matters waited until later in the day?

'Stay to breakfast, my good man, stay to breakfast,' he said genially, and at least did not suggest, though the temptation arose, that Baum might prefer to go round to the trade entrance and have breakfast in the servants' hall, where no doubt at this time of the morning it was available. He remembered in time that it was the Prince's friend and financial advisor Ernest Cassel — recently made a Knight of the Grand Cross — who had recommended Mr Baum to Robert as a shrewd and reliable financial counsellor and solicitor, with a background in mining and a good grasp of current commercial and financial matters. A good choice to manage the Dilberne financial estate, which in his Lordship's own description was in 'rather a jolly mess'.

But then Cassel knew well enough how to conduct himself as a gentleman, whereas Baum had just evidenced that he did not. Gentlemen wore their hats when out and about, were smartly attired, did not wear ridiculous fashions, or run through the streets in a panic to disturb other people's slumber, and then sit gloomily upon their damp front steps.

Cassel was urbane and self-deprecating. 'When I was young,' he'd said to his Lordship, 'people called me a gambler. As soon as the scale of my operations increased they called me a speculator. Now I am called a banker. But I have been doing the same thing all the time. You need someone reliable with an eye for detail, like young Eric Baum.'

But now Baum's preoccupation with

detail was running out of control. He seemed unable to stop babbling: her Ladyship had a good head on her shoulders and needed to be involved; the children needed to stop running up debts, Master Arthur's tailor's bills were now a matter of real concern with Mr Skinner from Savile Row contemplating legal action, and Miss Rosina had written a cheque to the Women's Suffrage Movement, which Mr Baum was sorely tempted to deny. Suffrage would do women no good, they would all simply end up as work drudges, and men feeling no responsibility at all for their welfare, but to what degree was Mr Baum to use his own discretion in such matters? The bills came in to him and if he did nothing, nothing was resolved.

'And these are the least of my worries,' said Mr Baum, 'I regret to say. What I have to tell you concerns all the immediate members of your family. All being signatories, all must hear it in person, in case of any future dispute. It is of great significance to all of them.' Robert frowned; he was no more used to being told what to do than he was to opening his own front door. 'Your Lordship . . .' he heard Baum's voice as though from far off.

He sighed. The debtor, it seemed, must

not only be servant to the lender, but give the lender his attention. There was to be no escape. He rang for Mrs Neville, who summoned Grace, who roused Lady Isobel and the children with the advice that they were expected down to breakfast with his Lordship and Mr Baum at nine o'clock. In the kitchens Smithers complained and abandoned the staff breakfast. Elsie, who had at least managed to have the morning room fire burning brightly, ran to bring Cook down from her attic to help achieve a formal upstairs breakfast for five including a guest, one hour earlier than normal. In the meanwhile his Lordship left Baum to cool his heels in the library and went out to the mews to check that Agripin was getting the treatment he deserved.

The horse was a promising four-year-old bay Robert had recently won in a wager with the Prince of Wales. The Prince could well afford the loss, having backed Cassel's Gadfly for a win in her maiden race, to the tune of five hundred pounds at seventeen to one. That win had been at the October meet in Newmarket. There had been eighteen in the field. The Prince liked to win at racing just as he liked to win at cards. It cheered him up. Agripin would need to be farmed out to Roseberry's estate in Epsom for John

Huggins to train, an expense Robert had not reckoned on at the time of the wager, but it was surely a good investment. You only had to look at the creature to tell he would eventually make someone a fortune, and at this particular time it would be just as well that he was that person, and that it should happen rather quickly.

The only reason he had transferred most of his, and Isobel's, wealth — and indeed what was left of the children's nest eggs — into the gold mine in Natal was that the seam was nearer the surface and a great deal quicker and easier to bring the ore to the surface than the diamonds in which so many of his landed friends and colleagues had invested. He hoped, rather against hope, that the news Baum brought was not to do with yet more trouble from the wretched Dutch Boers. The Modder Kloof mine was a few score miles to the south of Ladysmith, but so great was the British military superiority in arms and numbers the place had seemed safe enough. More, the Boer treatment of the natives was so appalling that loyalty from workers could surely be expected in the many British enterprises springing up in the area, providing employment, wealth and culture to a benighted land. Mind you, he supposed, that was probably the same assumption made by the Romans until they found the Iceni under Boadicea sacking Colchester and Londinium in 60 AD. What, after so much we have done for them — roads, rule of law, wealth, trading opportunities — still yet they can hate us?

An Early Breakfast

8.15 a.m. Tuesday, 24th October 1899

Grace, in her attempts to bring the family down to breakfast an hour too soon, approached Arthur first. He stretched a long lithe arm from the bed and tried to grab her ankle — but that she knew was merely from habit. When he had been fourteen and she, at eighteen an agreeable, pretty and willing young thing, his enthusiasm had been greater. Now she could pull away easily enough; he remained, she thought, essentially a child, while she had used the last dozen years to grow in dignity and pride. Then she would have engaged in an unseemly tussle, giggling the while, but the passage of the years somehow dried up the capacity to giggle. The more one knew of the world, the less frivolous existence seemed. She could only assume Arthur still knew very little of the world. Men took longer to grow up than girls, and the upper classes were slower than the lower. He could afford to stay an innocent.

All she had to say was, 'Stop that, Master Arthur,' and he did. She thought there was probably some hope for him yet. By the time he took over the title he might become as good a man as his father.

'Breakfast, with Pater? Why? Is there another tailor's bill in the post?' he asked her now.

'Worse than that. That solicitor is here,' she said. 'Mr Baum.'

Arthur groaned and got out of bed. He was naked and beautiful, his skin a kind of golden brown wherever hair grew. Grace shielded her eyes from his parts. She knew them well from of old, of course — and she couldn't help noticing now that they had grown even more impressive as he grew to full maturity — all the same she felt he might do her the courtesy of some small gesture to protect his privacy. The one thing which might lead her to take the jump, leave the safety of service and join the work force — she had savings which would enable her to take a course as a lady typewriter, and there were good hostels where working girls could live respectably and cheaply — was the sheer indignity of being treated as no different from a pet cat or dog, as another species altogether, so that their betters could perform their own animal functions — have sex, excrete, urinate, give birth, get drunk, vomit, quite freely in their presence. If the servants were young and pretty sexual favours could be expected from them, and no extra pay given, as if their bodies as well as their souls were owned. And though her experiences with young Arthur still loomed large in her mind, she suspected that he had hardly given the matter any thought at all in the last ten years.

'But why at this hour?' asked Arthur.

'I have no idea,' said Grace. 'I saw him from the window. He looked like a bird of bad omen. He had a yellow vest, like Miss Rosina's parrot.'

Miss Rosina kept a yellow-vested Senegalese parrot in her rooms, to the great annoyance of the servants. This bird was allowed to fly free from its cage, and scattered the floors with bits of fruit and vegetable matter and shat at will. The servants then had to do the cleaning up. Rosina had trained the bird to squawk *Votes for Women* at any man who approached. Grace thought it was quite funny but down in the servants' hall Mr Neville took it amiss.

'All this fuss,' he said. 'Women! They'll only vote the same as their fathers and husbands, so what's the point? Waste of bloody time.'

Grace Wakes Rosina

8.25 a.m. Tuesday, 24th October 1899

Grace went next to wake Rosina. She was a light and nervous sleeper, and never quite seemed to stop thinking, even when her eyes were closed. Her sleeping eyelids trembled. You could almost see the thoughts crossing to and fro just beneath them. Grace tapped on the little, white, long-fingered hand with her rather large and work-worn one. Rosina sat upright in bed, instantly. Like her brother she slept naked, but from principle rather than general carelessness. She was a member of the Rational Dress Association. She had little white breasts and pink nipples, which she made no attempt to cover up on Grace's account. She liked to sleep with the windows open at night, which was all very well in the countryside, but, as everyone knew, the night air of the city was poisonous.

It was a great waste for such a graceful

body to be unmarried, Grace always thought, but it was not her place to be Rosina's friend. When Rosina turned eighteen she had declined the opportunity to have her own lady's maid, saying she was perfectly able to wash, brush and dress herself, thank you. All the same, she was not above borrowing Grace from her mother from time to time and requiring Grace to mend, wash, iron and even accompany her to rowdy public meetings, should she prefer not to go to them alone. Thus she added to Grace's workload but not her income, matters the gentry seldom thought about while pursuing their lofty principles.

Now Rosina got out of bed and looked around for her wrap. She was all long, pale, smooth limbs and slender body, centred by a copious reddish blonde bush of curly hair between her legs. She was as tall as her father, who was well over six foot, and she was a little taller than her brother. Her jaw was too strong and her brow too prominent for real beauty. Her tongue was harsh — she spoke her mind and spoke the truth, careless of the feelings of others. She had refused to do the Season as girls of her class were required to do.

'I am not a prize cow at a market,' she had said at the time, 'to be stared at and valued. I am not a slave girl at an auction to be bought for my body after due inspection. That is all the Season really is, that and an opportunity for the mothers to show off their jewels. I will not be part of it!'

Lady Isobel had remonstrated and then given it up. She had once remarked to Grace that God had blessed her with a handsome, cheerful and obliging son, then tried her with an unbiddable daughter. She must be thankful for what she had. Perhaps one day some brave man would come along and take Rosina off her hands and tame her.

Grace thought there was something not quite right with the connections in Lady Rosina's brain. Most girls could bend their will to the demands of society, whether they were the gentry or in service. She herself found it difficult. She recognized the problem in herself — she was too clever for her own good, too ready to take offence for her own comfort. Why did she object to the way Lady Rosina now let her wrap slip to the floor? Why did she find the girl's lack of self-consciousnesses offensive, get so upset if others felt free to behave as they wanted to, not as custom suggested? Yet she did. She had, she supposed, been marked by her own strict upbringing. Some reactions had been engraved into her being, and no matter how her mind argued with them, they had become part of her. She wondered if anyone would ever find a way to unpick these habits of thought and supposed not.

She picked up the wrap and handed it to Rosina, and felt a surge of relief as, in the interests of warmth rather than decency, she covered herself up. But Grace worried that she would never manage to find herself a husband. The girl did not have the right instincts. Arthur had no shortage of girls who saw him as an ideal partner, though none so far had seemed to particularly interest him. Rosina went to public meetings and took notes, but scuttled in and out, and didn't stop to make acquaintances, as other girls would. For all her brave front she was nervous in crowds, and did not speak in public. She tried once and complained her voice rose an octave so she squeaked and the men around her shuffled and laughed in embarrassment and impatience until she stopped. So she did not try it again.

'I don't want breakfast,' she said now to Grace. 'I'm not hungry. I'd be content with a glass of water and some of Pappagallo's nuts. What's going on?' Pappagallo was her parrot, who lived on a diet of sunflower seeds and pine nuts, hardly food for humans. Though Rosina was capable of arguing otherwise. She was a member of the Theosophical Society.

'Mine not to reason why,' said Grace, as she went through Rosina's wardrobe and laid out suitable morning apparel, choosing the least eccentric articles of clothing she could find. 'But Mr Baum is here. You are required to be there.'

'I don't see why I should,' said Rosina. 'Horrid little man.'

Rosina was also a member of the Costume Society, the Aesthetic Society, and the Rational Dress Association, so few of her clothes were conventional or did anything for her figure. She liked to go corset-less but hated sessions with the dressmaker, so was reduced to visiting stores and buying ready-made clothes, which tended to hang in folds around her bust, and grip her around her waist. Some of the new Liberty Style fashions fitted her, but tended to be draped in a flowing Grecian way or were quaintly old-fashioned and simply not suitable for breakfast. Grace in the end picked out a pair of brown velvet pantaloons and a frilly-collared floral silk shirt, and laid them out.

'Pantaloons! Very daring for you, Grace,' said Rosina, but she put them on.

'Ours but to do and die,' Grace murmured.

'Oh, Tennyson,' said Rosina. '*The Charge of the Light Brigade.* You are very knowledgeable, Grace, in spite of being so backward in many ways. I suspect you know more poetry than I do, had a better education at your Ragged School than I ever did at Miss Broughton's Academy for Young Ladies. Father sent Arthur to Eton, but I was only a girl so Miss Broughton's and a spell at a finishing school was good enough for me.'

'There's misfortune and misfortune in life, I daresay,' Grace said calmly. She had been destined for service from the beginning: a foundling, taken in by Dr Barnardo, and sent to a good Ragged School where because she was clever, she was kept until she was sixteen. She was not taught shorthand or typing, her Headmaster believing that the skills were dangerous to society — the presence of unmarried girls in the office would lead to the collapse of family life — what married man could resist the temptation? She had no savings or family to support her, so her choice was a career in service, where if you were diligent, honest and pleasant, you could rise from kitchen maid to housekeeper, or factory work, which meant you could end up somewhere like the match works, where your skin turned yellow and your jaw got eaten away from the phosphorous, and you never got your full wages if you so much as dropped a match on the factory floor. Service was certainly preferable; the Dilbernes were good employers and kept a good table. All the same she found it hard to sympathize with Miss Rosina's troubles. Grace went to the master bedroom to attend to her Ladyship.

HER LADYSHIP'S
TROUBLED MORNING

8.45 a.m. Tuesday, 24th October 1899

As it was, even without the annoying arrival of Mr Baum, Isobel anticipated a busy day. There were eighteen to dinner and Rosina had upset her seating plans, deciding the company was not interesting, and had found a meeting she *had* to go to at a new ladies' club in Bayswater, this one in support of the movement for the peaceful settlement of international disputes. Pleas from her mother merely hardened Rosina's resolve. Isobel sometimes complained to her husband that Rosina had stuck at the age of sixteen, when girls were at their most wilful and argumentative. Isobel would rely on Grace to help her with the seating and the place names. Grace had her finger on the pulse of society, on the many-tongued gossip which travelled from lady's maid to lady's maid, concierge to concierge, footman to footman all around London: only

44

butlers could be relied upon to be discreet. In any case that was the common perception.

At least the Prince of Wales had not been invited, as Robert sometimes threatened. Then the seating would become a nightmare, though Grace could be relied upon to know who would be welcome sitting next to the Prince, and who had best be kept at the further end of the table. And, after a great deal of fuss and bother, news might come in any case that he was unable to attend after all. In the same way as Rosina was so good at finding meetings that simply had to be attended or her very life would collapse, so the Prince would find his mother the Queen had summonsed him, or affairs of State had arisen that needed his attention. Or perhaps he would decide suddenly that his wife demanded him by her side. Not that this courteous and well-mannered woman caused her husband any trouble unless she felt his reputation was in danger.

It was not the expense of royal dinners that worried Isobel — though the Prince was a hearty eater — but extra agency staff would have to be brought in, usually undertrained and prone to spill food and chip plates in return for outrageous wages. Robert worried about large sums of money but not the small, assuming that the normal workings of a large household came to him by right and were therefore free of charge. Isobel had been brought up by a mother from the North, who would say things like 'many a mickle makes a muckle' and 'look after the pence and the pounds will look after themselves', and her daughter knew it to be true. 'Come round to dinner,' his Lordship was quite capable of saying to the Prince, but instead of the pleasure and pride that a normal dinner party would avail, the inclusion of royalty brought only anxiety and tension. She reflected that the way Robert dealt with problems was first to invite them and then deny them. When Grace called her she was already fully awake. After his Lordship's earlier attention she felt languid and relaxed and her bed more comfortable than usual.

Her ladyship protested when roused that she saw no reason why she should be summoned early to breakfast just because of Mr Baum's presence. He was just a trumped-up tradesman who dealt in *money,* not even goods. He did not know how to behave. Coming to the door so early was not the mark of a gentleman, nor was asking himself to breakfast. She could not for the life of her think why his Lordship put up with Mr

Baum and did not send him packing,

'No, ma'am,' said Grace, whose normal role was to agree, receive information but not comment on it. His Lordship put up with it, thought Grace, because the Prince had recommended Mr Baum, because his Lordship was in all probability quite heavily in debt to Mr Baum, and because the children's affairs were — rashly, in Grace's opinion — dealt with by Mr Baum, which was why their mother needed to be in attendance. But hers not to reason why, let alone offer an opinion, just to decide what her Ladyship was to wear that day.

For Lady Isobel's immediate morning wear Grace picked out one of her new health corsets, which did not grip the waist and force the bosom up, a mere four layers of petticoats, to be topped by a loose brown woollen dress that did not sweep the floor but approached the ankle, with a high collar in cream lace to frame the face. She twisted her Ladyship's long, thick, fair hair into a simple top-knot. She needed no jewellery. It was merely a breakfast, after all. Only when her friend and rival the Countess d'Asti was in the offing, Grace knew, did her Ladyship worry greatly about her appearance. Then she had be firmly laced, encased in vast masses of expensive and heavy fabric, hair

47

tonged and tortured into fashionable shapes, simply so as to keep up appearances with the Countess. Grace thought Lady Isobel looked even more lovely and youthful when simply dressed, as now. She might be the child of a coal mining family but there was nothing dwarfed or rickety about her, as there was, frankly, about the Countess, whose invitations were so eagerly sought after by all London society. The Countess was witty, mean, and, Grace always felt, slightly fraudulent. Why her Ladyship took the woman so seriously Grace could not imagine.

Her Ladyship, once dressed, shook off whatever mood had been oppressing her and remarked that times were changing: these days the doctor came to the front door not the servants' entrance, and no one showed surprise — though some felt it: and if the Queen's son could make the banker Cassel his confidant, friend and apparent equal, and invite him to State dinners? She supposed she must move with the times.

'At least Mr Baum is only coming to breakfast,' remarked Grace, 'not dinner.'

Lady Isobel allowed the comment, and even smiled a little. Grace was a favourite. The poor tended to be misshapen and vengeful at worst, pimply and sullen at best

— but Grace was tall, slim and fair and an excellent lady's maid, quick, reliable, clean and willing. She seemed to have an instinctive eye for fashion. The Countess d'Asti had tried to poach her, but Grace had not been tempted away. As a result Isobel had raised her wages from twenty-four pounds to thirty the year: reproachful friends had told her this amounted to a betrayal. For one thing, if you paid more, other servants would feel entitled to more. For another, give them more, and they felt not that you were being generous but had underpaid them in the past. But Grace would use the money to buy card and water colours, and had decorated her room with really quite pretty little landscapes, and Rosina had claimed to have seen *The Rubáiyát of Omar Khayyám* and *The Collected Works of Tennyson* in her room. Grace's parentage was of course unknown. Rosina sometimes speculated that Grace's father was a famous artist and her mother his model who had left her illegitimate baby on the doorstep of the Foundling Hospital in Coram Street. Lady Isobel said Rosina must be responsible and not put these silly melodramatic ideas into Grace's head: it might make her feel sorry for herself when actually she ought to be extremely grateful. She had been promoted

49

swiftly through the servant ranks from kitchen to parlour to lady's maid, and now had a good place.

It would be bad for Grace, and certainly bad for Lady Isobel, if the girl got ideas into her head, and decided to leave service and seek employment as a seamstress, a milliner or even a lady typewriter as had Rose, Fredericka the Countess d'Asti's lady's maid. Rose had simply left without giving notice, and had been seen working in a Bond Street milliner, leaving poor dear Freddie altogether in the lurch with a big ball in the offing and no one to do her hair. These days, staff showed alarmingly little loyalty.

'Well,' said Rosina, with the lack of pleasantry and tact which marked her, and was another reason, her mother supposed, that the girl was nearly thirty and not married, 'I suppose if people are going to go on referring to you as "a beauty", you're going to need her services more and more. You are nearly fifty. You could try paying her more.'

'I have done so,' said Isobel, stiffly. 'And it might be a good idea not to invite Grace in to your various meetings. God knows what ideas these peculiar speakers put into her head. Let her wait outside in the carriage.'

'I daresay Mr Baum is going to be boring and scold Arthur about his tailor's bills,'

50

said Lady Isobel to Grace now. 'Poor Arthur must have something to cover his back. Tradesmen should know better than to try and sue for their money through the courts. Whoever is going to want their services if they make a nuisance of themselves?'

Grace did not mention what was common, if possibly inaccurate, knowledge in the servants' hall, that his Lordship's debts were out of control and that his close acquaintance with the Prince of Wales did not bode well for his marriage. Mr Neville kept an eye on the newspapers: agricultural rentals had struck an all-time low and the price of land had plummeted; and had not many thousands of Dilberne acres been sold off at a bad time to help pay 'debts of honour'? That is to say, his Lordship had been gambling and it was possible that what he was losing, the Prince was gaining. So much was known for sure, and a great deal more rumoured. Documents that Reginald had glimpsed on his Lordship's desk suggested that much of Lady Isobel's inheritance from Silas Batey, her coal mining father, now deceased, had already been mortgaged to pay the Dilberne debts.

She feared Mr Baum's attack upon the front door was likely to be of more importance than the clothes on Arthur's back. A very handsome young back, Grace would be the first to agree; the vision of his golden hairiness this very morning was hard to forget, and with it came a churning sense of the awful injustice of the ways of the world. Grace found herself humming as she left the room and went down to breakfast. A hymn was running through her head.

The rich man in his castle
The poor man at his gate,
He made them high and lowly,
He ordered their estate.

Really? Did He? Why?

When she got down to the staff dining room, everything was in disarray. The downstairs staff breakfast had been abandoned, cancelled. Upstairs must take precedence.

A WHOLE DAY TO BE REORGANIZED

9.00 a.m. Tuesday, 24th October 1899

By nine o'clock a light breakfast was in the chafing dishes on the morning room sideboard: the servants would have to go without their pork stuffing patties for the time being. When she could find the time Cook would serve up what was left from the upstairs table. A whole hour had been stolen by Mr Baum from the day's routine: and the staff thought the less of him for it. Between them, Smithers, Elsie and the sleepy Cook had within half an hour prepared porridge, haddock, bacon and fried potatoes, brown loaf (yesterday's, the range's oven not yet being sufficiently hot for baking), toast and honey, cold tongue and apples, kippers and buttered eggs. A dish of warm scones, cream and raspberry conserve had been purloined from the Austro-Hungarian Embassy at No 18 — Reginald was wooing the parlour maid there, and also — or so Smithers put it about — Janika von Demy, the Ambassador's niece.

But Smithers' stories had to be taken with a big pinch of salt, she being sweet on Reginald who never so much as looked at her, preferring, as she lamented, 'the fine-boned type'. Nevertheless it had to be remembered Janika *was* foreign and so might quite possibly not know how to behave — Queen Victoria herself had married Albert, whom everyone knew was the bastard son of a German groom by his mother, the scandalous Louise of Saxe-Coburg and Gotha. Reginald's sons might yet end up vons, if not Princes. Love, just occasionally, won over the basic laws of an ordered, God-fearing society, where the rich man in his castle and the poor man at his gate did indeed know their proper place.

When all were finally seated upstairs and Mr Baum felt he could at last open his mouth to speak, the Earl of Dilberne said shortly: 'Breakfast first, then business.'

Mr Baum, silenced yet again, felt truly affronted, and now he didn't care if it showed. His own wasted time meant nothing to them. It was a full two hours since he had run up the steps and rung the bell, since when he had been kicking his heels while his Lordship attended to his horses, the son to his automobiles, and the ladies to their dress. He had tried to be a friend, had hoped to be included, had put himself out for both father and son — the Skinner court case, which he had settled out of his own pocket, would have brought disagreeable publicity and it might have emerged that his Lordship owed his tailor even more than did the son — yet they continued to treat him like a glorified servant. Well, they would learn. They had gone too far. What was that line from *Hamlet,* which Mrs Baum had insisted on dragging him to — *One may smile, and smile, and be a villain?* Why had that come into his head? Sarah Bernhardt, a woman, had played Prince Hamlet — it had been most unnerving. Mrs Baum said it was because Hamlet had many feminine qualities, which he supposed to be true enough, in that Hamlet seemed to be confused, moody and much taken up by his own wrongs. His own view was that people went to see the play simply for the novelty value of seeing a woman playing a man, a mere fairground trick. Mr Baum composed his face to display a more friendly countenance. A man may smile and smile.

Lady Isobel was picking at toast and

honey, having greeted Mr Baum coldly and failing to ask after his wife. Naomi Baum had met Lady Isobel briefly at a Charity Tea, and now lived in hope of receiving an invitation from the Dilbernes, any invitation. She could not hope for dinner, of course, but a simple 'At Home' one morning would help her into society, where she deserved to be. Naomi went to plays and concerts and had twice the wit and artistic sensitivity of any of the Dilbernes. Yet no invitation arrived. Mr Baum's sorrowful brown eyes darkened at the thought, temporarily dimming the smile. There was a new determination, a new hardness in his heart. Why did he put himself out for these people?

He watched the daughter eat an apple, some scones and all the strawberry jam; she simply acted as though Mr Baum was not in the room. Rosina was a very strange girl, too clever for her own good. It was unfortunate for a woman to be born intelligent: it deprived her of essential womanly skills. Mr Baum, tall, melancholy, and not unattractive, was accustomed to having a response from young women, if only the second look, the glance held an instant too long. It was noticeable that no response at all came from Rosina. Her mother, on the other hand, responded, if only with an all-purpose haughtiness. At least, he thought, the girl had not brought her ghastly unhygienic parrot to the table, which practice had disturbed him more than once in the past.

Arthur ate hugely and happily, helping himself to all the fried potatoes and bacon left, and leaving none for Mr Baum, who was still picking bones out of his haddock. Had Mrs Baum served haddock for breakfast, Mr Baum thought, there would not have been a bone left in it. He would not have eaten the bacon, of course, but he would have liked some of the fried potato.

Arthur was at least talkative, smiling at Mr Baum with jovial, confident eyes, assuring him that he would get his 'pound of flesh' in due course. Indeed, he said, Mr Baum could fry it up for the tailors' dinner if he felt like it, or his own dinner, come to that, though that might go against the Jewish religion. Mr Baum managed to laugh, sharing the joke. It seemed to be innocent fun, but how could Baum possibly be complicit in it? He felt teased and humiliated. Why was he even in this country, where insularity, stupidity, and xenophobia ruled? He would be in America by now had not his parents, impoverished and knowing no English, in flight from the Odessa pogrom, been put off the boat at Cork, when they had paid to be taken to New York.

The Earl of Dilberne seemed genial enough, and made a point of sharing the scrambled eggs with Mr Baum who, still hungry after his morning rush, treated himself to the remaining kipper, picking the bones out of the bright orange smoked flesh with scrupulous, silent care. At least in kippers one expected bones.

Elsie, hovering in the background, serving coffee and tea as required, realized there would be precious left of this meal for the servants. Leftovers would be nothing better than porridge, yesterday's brown loaf and picked-over scones and jam.

'Well,' said his Lordship finally, dabbing his mouth and putting down the napkin. 'Get on with it, old chap. Breakfast was the good news, now let us broach the bad.'

THE BRINGER OF BAD NEWS

9.40 a.m. Tuesday, 24th October 1899
Mr Baum murmured that it would be wiser if the conversation they were about to have were conducted in private, but they did not even deign to respond. They were unworried by the maid's presence. He had spoken out of turn, he realized, the servants being as of little interest to these people as the furniture.

'Lord Dilberne,' said Mr Baum, 'news has come that Ladysmith is besieged by Boer troops. It was thought they would be already fully stretched at Mafeking but apparently not. They are well organized and have men and equipment to spare.'

Arthur filled in the ensuing silence by remarking that in his opinion, whatever anyone said, the Boers were an undisciplined rabble of farmers, that Kruger was no leader but a bible-thumper who believed the Earth was flat, and that he, Arthur, had it on good authority from army friends that the garrison in Ladysmith numbered at least five thousand disciplined and trained troops and was well prepared to withstand any attack. They would give the enemy a good thrashing into the bargain.

'Ha,' said his father, eventually. 'Hum. I admire your patriotism and spirit, Arthur, but it is a mistake to underrate an enemy just because you don't like him. This is hardly good news. Having no concept of the rules of war might turn out to be to the Boers' advantage.' He pointed out to his son that though Ladysmith was probably safe enough, five thousand troops trained in tight formation fighting and armed only with single-shot rifles might do well enough to repel savages and their spears, but the Boers would no doubt have Mauser magazine rifles and Krupp field guns. It was certainly an unsporting way of fighting — simply mowing down an enemy — but highly effective when it came to it. Lord Lansdowne at the War Office had assured the House that Lee-Metford bolt action rifles would soon be on the way to Natal, but 'soon', when it came to army procurement, could drag on for a long, long time.

Lady Isobel looked at her husband admiringly. He spoke fluently and so well; he was turning into a politician. Even his brothers would come to think well of him.

'You describe it as "unsporting", Father,' said Rosina. 'How can you describe it in such a way? It is savage; it is barbarous. Is it not bad enough to kill young men one at a time — but ten at a time! Though I daresay young women will get along well enough without them, if that is what they have to do. Men have only themselves to blame.'

'Rosina,' said her mother, somewhat acidly, 'please leave such sentiments for your parrot to preach.' Cook had left bones in the haddock. That was shockingly careless, but the kind of thing that happened if normal household timetables were disturbed.

'Well, Mr Baum,' said her husband, putting down his napkin and preparing to leave the table. 'I am sure this is all very interesting, but as things stand there is very little we can do about the situation in Ladysmith. We'll just have to leave it to the man on the spot to deal with — Sir George White, I believe. But thank you for coming in such haste to bring up the dire news. No need to panic — and the signing of documents can surely wait.'

'The report is that Sir George is trapped inside the town with his forces, sir,' said

Baum, still smiling. 'And that not only Ladysmith, but the area for thirty miles around is in enemy hands. That area includes the Modder Kloof mine.' His Lordship returned to the table and sat down. Elsie sighed. Now she ought to replace his napkin with a clean one, but had come to the end of the pile. Perhaps his Lordship would not notice. He was speaking genially.

'Why didn't you say so at once? But White is a most reliable fellow. Won the Victoria Cross in Afghanistan. He is smart and a brave fellow: I have no doubt but that he'll fight his way out and clear the area. It won't hold up production at Modder Kloof for more than a week or so at worst. He'll be looking out for Syndicate interests. And if White does fail, and I don't see that he can, I believe General Buller is waiting in the wings. Remember Redvers Buller, Isobel? Came to dinner once. Much appreciative of the grouse. Got a mouthful of shot. Tall chap? Went shooting with him once or twice. Bit of a ditherer, true. Managed to shoot his own dog. That went the rounds. But nothing wrong with him as a soldier. He has a VC.'

'Robert,' said her Ladyship, 'I have a very busy day ahead of me. We have a dinner tonight. Mr Baum brings us serious news, though I rather think it could well have waited until later in the day. Indeed, I daresay we will read it in tomorrow's *Times*. But is this the news you have been trying to tell us with such urgency, Mr Baum? Or is there more? Is it possible that our gold mine has been compromised in some way and you are reluctant to tell us?'

'That is indeed the case, Lady Isobel,' said Mr Baum. 'I too am to have a busy day. The Modder Kloof mine, a considerable part of your family investment in the Midas Gold Syndicate, in which I too I may say have a significant interest, has been sabotaged, looted and I believe flooded by criminal gangs of natives egged on no doubt by the Dutch rebels. All production has ceased and the native workforce has fled.'

The delectable Lady Isobel, removing the silver fork carefully from her delicate lips, had paled slightly at the news, but otherwise let no emotion show on her face. Mr Baum was sorry for her sake that this had happened, but he had warned the Earl of the risks, though with hindsight perhaps not strongly enough. The Earl had been in a hurry to raise funds. Initially he had been lucky, as his Lordship so often was, and a promising seam of gold was struck at Modder Kloof almost immediately the mine was opened. The financial danger — at the time simply that a mine could be opened where no gold was, and the investment lost — had been averted. The geologists had been proved right; the sandstone and shale layers had opened up and revealed their glitter. The future had seemed assured. The Dilberne fortune safe. Now this.

Well, he had done his best. He was just the money man. What did he know of war and politics? Dilberne, with his close connections at both the Colonial and War Offices, should surely have anticipated what would happen next. True, the Transvaal bristled with troops protecting the interests of British investment in diamonds and gold, following Cecil Rhodes and de Beers wherever they led, but perhaps their Empire was not after all as invincible as they assumed? As for my loan, thought Mr Baum, that will be the last of their considerations. They will think only of themselves.

'I have to tell you that the dividends expected yesterday by telegraphic transfer did not arrive in the bank,' said Mr Baum. 'I hoped it was some technical error but after today's communications I fear it is more than that. Gold has been stolen rather than shipped, and production had been halted.'

If Mr Baum had hoped for cries of alarm and despair he was disappointed. All that happened was that the whole family stared at him with slightly raised eyebrows, as if he were in some way out of order, had committed some grievous lapse in taste. Then his Lordship stood once again, smiled and spoke gently but firmly.

'As I say, thank you for bringing us this news, Mr Baum. And now you must have a very busy day in front of you.' He remained standing, giving Mr Baum no option but to get to his feet and leave. His Lordship's napkin fell to the floor as he stood. It was unused and Elsie thought she could get away with folding and smoothing it and putting it back.

Baum reached the door and then turned back.

'Good breakfast, what!' said the Earl, still smiling.

'It may be necessary for me to call in your debt to me,' said Mr Baum, still smiling. He was learning fast. 'Because I too am of course affected by the news.'

The Earl's smile remained unaffected. Mr Baum left.

Elsie went with him and showed him out. By rights she should have fetched Reginald but the circumstances seemed to be such that a quick exit seemed appropriate.

'*Goyim*,' Mr Baum muttered. 'All insane!' and actually spat on the steps. Elsie ran downstairs and gave the servants' hall the news of the Dilberne's downfall. William the groom, a London man, newly employed, was fetched from the stables to wash down the front steps. The Dilberne servants saw no reason to expose themselves to unpleasantness when Londoners were available. Smithers went back up to the drawing room to help Elsie clear away and find out what was going on.

'Smithers,' said the Countess of Dilberne, 'kindly ask Mrs Neville to deduct sixpence from Elsie's wages. His Lordship should have been handed a fresh napkin when he returned to the table.'

'Yes my Lady,' said Smithers. She would of course do no such thing. Her Ladyship would soon enough forget all about it when she returned to her usual sunny mood, and Elsie was tried enough by circumstance as it was.

Après le Déluge

9.50 a.m. Tuesday, 24th October 1899

The Dilbernes remained sitting at table in silence after Baum had left.

'Should you not be off to the House, my dear?' enquired Isobel eventually. 'You mustn't let your day's work be unravelled by that appalling little man.'

'Not worth going. Fitzmaurice is speaking. He'll use the opportunity to gloat over the Ladysmith news, and blame the ghost of Gladstone for everything. There's the first reading of the Exportation of Arms Bill but Salisbury will have it thrown out. The majority will be narrow but it will be enough; I am not needed today.'

Rosina enquired as to what murderous end this particular Bill had been devised and her father replied it was the first reading of a bill to restrict the export of arms and materials that might damage the interests of her Majesty's forces abroad. If Salisbury had it thrown out it would be in the nation's interests: its terms of reference were too wide; it could for example interfere with the sale of coal abroad, coal being used to fuel enemy warships. Rosina should not look for bad intentions where they were absent.

Rosina remarked she did not care at all for the dealers of death and destruction and the sooner the bill was passed, the better.

Arthur said it was just as well women didn't have the vote: if Rosina did she'd only vote Liberal, just to annoy. Women were so emotional: they let nice feelings get in the way of practicality.

Her Ladyship then said Rosina should put loyalty to her family before loyalty to the variety of eccentric causes she espoused. She asked Robert what the Prince's view on the Arms Bill was, and her husband replied, with unusual asperity, that he didn't see what that had to do with anything.

Isobel remarked, lightly, that she would not want her husband's friendship with the Prince to influence his political judgement in any way. Nor would she want that friend-ship to have anything at all to do with her husband's ability, at a time of coalition, to veer the House's decision one way or an-other. It seemed to her that the voting might be rather marginal.

'My dear,' said her husband, 'leave politics and financial matters to me, and concern yourself with the arrangements for tonight's dinner, will you?'

It was as near as his parents had ever come, at least in Arthur's presence, to having what the lower orders — or so Grace had once told him — called 'a row'. He had been thinking of his breakfast more than the consequences of the news the lawyer bought and had switched off as soon as he realised his own debts were not the subject of any particular upset. Something about the gold mine outside Ladysmith? Looted, flooded? But it was abroad; obviously things would not go smoothly there. His father was always indulging in mad, impractical schemes, and always oddly out of date. The diamond boom was over; gold was a flash in the pan. The future was in mechanisation, but the older generation found it hard to understand change. When his father died and he came into the title he would probably get rid of yet more estate acres, they being no source of income at all in the face of food imports from abroad, a trend he could see steadily increasing. Though he could see a future in setting up an off-road circuit for auto racing and using the surplus acres for a track. Road racing had already been banned in France — too many fatalities, over which people made a dreadful fuss — but would eventually overtake horse racing in popularity.

He would keep Dilberne Court, of course, whatever happened: he had that much sensibility of family in him, whatever his father thought. Pater saw him as a frivolous idiot, and for some rather perverse reason of his own, he, Arthur, had enjoyed playing up to the role. Now that it seemed his father was the idiot, investing the family money in some harebrained scheme, he might need to present his serious side. Why on earth had Mr Baum been chosen as an advisor? Was his father so influenced by his new friend the Prince that he must take his advice in everything? Baum was good enough when it came to trivial matters like tailors' bills and gambling debts, but mightier matters should surely be left in the hands of experienced Christians. Cunning was no match for wisdom. And his mother, she was the one with her head screwed on properly, not his father. He marvelled at her diplomacy: now she just smiled equably and 'the row' dissipated.

The brief burst of animation over, all fell silent. Elsie returned to the room and started clearing the remaining dishes from the sideboard with the kind of clatter that suggested everyone should vacate the room and get on with their lives. Nor, to Arthur's surprise, did his mother reproach her or mention the matter of the missing fresh napkin. Maids had been fired for less.

'Very good, Elsie,' said her Ladyship. 'There is a very great deal to be done today. Please ask Mrs Neville and Cook to see me later in the morning room, and send for Grace.' Elsie went. Again silence fell.

Grace, thought Arthur. She was his mother's favourite and rightly so. She was intelligent, useful and loyal. He did not think he had behaved badly to her. She had more or less offered herself: he had not seduced her; she had been more experienced than he was: he was fourteen and just discovering the joys of sex: she was fifteen, and in the silly, daring patch girls could go through, of whatever class. One thing had led to another, over a summer. He'd gone off to Eton, she had been promoted — or so he supposed: now she wore a starched and fluted cap and opened the front door instead of a plain floppy one in which she made the beds and emptied the pots — and had become stiff, formal and unwelcoming. The event was never referred to after that by

71

word or glance. Perhaps she had realised, as he had, what she had to lose. She had certainly seemed to stop giggling over the years. He stopped thinking about Grace. He would rather think about combustion engines; they were less puzzling than women. He couldn't wait to get back down to the garage.

Robert's hand stretched out to take Isobel's. She closed hers on his. The children looked in wonder at such a rare demonstration of love and trust.

'One assumed,' said their father, after a little thought, 'that the area was well defended. We should have bought arms in from Krupps and Mauser when we could. I told them. Lee-Metford bullets are too soft: they stop no one. As well hit the enemy with bags of flour. Armstrong-Whitworth would have done better and we could have re-armed sooner. But one saw an advantage in buying arms from British sources only. Free trade when it comes to arms, is well known to have most malign consequences.'

'Old Willie Armstrong is hardly concerned with consequences other than for himself,' said his wife. 'He supplied both sides in the American Civil War.'

'Mere rumour,' said her husband. 'And that was a different time, a different world.

I think we are beyond such niceties. Let trade follow the flag.'

Another silence.

'A pity you did not at least consult me,' said Isobel. 'Working with servants as I do, I understand the concept of sabotage. How dinners get spoiled and mines get flooded, when least expected. But men work from theory and women from experience. I daresay that is the case.'

It was the only word of reproach on the matter her children heard her utter.

'And I take it that what remained of my, and the children's trust funds is lost as well? All that was left of my father's wealth?'

'The Prince has money in the syndicate as well,' was all her husband said.

'Had,' said his wife; and then brightly: 'So. We are ruined. What is to be done?'

His Lordship turned to Arthur and said, 'You are the son and heir. You answer your mother. What is to be done?'

Arthur, taken aback at so direct an approach, said that if his father sold off the Mews and got rid of the horses, he could start a garage specialising in steam cars. He would make a fortune. Isobel explained that the Mews were leased not owned, there was no question of money from a sale. Arthur shrugged this off, with the replacement suggestion of selling off some more of the farms. His father said the automobile would never replace the horse. Rosina, though not asked for her opinion, said steam engines might amuse schoolboys, but were always frightening horses. She personally, she added, was going to train as a doctor and support herself. She wanted no part of the old world. Ignorance, illness and poverty were the source of all human ills. Abolish these and humanity would be reborn. So perhaps, on second thoughts, not a doctor but a reformer. She would start with the condition of many of the farm cottages on the Dilberne estate. They were damp, run down, crowded and unsanitary. Tuberculosis and any number of fevers were rife. It was a disgrace. She would build a model village and people would come from far and wide to see and admire, and the profits could be ploughed back into the estate.

The Earl protested and said he had spent unconscionable sums improving the land over the last five years. If the tenants could stir themselves out of their idleness and torpor to pay their rents on time they might find themselves better off. Rosina said that torpor was largely caused by poor nutrition and if the political classes could stir themselves to abolish free trade the poor might at least be able to afford something to eat. Robert pointed out to Rosina that the problem was holding on to Dilberne Court and the estate at all. Arthur said he would be sorry to see the old place go — tradition and all that — but he personally had no appetite for rural living, any more than his mother had. Robert looked pained that three centuries of hard work, dedication and *noblesse oblige* might be dismissed as 'tradition and all that', and Arthur felt suitably chastened but at a loss to offer any further solution.

Rosina said, with a rare show of self-interest rather than principle, that perhaps they had been foolish in not showing themselves more civil to Mr Baum, who presumably held their future in his hands. 'If Pater has gambled our patrimony away, and got himself in debt to this moneylender — the least he should have done was to be agreeable to him. Moreover, Mother, I do not think you should refer to Mr Baum as an appalling little man, even in his absence. He does not know how to behave, it is true, but very many perfectly worthwhile people do not. He is only making a living, as people must.'

'Rosina,' said her mother, 'the sooner you get married and stop telling other people how to behave the better.'

'I don't see at all why one would be a consequence of the other,' said Rosina. Still Isobel kept her temper. Arthur thought how important it must be to marry someone of equable temperament. He wondered if it was possible to ensure that his future wife gave birth only to sons, but he supposed it was not.

'Rosina is right,' said her father, who often took a more kindly view of his daughter than did the mother, or indeed the brother. 'It might have been wiser for all of us to have shown more civility to Mr Baum. Arthur, you should not have been witty at his expense.'

'Sorry and all that, Pater,' said Arthur, 'but sometimes the tongue outruns the mind. I really must be off. I'll leave you to sort this out. I'm needed in the garage. I don't trust William with the boiler of the Jehu. The man's a good mechanic but does not quite understand the power of steam.'

'I would prefer that you stayed, Arthur,' said his father. 'You are to inherit the title, the trust fund is empty and you are perfectly old enough to give the matter some attention. The future of the steam car is neither here nor there. It is an absurd contraption, and dangerous as well. As for you, Rosina, you yourself scarcely acknowledged Mr Baum's presence.'

'All I did was ignore him,' said Rosina snappily, 'I didn't make fun of him. So all of a sudden I am the one expected to be nice to someone Mama dismisses as a dreadful little man. I'm glad there is a Mrs Baum, or next thing you would be asking me to marry him.'

Both parents looked at her speculatively. Isobel said, 'Well, my dear, it is a great luxury for a girl not to marry, one you may not be able to afford. The younger she marries the better her prospects in the world. With every year her charms wane. So I suggest you get on with it, for you have no dowry other than your looks to offer.'

'Plainly spoken, Mother,' said Rosina, bitterly. 'I am sorry to be such a disappointment to you. Let me just say that I am surprised that so much of the family fortunes was trusted to a hole in the ground.'

'Mines can be drained,' said Isobel. 'We must see this as a setback, not a disaster.'

'What, drained, with hostile forces in the area?' asked her husband. 'After a mere two weeks wooden pit props rot under water. Iron fixtures corrode and rust. The Boers resent all mining, whether gold or diamond, in what they fancifully see as their territory.'

'I think I should have been consulted,' said Rosina. 'You mentioned investing in South Africa, Pater, but no one said anything about *mining*. The conditions down the mines are shameful. It is no better than slave labour. Workers *die*.'

'Rosina, please do try not be so disagreeable,' said her mother. 'It is hardly surprising if your father keeps some things to himself.'

'A gold mine?' It was Arthur's turn. 'We have interests in a gold mine? Why? Diamonds I can understand, you can use them in machines to cut other things with, but gold? It's so soft. What can you make out of it, other than ladies' jewellery and spare teeth? If there was money to spare, it should have gone into automobiles.'

'Paper money will lose its value,' said their father. 'It is an invention, an abstraction, numbers on a piece of paper, a concept. Gold is real; it is not smoke and mirrors: you can see it and touch it. It is in scarce supply in the world and so can be used as a base from which to value other things. Gold is a wonder.'

'You are such a romantic, dear Robert,' said their mother. 'You see only the glister, you forget about rotting pit props, strikes and sabotage. As for you children, when you gave your father power of attorney it was so that you, Rosina, could devote your valuable time and energy to improving the world, and you, Arthur, to the workings of the steam automobile as opposed to the petrol engine. You chose to do so and are in no position to complain.'

Arthur put some honey on his bread and ate it and said nothing more.

'I am glad the mine is flooded,' said Rosina. 'It spares me from belonging to a slave-owning family.'

His Lordship said Rosina was at liberty to leave the room, there was too much chattering which precluded necessary thought. 'I really cannot put up with any more annoyance than I have already had today.'

'So Arthur is to stay and I am to go?' enquired Rosina. 'Yet I am the elder? The laws of primogeniture reach everywhere!'

So Rosina flounced out of the room and went to find Grace, whom she asked to help her compose letters to such medical schools as accepted women as students. She did not intend to marry anyone. Marriage was slavery, a woman offering domestic and sexual services in return for her keep, George Bernard Shaw had said so.

'Yes,' said Grace, 'that's as may be, and we all know him to be a very clever man, though some think if he were not a vegetarian he would speak more sense. But marry the right person and at least you can afford to get someone else to do the domestic servicing. The sexual servicing, in my opinion, can be quite enjoyable.'

'Ugh!' said Rosina.

Back in the breakfast room Robert suggested to Isobel that it might be wise to invite Mrs Baum to an At Home or whatever it was the ladies did to be hospitable. His wife should remember that times were changing and that these days those who were once powerless now had power. Isobel raised her elegant eyebrows and refrained from remarking that it was in male nature to look for their own faults in those most near and dear to them.

Robert had kept his composure remarkably well so far, for which she was proud of him, but she knew by the twitching of the vein above his left eyebrow that at any moment he might start shouting at either herself or more likely Arthur, who sat sulking at being prevented from going to rescue his new steam car from destruction by an over-pressured boiler; or he might start banging the furniture or the doors, simply to ease his tension.

'I quite agree. Mrs Baum is pretty and noisy,' said Isobel, 'although she wears too much jewellery in the morning. I daresay she has a good heart, and I wish her no ill. But it would be an unkindness to her to set her down in real society. They would tear her to bits.'

'Even so,' said Robert, and his voice was rising in scale. 'If Baum forecloses on my debt to him, we will have very little but the clothes we stand up in.'

'I hardly think it will come to that,' said Isobel. 'Or that Baum will actually foreclose. We have friends in high places. And Mrs Baum will have an invitation from me by tomorrow's post. Though only to one of the less important "At Homes".'

'Thank you, my dear,' said Robert, and the vein in his forehead ceased throbbing. 'Perhaps the Prince could be persuaded to buy his racehorse back.'

'My dear,' said his wife, 'I don't advise any approach to him at the moment. To them that hath shall be given. Not to him that hath not. Are you listening, Arthur, or still sulking?'

'I am listening if that's what you prefer, Mother,' said Arthur. He was a handsome and charming lad: even when sulking he could not hide the agreeable curve of his lips, or the brightness of his smile, when he chose to use it. 'Anyway they say the Prince is up to his ears as well, and since the Queen won't finance him because of the latest scandal — he being too closely associated with Agnes Keyser for Her Majesty's comfort — he has gone to his friend Cassel for money. Which is why the fellow has scrounged a KCB.'

'Arthur, that is a foul calumny,' said his father, his vein throbbing again. 'The Prince is not to be bought.'

'It is only what the servants say, Pater,' said his son. 'I am not saying it is true.'

'Be that as it may,' said his wife. 'Arthur is only reporting back what is widely held to be the case. I would advise against spreading the news of our financial difficulties abroad. See them as merely temporary, and they will be. Poverty is seen to be as catching as the smallpox, and people flee from it.'

'What about my tailor and his beastly letters?' asked Arthur

'Carry on spending,' said his mother, 'as if nothing were amiss. Carry on running up bills. Defy the sorry rogue to go to court, and he will not. On no account offer him part-payment, or he will take it into his head to demand the lot. *"Let the fear of poverty govern your life and your reward will be that you will eat, but you will not live."* ' She spoke with vehemence, as one who knew.

There had been times when the lawyers of her father's legal wife had prevented money reaching them, and little Isobel and her actress mother had gone hungry.

'I only hope you are right, my dear,' said the Earl. 'I hope you have not learned too much from me. Heaven knows how I have got us into this mess.'

How the Earl Got Them into This Mess

His wife knew well enough. Robert loved to take a risk: he loved to gamble. He was wily, but trusted too much. His impulse was to keep up with whoever was around to keep up with and keeping up with the Prince of Wales was no easy matter. So far as she knew his Lordship did not accompany HRH to the brothels of London but kept to the gaming clubs, though they were alarming enough: the most charming and attractive girls of loose morals gathered there in the hope of a little excitement and if they were lucky a protector. But she trusted him — he seemed too fond of getting back to his wife to succumb to any folly. Also, her Ladyship was well aware how hard it was to be anonymous in current London society. Servants carried news from household to household, hotel to hotel, stable to stable.

Just as well, Isobel thought, that her

beloved father Silas was not alive to crow over Robert's present predicament. Silas had warned her against the marriage.

'Marry that young man,' he said, 'and you'll end up poor.'

Thirty years later and Isobel could see that it might be true. The upper classes were up against it as never before. It could only be in desperation, Isobel thought, that Robert now surrounded himself with unsuitable advisors. Silas, who had started life as a coal miner and ended life as a coal baron, had foretold it. Land as a source of income was finished.

'Where there's muck there's brass,' he'd said. 'Where there's sheep there's nought but wool, and who wants wool now cotton's here? Your young man's a second son, he won't inherit. He's not in the habit of earning a living. All he can do is chatter and look down his nose. It's a good nose — I'll grant you that — for looking down.'

'He loves me, Father,' said Isobel. 'His father will set him up as Member of Parliament.'

Silas had snorted. 'Then he'll die even poorer. Tell him he'll get not a penny from me and see what he says then.'

She told Robert, and though he blanched just a little, he said it made no difference, he loved her, and meant to marry her.

Isobel was Silas's youngest child, and born out of wedlock. Her mother was a young widowed actress, Fanny Bridie, a member of the London *demi-monde,* that frivolous fringe of society where artists, musicians, poets and theatre people clustered together, talked, fornicated and chatted freely and all without any apparent sense of guilt.

Silas had married his cousin Nell when he was twenty and she was sixteen, and left to her own devices by him when she was thirty, already the mother of five boys who'd burst from her like peas from a pod, and who, like their mother, struck Silas as plain, dull, worthy and without special merit. Nell made no objection when her coal baron husband vanished from home for weeks at a time to cleave to pretty, lively, silly Fanny, the London actress. Nell was relieved that there would be no more babies, and that she could reap in peace the benefits of her husband's ever-increasing wealth and status in the world. The fact that he had a mistress was no secret but seldom referred to.

When Isobel was born Silas thought that at last he had a child worth having — a bright, lively, pretty little thing, who could read when she was three, speak Latin when she was four and by the time she was fifteen was writing poetry, had been painted by Rossetti (some say she was the model for *La Castagnetta*), and keeping company with members of the Garrick Club, who often visited Fanny at her home, and who took her child up as a kind of mascot and wrote poetry to her, sometimes romantic, sometimes lascivious and often bad.

Within a few years Silas had replaced Fanny with another, but continued to support her and her daughter in some comfort and style. Fanny could never be accepted in bourgeois society of course, let alone in high society, but the handicap did not worry her. While there was food, drink, conversation and the thrill of the theatre, who cared? Her little girl grew and flourished on the edges of society where the rich and powerful mingled with the bohemians; she took good care to preserve the girl's virtue and was rewarded when the young Robert Hedleigh wooed and won her.

The eldest son and heir to the Dilberne title would never have been excused such behaviour, but a second son was allowed more latitude, and Isobel's charm was great and her manners perfect, so the imprudence of the marriage was all but overlooked, though some Hedleigh eyebrows were raised. But when it was rumoured that Silas had settled one hundred thousand pounds on the girl, so that she was, in fact, an heiress, society marvelled at the romance of it all. When Robert's father and eldest brother were killed in a yachting accident in a storm off the Isle of Wight, and Robert stopped being 'the Honourable' and became an earl and she became a Countess overnight, Isobel's origins were quietly overlooked. She seemed born to the title, preferred the town to the country, gave excellent dinner parties and lavish balls and her invitations were eagerly awaited by anyone who mattered. And who mattered in today's Society was increasingly decided by Isobel, Countess of Dilberne.

Silas was a frequent visitor at Dilberne Court, and rubbed along well enough with his son-in-law while continuing to believe that the man had no head for business, though saw that perhaps he did for politics. He was of the view that few politicians died rich unless they were corrupt; and the landed gentry saw corruption as beneath them, though how long their principles would stand fast against hard times was anyone's guess.

Alas, Robert had spent money he did not have on the lavish refurbishment of Dilberne Court. He had for long done what he could to avoid using his wife's money. In the end he had asked Baum, a young solicitor recommended by the Prince's friend Ernest Cassel — albeit that the latter was described by his enemies as a Shylock and a moneylender — for a loan to pay the builders. There were a couple of bad harvests. Soon he was eating into his wife's money, and his children's. He had no option. His Lordship gambled, the sooner to pay Baum back, and lost yet more.

Robert turned to Silas. Silas refused him cash but gave him free advice. Robert should grit his teeth, tighten his belt, sell off the less productive farming tenancies, and a couple of the villages — times were such that overdue rentals were running at atrocious levels — pay off Baum and the gambling debts: these money people were not tradesmen to be ignored but were dangerous — and invest the rest in the productive Welsh coalfields. Baum's advice was different: forget coal, invest in the diamond mines of Kimberley.

Robert sold off a third of the Dilberne estates — which enraged his two remaining siblings, Alfred Hedleigh, the third son, who was an army officer in India and Edwin Hedleigh, the fourth, a country parson and amateur architect. As the eldest surviving son he had inherited the land outright — but the other two had their principles. Robert did not have the moral right, they claimed, to sell off land which had been in the Hedleigh family for generations. Robert was surely unduly influenced by his wife. Such a marriage could never have been expected to turn out well. He was landed aristocracy; she was trade, and a by-blow at that. Old wealth and new wealth would never speak the same language.

Forget that the unproductive Dilberne acres were sold to an idealistic developer who wished to create a self-contained garden city of ten thousand souls; to clear the tenants' debts and rehouse them in better conditions than they had ever dreamt of; forget that much of the profit from the sale was to be set aside for improvements to the two thirds of the land and tenancies that remained: the Hedleigh brothers were not appeased.

The sale went ahead and notification arrived that the cheque had reached the bankers. His Lordship havered. Coal or diamonds? It just so happened that on the very day the cheque was safely in his Lordship's bank — his Lordship now banked with Ernest Cassel himself, banker to the Prince of Wales — Silas was visiting his daughter

Isobel. She was the only one of his many children whose company he sought, though when he did visit he had to put up with a son-in-law who was too pleasant a fellow fully to understand the world, and a grand-daughter Rosina who was too self-righteous to make concessions to it. Silas didn't object to Arthur because they were both interested in engines.

But Rosina, then aged twenty-four, at the time much exercised by reports of two hundred and fifty deaths in the terrible accident at the Albion mine near Pontypridd that very day, had a heated argument with her grandfather over the morality of coal mining.

'It is a disgrace,' said Rosina. 'That so many should die to make a few rich men even richer. The owners knew the mine was dangerous but they did nothing to make it safe.'

'So a few people die that many will be warm?' said old Silas, snappily. 'It is not so bad a bargain.'

'Coal is nasty, filthy stuff,' said Rosina. 'God put it underground, there it should stay, and not be gouged out for reasons of profit.'

She was young but argumentative. Silas, who had started as a miner himself and ended up as one of the wealthiest men in England, who saw very well the benefit to himself, to his family, to this household, to his very country, of digging coal out and burning it, felt such a spasm of anger that, in the words of Elsie who was there to witness the event: 'The poor old man just grabbed his heart, fell down in a faint and passed away there and then.'

'All I did was speak the truth,' said Rosina, over and over into the uproar, as doctors, police and lawyers gathered round the sofa where the body lay. Robert had been sent for. 'Coal is nasty dirty stuff.'

'Just be quiet, Rosina,' said her mother, through tears. 'For heavens' sake, just for once have the decency to keep your theories to yourself.'

'But it's true,' said Rosina.

'You killed him.' Isobel turned on her daughter and slapped her, short, fierce and hard against the cheek, and though after that mother and daughter were civil to one another, neither one ever really forgave the other. Some things once said cannot be unsaid.

'Nasty, dirty, dangerous stuff,' said Rosina but under her breath, out of the hearing of her mother who knelt beside the body, her head resting on the still chest. Rosina looked at her grandfather's body with cold detachment. Already the white hairs of his beard were taking on a wiry appearance, the skin a marbled solidity.

'My goodness,' Arthur remarked at the time, 'you don't give in easily, do you, Rosy.'

'Your difficulty in life, Arthur, is that you have no principles.'

'And your difficulty, and ours, is that you have,' said Arthur.

The love between the two siblings was fitful at the best of times. Rosina was her father's daughter, Arthur his mother's son. Conversations held over dead bodies carry considerable weight and are not quickly forgotten.

Silas's will left the majority of his wealth to his wife and legitimate children, a mere fifty thousand pounds in trust to Isobel and her children — Robert could understand that, because when it came to inheritance the true line must be respected — and an equal amount to a coal-miners' charity. Still, the fifty thousand pounds was a useful capital sum.

The choice remained, coal or diamonds. Public outcry over the Albion disaster was such that any mining venture at home, when one's own countrymen were involved, seemed distasteful. Silas was no longer around to argue for it. It seemed a waste to pay Baum off — the gambling debts likewise — when the money could be more profitably invested. Baum was not pressing for repayment. It seemed he had connections to the South African diamond business. All the same some instinct, some sense that diamonds were too purely commercial, too distant from the day-to-day business of an English gentleman to be properly respectable, kept Robert havering.

'Do make up your mind, Robert,' said Isobel. 'You will fritter everything away.' By frittering she meant gambling. He was back at the tables with the Prince. 'At least set the money to work; if it sits in the bank it may simply lose value.' She was grieving for her father: angry with her daughter, upset by not having been able to go to Silas's funeral. She accepted that this right must be left to the legitimate family, but she was left with an agitating sense of unfinished business, of impending doom and Robert would come home in the early hours from his jaunts with the Prince, over-exhilarated by winning, downcast by loss. At night, alone, it seemed impossible for her to keep warm.

Robert's response to her gloom was to set

about putting central heating into the Belgrave Square House, at huge expense, regardless of the fact that since the property was rented, not owned, no value would accrue to him. Isobel did not object too much. She liked to be warm. She cheered up.

Then Baum came up with another alternative. Gold. Nobody surely could fault gold. He put a prospectus from the Ladysmith Syndicate under his Lordship's nose and enthused: the idea was to mine in a spot in the Modder Kloof region of the Transvaal, clearly a sure-fire proposal. A ridge of shale and sandstone intersected with promising veins of quartz, ripe for mining, had recently come to the notice of geologists from the Royal Institute. Now the Transvaal was safely in British hands the place swarmed with prospectors. Gold was a safer proposition even than diamonds, which had already made many a humble Briton rich. Why should not gold do the same for the landed gentry? Or platinum? The quartz might contain pitchblende which could yet prove promising. It contained an element called uranium and traces of a strange new substance called radium, an almost pure white alkaline earth metal, which turned black on exposure to the air but emitted a strange blue glow.

His Lordship consulted the family. Their money was at stake as well as his own. Isobel made no objection. 'Just put it where you can't get at it,' she said. Robert could see the wisdom in this.

Rosina was by now too absorbed by the weekly meetings of the Fabian Society to give the matter much thought.

'If I argue you'll fall down dead like Grandfather,' she said, 'just to pay me out for being a woman and having a mind of my own. Do what you like.' Which her father took as assent.

Arthur had more important things to think about, such as getting down to Nice in France for the 'Speed Week' auto race in March, properly outfitted by a new and trusting tailor. His boots and gloves were to be made of sealskin, which was expensive, but light and supple.

'Go for gold,' Arthur said. 'If the decision is Wales or Natal, go for Natal. The weather is better and labour is cheaper. Benz and Daimler are exporting there: we need to get into the market too. Do what you think best, Pater.'

So Pater did. A generous seam of gold was unearthed in the very first weekend and profits began to flow from the Modder Kloof mine. All rejoiced. They were to be rich; the Dilberne family fortune seemed assured.

The British had learnt how to mow down Zulu hordes, but the irregular tactics of the determined Boers were new and surprising. No one had reckoned on the flooding of the mine by white enemies armed with Mausers and field guns.

A Solution is Found

11.50 a.m. Tuesday, 24th October 1899

'The problem now, surely, is less how we have come to this pretty pass but what are we are going to do about it,' said Isobel. Robert, Isobel and Arthur remained sitting around the breakfast table, indifferent to Elsie's suggestion, expressed in body language rather than words, that she should be allowed to get on, that there was a lot to be done before the dinner tonight, and the early breakfast had already upset the order of things. 'If Mr Baum is not the best person to be indebted to, he is not the worst. I do not think he would dare foreclose. Imagine Dilberne Court passing into the hands of Mrs Baum, who knows even less than her husband how anything should be done.'

Her husband smiled at her joke. 'Of course that won't happen. But you should not judge poor Mrs Baum too harshly since we know next to nothing about her.'

Lady Isobel said she had encountered Mrs Baum occasionally at charity events organised by Freddie, Countess d'Asti — she had seemed pleasant and pretty enough, though a rather timid young woman, over-dressed for the occasion. Alas, Mrs Baum had tripped on her own dress, stumbled, and in saving herself had broken a valuable Lalique glass lampshade, and then had not had the wit or self-command to simply move her cut hand so that the blood would drip on to the parquet floor rather than a white tufted rug recently imported from China, and especially precious to the Countess. The rug, though instantly treated with white wine and salt, had never been quite the same again and had to have an occasional table placed over it to distract the eye. The wound had bled quite profusely before bandages could be fetched. Mr Baum might plead for a Dilberne invitation all he liked, but it would not be forthcoming. Her Ladyship valued her possessions too much.

'It is sometimes easier to wander off into trivia,' observed Isobel of her own discourse, 'than to face the problems at hand. I can see, my dear, that we are in dire straits, and that I am blaming not even the bringer of bad news but the wife of the bringer of bad news. We could always sell Agripin.'

'Oh for Heaven's sake!' said his Lordship.

'Do we even have enough to renew the lease of this house, which I believe is to expire in some eighteen months?'

'No,' said his Lordship.

'Nor can we sell what antiquities and paintings we have without word getting round that we are to be pitied and sold up?'

We cannot,' said his Lordship. 'Nor would my brothers allow it. I suppose I could throw myself beneath the new tram to the Elephant and Castle, Arthur, and leave you to deal with your uncles.'

'I sincerely hope you will not, sir,' said his son, alarmed.

'Please try to keep to the matter in hand, both of you,' said Isobel, 'namely, what is to be done? What are our assets?'

'Sometimes you show a clarity of mind and an ability to speak it that quite daunts me. You can be more frightening than Salisbury,' said her husband.

'I am always more articulate when Rosina is not in the room,' said Isobel. 'She takes up so much of the moral high ground I tend to topple right off. Our assets, my dear, are our children. They have looks, breeding and manners.'

Arthur, at first taken aback, laughed heartily.

'Rosina? Looks, if one can overlook her height, and breeding, but manners? She terrifies men out of their wits. She killed her own grandfather with a couple of sentences. Word gets round.'

'I wish you would be serious, Arthur,' complained his mother.

'Even Kate in *The Taming of the Shrew* found her Petruccio,' said Robert. 'But I can see Rosina might present a difficulty. She will be off our hands eventually, I daresay, eventually find some penniless artist or poet willing to marry her. Together they can pursue Utopia and I hope they will be happy. But Arthur, I agree, my dear, is a different matter.'

'I'd rather you did not take my name in vain, Pater. I don't like the way your minds are working,' said Arthur.

'Lord Curzon's wedding to Mary Leiter was a magnificent affair,' observed Isobel, 'and much approved by Society. Mary being American and her father being in dry goods was scarcely mentioned. Curzon was penniless at the time. And now look at him. Viceroy of India. And she is a most splendid vicereine. All on her father's money.'

'Just think of it, Arthur. Viceroy!'

'You are teasing me,' said Arthur. 'I will not marry some fat plain American heiress for money.'

'She need not be fat and plain,' said his father. 'Mary Leiter is a beauty, and made a most fetching bride.'

'I can discreetly ask around,' said his mother.

'You will not, Mother,' said Arthur, and went downstairs to ensure by his supervision that William did no irreversible damage to the boiler of the new Arnold Jehu.

THE EARL WALKS TO THE HOUSE OF LORDS

12.30 p.m. Tuesday, 24th October 1899

The Earl of Dilberne decided he might as well go to the House of Lords as not. The crisis in South Africa certainly demanded some attention, and he felt what he realized to be a childish need to be looked on favourably by as many people in high places as possible. The wealthy could afford to be haughty: the poor needed friends, and the more influential the better.

His walk took him down Constitution Hill towards the Prince's residence at Marlborough House, around Buckingham Palace and then down Birdcage Walk to the Palace of Westminster.

The cabriolet, driven by Reginald, since William had been purloined by Arthur to work on the Jehu, followed close behind in case his Lordship encountered mud, embarrassment, or violence of any kind, though the area was both well paved and policed.

Since all at 17 Belgrave Square was at sixes and sevens as the household prepared for the evening's dinner, Reginald was happy enough to get out of the house.

On a corner near the Palace they encountered a flower girl who, unusually, had not been moved on by the police. The law liked to keep the area clear: there was always the possible, though unlikely, danger of an assault on the Queen by the mentally unhinged or an anarchist terrorist. The child was a pretty little thing, about twelve, perhaps, bare-footed and thin, none too clean, but with golden curls and a sweet mouth. She was selling decorative greenery from her basket — the kind with which Isobel liked to ornament her dining room. Robert remembered the Hans Andersen story of the little match girl, and when he arrived at the House told Reginald to stop on the way home, buy greenery for the house, and pay the child handsomely.

What did the Bible say? *Cast thy bread upon the waters: for thou shalt find it after many days.* Robert felt that lately he had cast so much bread upon the waters that it was high time some divine munificence came his way.

'Good *karma,*' his brother Alfred would say. Alfred had spent time in India.

It was a pity Robert's relationship with his brothers remained so bad — when they found out about the Ladysmith fiasco, and his involvement with the project, it would certainly confirm them in their low opinion of his managerial competence. They would have assumed he'd at least put the profits from the sale of their ancestral land into the Welsh coalfields. These were currently booming — those who had chosen coal over diamonds and gold had done well.

On his way into the House his Lordship passed under a workman's ladder and found himself crossing his fingers for luck. Or was it to avoid bad luck? He couldn't remember. Isobel would know. At least he had Isobel. He was sorry for the Prince; married to a deaf Danish woman at his mother's bidding. But he could not cheer up his Highness for ever. There had to be an end to gadding about. It was just too expensive.

ARTHUR PROPOSES TO HIS MISTRESS

12.40 p.m. Tuesday, 24th October 1899

Even as Robert crossed his fingers for good luck, his son, Arthur was proposing to his mistress. She lived a mere ten minutes' walk from Belgrave Square, in the opposite direction from the House of Lords. Many in the Lords enjoyed the stroll to Shepherd Market, with its cobbled streets and pretty little houses, after the close of business for the day. The brave, most agreed, deserved the fair, and the sons of the brave likewise.

'Will you marry me, Flora?' Arthur asked.

'Don't be silly,' said Flora indulgently. She was a plump big-bosomed girl with wayward tendrils of blond hair, blue-eyed and pink-cheeked: her mouth was generous and kind and she wore lipstick, which marked her for the kind of woman she was — that is to say, not the kind cut out for matrimony. She was wearing a yellow satin wrap which fell apart at any excuse to reveal her right breast, swelling, silky to the feel and with a small pink-tipped nipple.

After Arthur had checked that the Jehu was not going to blow its boiler, he had walked the quarter of a mile to 5 Half Moon Street, knocked on the yellow front door with the brass knocker and roused Flora from her slumber: he felt entitled to wake her since he paid her rent, and her drink bills, and paid her a small allowance on top of that, on the understanding that she would offer Arthur, and only Arthur, her most agreeable hospitality.

'How is that silly?' he asked, offended. 'If I'm already married they can't ask me to marry someone else.'

Flora just laughed, and her bosom shook and the yellow wrap fell yet more open. The satin was appliquéd with velvet splashes of red flowers, Japanese style.

'I have my pride,' she said. 'Run along little boy and marry someone suitable. It needn't make any difference to you and me. You can still come and visit me.'

'It doesn't seem much to ask,' he said. 'Considering how much you have from me each week.'

He ran his hands up beneath the wrap. She was wearing silk knickers with no crotch and his fingers encountered a soft fringe of curly hair.

'You've only bought bits of me,' she said, 'not all of me. You've bought my body not my soul. One day I'll meet a man who'll really marry me and take me away from all this. Then I won't need you any more.'

It was every whore's fantasy, he knew that, and most unlikely to happen, but still panic rose in his throat. He could not do without her.

'Perhaps I have already,' she said, pouting.

It occurred to Arthur that he hadn't seen the silk wrap before. He knew nothing about women's garments but it looked expensive. How had she managed to afford it? He'd seen his mother wear one vaguely like it.

'Is that new?' he asked.

'Of course it's not new,' she said, 'you've seen it a hundred times. It's a gift from long before your time.'

'It had better be,' he said, darkly. 'Or all this stops.'

'All this,' Flora said, 'all this! A tiny little rented house in Mayfair?' And she said he wasn't the only one in the world: others would be happy to take over from him. 'The Prince built Lily Langtry a most splendid house at the seaside, where they could be together at weekends: he loaded her with jewellery and introduced her to all his fine friends. When I look at this little wrist I see not a single diamond upon it. It is a disgrace.'

'You are not Lily Langtry,' he said.

'They say I look very like her,' Flora said, tucking her left breast back beneath the yellow wrap so a red flower showed in its entirety. 'Except I'm not so thin and pale.'

Arthur fell upon her and steered her back, giggling and cooperative, towards the crumpled bed. He saw no sign that anyone else but she ever occupied it. He wrenched the wrap aside and if he tore it he was glad. It was not of course that he loved her; she was only a whore, he told himself, and that he did not want to be cheated. If you had a title and money people lined up to cheat you. You had to be careful. Flora had promised exclusivity, and she should keep to it.

'But you know,' she said, as her lovely warm wet mouth groped for his intimate parts, 'I should like a bracelet — not diamond. Diamonds are for wives: icy and sharp. Rubies are best, warm and passionate. I'd do a lot for a man who gave me rubies.'

Bet you would, he thought, as her mouth closed and pleasure stopped thought and prudence both. It occurred to him as he went under that if he did marry some rich heiress he would be able to afford ruby bracelets for his mistress. If the Prince of Wales could have an official mistress whom his Danish wife apparently quite liked, really one could do anything without anyone getting upset.

LADY ISOBEL INSTRUCTS THE STAFF

12.40 p.m. Tuesday, 24th October 1899

At the same time that Robert was crossing his fingers, and Arthur was counting out the cash for Flora after proposing to her, Isobel was talking through the final touches of the evening's dinner party with Cook and Mrs Neville. Both women were well trained and reliable: Mrs Welsh was a particularly fine cook, as was evident from the fact that her Ladyship had had to ward off several offers to buy her services, noticeably from the Countess d'Asti. And Mrs Neville the housekeeper, when helped by Grace, could achieve a most attractive table, napkins fluted, cloths spotless and starched, silver and glassware polished and sparkling, centrepieces elegant and of the moment.

Impressions of her Ladyship's dressed dinner table had even been sketched once or twice and published in the *Illustrated London News*. The Prince himself was

111

happy to dine at 17 Belgrave Square. Once Princess Alexandra herself had been a guest, a rare compliment.

Grace sat quietly taking notes, which her Ladyship would later consult, the better to judge the success of the menu. A responsible society hostess left nothing to chance. This morning her Ladyship showed a degree of anxiety in the slight tremble of her fingers and a high colour — not in the apple of her cheeks, which would have been becoming, but around her nose, which was not. Grace wondered what news Mr Baum had brought. Elsie's garbled ramblings in the servant's hall about the African mine being flooded and the family ruined had been dismissed as hysteria, and Grace was inclined to agree. The rich stayed rich. Mr Baum had been the one to be upset, muttering an imprecation and spitting upon the steps as he left.

Her Ladyship's discomposure, Grace concluded, was most likely to do with tonight's dinner. His Lordship had once on impulse asked the Prince to 'come round tomorrow for a bite to eat', greatly to her Ladyship's upset, since invitations for that evening's event had long been issued, a table plan drawn up, and a fitting menu organized, as his Lordship would well know.

To make matters worse the Prince had responded with a vague 'what a pleasure, unless of course something turns up', thus leaving her Ladyship in a state of uncertainty. Her Ladyship had tried to make a joke of it, asking if that meant Daisy Greville turning up and his Lordship said that was one way of putting it, and both had laughed, but Grace could tell that, like the Queen, her Ladyship was not amused. On that occasion the Prince had not turned up, and all had been well, but if his Lordship could do it once he could do it again, and this was perhaps what her Ladyship feared, particularly as tonight young Lady Peaburton was to be one of the guests.

Lady Peaburton was soon to give birth and the situation was delicate. It would hardly do for the Prince and she to be at the same table. In the servant's hall it was rumoured that the Peaburton child was a royal by-blow, and that the newly knighted Sir William Peaburton, whose fortune was in fisheries, had been bought off to marry the mother.

There had been much discussion as to whether her Ladyship was doing the right thing in receiving the pair at all. 'Lower your standards and where will it end?' Smithers had demanded. 'I don't want to be emptying the slops of those what don't deserve it. It will be guilty parties in divorces at dinner next.'

Her Ladyship's voice firmed as she went through the menu, and her hand stopped trembling. Her colour evened out as she spoke. Familiar tasks brought calmness. Minced sturgeon — the fish was new to Cook, a delicacy imported from the United States — lightly poached and garnished with parsley and lemon, its roe or caviar handled separately, served from silver bowls together with very finely chopped hard boiled egg and sweet onion, offered with paper-fine sheets of buttered brown bread. There was *foie gras* for those who might find the caviar too adventurous. (Her Ladyship certainly had no intention of economizing, Mrs Neville marvelled later: proving that the news that had brought the agitated Mr Baum to the door so early in the morning could not have been as bad as Elsie reported.) Clear mock turtle soup followed by turbot with horseradish sauce. Lark pie — Rosina alone to be served with chicken croquettes. (The girl had let it be known that she was repelled by the idea of gulping down a whole bird, while not apparently minding eating part of a big one.) Saddle of mutton with crab-apple jelly. *Pommes de terre rôties* and *choux de Bruxelles*. Marbled jelly, almond pudding, lemon ice cream. Cheeses and devils on horseback.

No fear then that the Prince would turn up, Grace concluded — if there had been her Ladyship would have improvised another two extra courses at least — lobster perhaps, a vanilla soufflé with a wine sauce, both favourites of his Highness, but easily prepared, and leaving the ovens free for their already daunting task. No, something had happened at the table after Mr Baum had left, and Miss Rosina had slammed the door as she left, to disconcert her Ladyship.

The menu had been settled a week back, and the sturgeon and turbot would be brought in by six in the evening to ensure its freshness. Otherwise all the ingredients were already in the pantry. The servants' dinner — to accommodate in addition two agency staff employed for the occasion — was to be served at five: upper and lower servants were to have the same: soup made from bones and trimmings with macaroni; roast ribs of beef with Yorkshire pudding and greens, followed by cheese. Cook's breath, Grace noticed, smelled slightly of sherry. Her Ladyship noticed it too and when the others left asked Grace to stay behind and asked her if she thought Cook

115

might have been drinking.

'If she has, your Ladyship, it will not be enough to imperil the dinner.' Which soothed her Ladyship's anxiety just a little.

ANOTHER TASK FOR GRACE

1.00 p.m. Tuesday, 24th October 1899
'There is something else, Grace,' said her Ladyship, 'it has come to my notice that you can use a typewriter.'

'That is so, my Lady,' said Grace.

'Such an incessant clacking,' said Isobel. 'To write with a machine seems unnecessary when God gave us perfectly good hands to write with, but I suppose we must move with the times. And it is true handwriting can be hard to decipher.' She remarked that the Countess d'Asti now employed a full-time social secretary to keep proper files and lists, not her usual scraps of paper in drawers, and added that though one would not want to go quite so far, it would be convenient if Grace extended her duties to take up a few minor secretarial tasks.

'By all means, ma'am,' said Grace, quite gratified. She boldly asked if her extra duties would meet with extra remuneration

117

and was told no, because Grace was quite idle a lot of the time, was she not, as her attendance at typing classes confirmed, and so her duties could not be seen as onerous. Grace murmured that Miss Rosina by rights would have her own maid, but she had to be looked after as well. Her Ladyship kindly said she would consider the possibility of taking on another girl to train up.

What her Ladyship wanted, it turned out, was a typed and carbon copied list of wealthy heiresses suitable for her son the Viscount, which Grace would help to compile.

Gossip and information garnered from the best servants' halls in the land, Isobel was well aware, tended to be more accurate than recommendations from friends, who would keep the best names to themselves: or would simply not know enough about possible candidates. The servants knew a great deal about the bad habits, disagreeable manners, and perversities of their betters. They made the beds, after all, and saw what soiled them.

Grace said she would be happy to do so, and could come back with names before the end of the week.

'The sooner the better,' said her Ladyship. 'And I suggest you start your enquiries in Kensington, though it may seem rather far afield.'

In other words, thought Grace, the d'Asti servants' hall. The Countess had two sons in their late twenties. They too would be seeking good matches, though presumably amongst the older aristocracy than the mercantile class. What the d'Astis needed was family rather than money.

'And of course your friends in Dover Street,' said her Ladyship. 'The *Oceanic* is due in soon from New York.'

The *Oceanic* was the latest White Star transatlantic liner, designed for beauty and speed: it could make the crossing in just over five days. Her Ladyship's friends would often stay at Brown's Hotel in Dover Street when arriving or leaving for Southampton, and Grace would on occasion be lent to help out with packing or last-minute sewing for hard-pressed travellers. Her Ladyship was always generous with Grace's services, if there seemed something to be gained from it.

'As Francis Bacon said, knowledge is power, and it applies as much in society as it does to politics. *Scientia potentia est,*' Grace had once overheard Lady Isobel say to his Lordship; he had wholeheartedly agreed and told his wife she was the best society hostess in the land and she had asked, 'Better than the Countess d'Asti?' and he had rather rashly replied, 'Not even in the same class, my dear, though one has to admire the woman's nerve. Not to mention her *embonpoint*.'

The Count and Countess had land near Piedmont, in the north-west of Italy, a singularly mountainous area far from Rome. They had come to live in London in search of a livelier and more cultural life than was available at home. They were seen as a little too colourful for comfort, their title inconsequential and dubious — Italian Counts were two a penny — and the connection to some foreign royalty which they claimed was somewhat opaque. But they were immensely rich, socially energetic, had a good table, and were indubitably good company. They did not shoot or hunt, however, and the Countess's new red brick house in Pont Street in Knightsbridge was considered a trifle vulgar and over-ostentatious. Where 17 Belgrave Square was grand and dignified, Pont House was vulgar and ornate: plaster harpies peered down at the visitors from its balconies, and passers-by could see into the bay windows. Nevertheless the thinkers and writers of today gathered at the d'Asti table.

The Dilberne's place in society was obviously more secure: they could offer the best shooting in the country and the best dinners in London; this was the true heart of London Society: the genuine thing; guests knew how to behave and could be trusted if ever a new acquaintance was to be made. The conversation might be duller behind the stone walls of Belgrave Square than the brick of Pont House, but it was safer. You would for example never have encountered Emile Zola, in flight from a prison sentence for what amounted to treason, at the Dilberne table. He had appeared three times at Pont House. Where the Dilberne's table was solid mahogany and could seat twenty-four comfortably and twenty-eight at a pinch, the Pont House table was of a light maple laced with mother of pearl and seated thirty-four with ease, in itself a sign of too much openness. All kinds of unusual people were these days being accepted from the lower strata of society — guilty parties in divorce cases, fashion designers, racehorse owners, Jews, actresses, Americans, architects. Who knew where it would end?

Her Ladyship was accustomed to keeping an eye on what went on at the maple dining table of her upstart rival, both from the relayed gossip in the servant's hall, and from, if only inadvertently, her own guests.

To this end she used Grace. If anyone was desperate for a competent seamstress — so hard to find, these days! — to sew a spray of diamonds onto black velvet for a special ball, or to let out a waistband, or as when the newly married Lady Peaburton needed to minimize her pregnancy, with a tuck here, a flounce there, Isobel would say 'Oh do borrow Grace! Grace is a miracle!' and Grace would catch the bus to wherever it was, and oblige, and bring back such morsels of gossip as she found interesting.

It was Grace who, back from the d'Astis' establishment in Pont Street, had informed Lady Isobel earlier in the week that marbled jelly in yellow and green with an ice sculpture table motif in the form of entwined white storks was quite the thing of the moment. This was to celebrate the success of the International Hague Convention, which was to limit the manufacture and exchange of weapons, and ban the dropping of explosives from balloons.

'But why storks?' asked Lady Isobel.

'I believe they are the symbol of the City of The Hague,' Grace had replied, and her Ladyship had thought for a little and then remarked that Freddie was really rather a silly woman and ice sculptures were all very well at the beginning of a meal, but by the time desserts were served were bound to have lost shape and definition, especially as white storks suggested a milk ice.

The Countess d'Asti, when not seeing to the proper display of her diamonds, or attending the theatre, the opera, or travelling to anywhere Mr Elgar, whom she much admired, was conducting his own work, had lately revealed herself as an admirer of Annie Besant, an earnest and influential mystic who campaigned for peace between the nations, the end of world misery, antivivisection and so forth. Isobel felt that allowing these worthy preoccupations to seep into the dinner table arrangements was a mistake. Who wanted their consciences disturbed while trying to eat dinner?

Her Ladyship had allowed the yellow and green marbled jelly on this occasion but banned the storks. Amelia Peaburton was on the guest list; she was a dear sweet girl, and would not want attention drawn to her condition. The fact that the stork was the heraldic symbol of The Hague might well escape her. She was charming but not renowned for her interest in world affairs. Amelia had been married for a mere two months but had clearly been expecting for several months more. Times were changing, one had to face it; and just occasionally they

changed for the better. Once Lady Peaburton would have tactfully gone abroad for a
year. Now it seemed totally possible to ask
her and her new, recently knighted young
husband to dinner, forget any possible
doubts about the baby's parentage — she
had been seen once or twice with the Prince
himself — and even look forward to the
girl's company. One did not go so far as to
invite Lady Peaburton's parents, even on
occasions when perhaps they should have
been, not because they had at first barred
the door to their own daughter and son-in-
law, and one disapproved, but because it
occurred to one that they were just, frankly,
irremediably old and boring.

The Countess d'Asti might go too far, too
fast, but Lady Isobel was the first to acknowledge that at least she moved in the
right direction.

And Grace understood by the reference
to the *Oceanic* that her list of suitable
candidates for the role of future Countess
of Dilberne could be stretched just a little:
that not to be English was not necessarily
to disqualify. Perhaps not even to be a
virgin. Though Arthur would have his own
opinions on that, and she, Grace, certainly
did. If one was going to be 'in service',
reciprocal rights and duties applied. The

least girls of the upper classes could do was stay virgins until they married. How else could they produce heirs with a lineage that made them fit for privilege? How did the Bible put it? *Leaders of the people by their counsels . . . wise and eloquent in their instructions?* Or as Smithers had put it: 'I don't want to be emptying the slops of those what don't deserve it.'

An Informal Party Comes and Goes

8 p.m. Tuesday, 24th–1 a.m. Wednesday, 25th October 1899

The dinner party went very well. Cook remained sober and no one noticed any shortage of courses. Conversation flowed easily. Rosina had relented and made an appearance, looking quite normal and indeed rather fetching in pale yellow silk and wearing a proper corset which made the most of her figure.

There was much speculation as to what the new century would hold.

It was unfortunate perhaps that when her father related that 'In the Prince of Wales' opinion, by the end of the new century everyone would be healthier, happier, taller and fatter, Rosina was heard to say: 'Only if the evils of poverty, illness and ignorance are removed from our streets and I don't see that happening for long time. And it isn't a new century at all, only a new year.

1900 is the last year of the nineteenth century. The twentieth begins in 1901.' But no one was listening at this juncture, as Lady Peaburton had been seized by a sudden faintness and was taken home early by her husband.

When the conversation resumed and turned to the stork motif in ice at the d'Astis', Rosina glared but did not deign to reply when her father, presumably from the influence of more glasses of wine than was his habit, teased her by saying that the Hague conference was a frippery inspired by Annie Besant and her friends, and the nations were only happy when at war with one another.

There were oohs and ahs over the caviar; and no one would have believed for one minute that the ancient family of their hosts was in grave financial difficulty.

Carriages were at one a.m.

GRACE PRESENTS HER LIST

10 a.m. Thursday, 26th October 1899

One way and another it was a full two days before Grace could come up with a reliable list of suitable heiresses. Lady Isobel had hoped for it within the day. But tact had been needed, as her Ladyship required, and no sense of urgency conveyed. The d'Astis were only just back from the Howards' place at Arundel Castle — 'Roman Catholics, of course,' remarked her Ladyship, doubtfully — and it had been Thursday before Grace could meet up with Sarah, the d'Asti lady's maid. Nor had Sarah been of much help. The d'Asti boys were careless of their inheritance, such as it was, and were as likely to marry outside their circle as in. There were no lists, no plans. Agatha, the lady's maid at the Austrian Embassy next door had a good list of the plainer girls, although most had been through three or four seasons and not yet been picked: and so not likely to appeal to Master Arthur.

'Leave that for me to decide,' said Lady Isobel, taking Grace's neat lists and folders, old copies of the *Illustrated London News* and *McCall's,* relevant portraits and photographs carefully ringed and flagged.

Grace's chief informants had been George, *maître d'hôtel* at the Savoy Grill, and Eddie, the head concierge at Brown's. The Savoy was awash with pretty girls ripe for marriage, even out of season, but none with noticeable fortunes.

Eddie at Brown's had a friend who worked for the White Star Line and had access to the First Class passenger lists of all the transatlantic liners. Grace did what she could to put him in a good mood, in the cosy little concierge's office just off the foyer. Eddie then divulged that the *Oceanic* had just docked at Southampton, but the only possibles were the O'Briens: they were wealthy enough, being the meat baron O'Brien's wife and unmarried daughter but he couldn't recommend them.

'Not right for our young Viscount,' he advised. 'Dry goods is one thing, meat's quite another, not so much barons in that world as mobsters. And from Chicago, not even New York, so no idea of how to behave.' The mother had snored so loud the next door cabin complained, and the girl was a looker but had the kind of past there was no overlooking. 'If they're looking for a title they'd best forget it.'

'What sort of past?'

'Moved in with a man and lived as his wife.' It seemed the Assistant Purser on the *Oceanic* came from Chicago, and so knew everything there was to be known.

Grace, respecting Eddie's sense of protocol, had failed to add Minnie O'Brien to her list of marriageables. Eddie was a man of many contradictions. He was a well-set-up, vigorous man in his middle forties, with a bright blue eye, a flushed face, unmarried, popular with the staff and respectful to the guests, while living a double life as a trade unionist and radical.

'I like to hedge my bets,' he'd say. 'Today's enemy is tomorrow's friend and vice versa.' He was rumoured to have accumulated a nice little nest egg arranging special services for male guests. Grace did not mind at all putting Eddie into a good mood when he so required, though both were usually pushed for time. At least this way she wouldn't join the pudding club.

Her Ladyship, of course, was not to know any of this. Having complained about the delay and received the nicely typed up and

thoughtful document from Grace, her Ladyship dismissed her to get on with her work.
Grace, who had hoped for at least a discussion on Master Arthur's like and dislikes,
on which she felt an expert, if anyone was,
was most put out.

Her Ladyship studied Grace's list at some
length, crossing and ticking, and then summoned Arthur to discuss his forthcoming
marriage.

ARTHUR PAYS ANOTHER VISIT

2.30 p.m. Friday, 27th October 1899

His mother's dinner party having come and gone without untoward incident, and quickly faded into history as dinner parties do, and since there had been no further mention of marriage from his parents, and the very best caviar had been served at dinner, Arthur supposed that one way and another the financial crisis had melted away. His elders had been panicking. Probably his father had been lucky at the Cheltenham races, or Mr Baum had changed his tune. At any rate, being of an optimistic turn of mind, Arthur decided he could well afford another visit to Flora. He paid for her flat by bank draft, but whenever he turned up to make free with her services it was a given that he eased her way with some pocket money.

She served him a delicious light lunch of French cheese, grapes and fresh white rolls, served with a Rhône wine, and made him comfortable in other ways; and when he was lying back on the bed satisfied and happy, watching her replace her garments one by one, almost as fascinating a sight as watching her remove them, just more relaxed, she said to him,

'I have been thinking it over and realize I love you very much. I agree to your proposal of marriage.'

'My what?' asked Arthur. He had forgotten all about it. 'Oh, that. No, no, that's water under the bridge, my dear. It isn't necessary any more. Everything is settled now. They were all just panicking. Things will go on as before.'

She looked at him sadly with quivering lip and tears gathering in the large blue eyes.

'You told me you loved me. You promised to marry me. You can't just change your mind. I will sue you for breach of promise. You have broken my heart and what's more there is the financial loss. I told Jim I was going to marry you and I sent him away.'

'Jim?'

Jim, it seemed, was a very nice rich gentleman Flora had met while walking her little dog in the park and Jim had offered to set her up in a little house in Maida Vale, much superior to the lodgings she currently had in Mayfair but she had said no, because she was going to marry into the Hedleigh family and her children would be lords and ladies. Now came this terrible denial, shock and disappointment.

Arthur's good cheer faded. He could not bear to lose Flora. He was not born yesterday: Jim was probably an invention. The 'breach of promise' threat was an absurdity. No one would take a whore's word against his own. On the other hand, and this was the really outrageous part, he realised Flora was perfectly capable of deceiving him with another man: assuring him too that he was 'the only one' while using the very bed he, Arthur, had paid for. Or more than one, as had happened to his friend Ernest Dowson the poet. Dowson's sweet all but pre-pubertal Cynara turned out to have a whole flock of admirers.

I have been faithful to thee, Cynara! in my fashion. Yes, but what about Cynara? What had she been up to?

You couldn't blame the girls: they had to make a living: fidelity was something a man had to expect to pay very highly for. Ernest Dowson had ended up marrying Cynara, and a very good wife she was proving, though hardly one who could move in any society other than the *demi-monde*. But

Ernest was a poet. Arthur was a gentleman. Different rules applied.

He should not care, but the thought of Flora with another man made Arthur feel ill.

Arthur fell upon his knees and begged Flora to stay with him, to be faithful to him, to ignore offers from other men. He offered to increase her remuneration. He might even have to sell the Arnold Jehu to be able to afford it. That a man should consider selling a car to keep a mistress happy was not in the ordinary run of things. This must surely impress her. Perhaps he did indeed love her.

Sobbing and plaintive, but already cheering up, Flora accepted his offer of three pounds a month more than the twenty pounds she already received, plus a rental of five shillings a week.

'I love you so,' she said. 'I want no one but you, and I never have.' She put her milk-white arms around him and dragged him back into bed. The sheets were exquisitely clean, exquisitely embroidered. Her little dog sat on its red velvet cushion and looked on: the canary in the gilded cage sang its joy in their passion. It was worth it.

Arthur's allowance was three hundred pounds a month. He owed his tailor Mr

Skinner of Conduit Street one thousand, eight hundred and fifty pounds. His father refused to pay off the debt, which Arthur thought unnecessarily mean. The Earl, Arthur had observed, could spend just as much on a night's gambling with the Prince, and though his father persuaded himself that the losses and gains evened out, Arthur doubted that this was the case. A gentleman's tailoring requirements were not trifling: he required not just a dress suit, a morning and an evening suit, but appropriate clothing for bicycling, riding, hunting, golf, and motor sport: white kid gloves were needed for evening wear and after one wear would have to be replaced. More, several copies of each garment would have to be made, since in the end brushing failed to remove dust, dirt and grease, and fashionable fabrics did not stand up to much washing, no matter how careful the laundress. Wardrobe life was short and garments went out of fashion. His Lordship had declined to provide Arthur with a personal valet, and Arthur got by, but it was a false economy.

The Viscount, as Grace had observed, kept his dressing room manageable by the simple device of handing over any garment which displeased him to Reginald and telling him to find a home for it. Over at the Austrian

Embassy, she had noticed, staff often appeared on their days off in Master Arthur's cast-offs.

So what really was another three pounds a month for poor Flora, whose hopes Arthur had so cruelly and thoughtlessly dashed? The qualities one looked for in a wife were very different from those of the girls one had fun with: nevertheless all deserved to be treated kindly and generously. God would provide if his father wouldn't.

Arthur assumed, as did his mother, that his father did not keep a mistress. Like her he took it for granted that though his father so often accompanied the Prince to the smart gambling houses of London, he did not go on to the brothels the latter liked to frequent as night turned to dawn. The Prince, a disappointment to his mother the Queen, was a man of prodigious fleshly appetites. The Queen had arranged her son's early marriage to Princess Alexandra both in the interest of affairs of State, and in the hope of quenching these appetites and so avoiding scandal. The plan had worked for a time. The unwritten understanding was that the prime duty of a royal couple was to provide heirs for the succession. After two males had been born to the virgin bride — one spare, in case of illness or accident —

what royalty did with their lives thereafter was at their discretion. Alexandra had six children in quick succession, but apparently stayed in love with her husband: at least no scandal had been attached to her. The Prince, however, very soon took advantage of the fact that fidelity was not required of him. He and Alexandra simply did not 'get on', as everyone knew, whereas the Dilberne marriage was surely a love match. Different and more exacting behaviour was expected from the Earl and his wife, especially by their children. Good husbands were not expected to keep their wives company of an evening, but must treat them with respect and not expose them to humiliation or shame. Gambling dens were one thing, brothels quite another. That was left to Royalty, who actually had little need for them, other than to indulge in the more extraordinary of tastes.

'If you make it five pounds a month more,' said Flora now to Arthur, 'I can think of even more interesting things we could do which you might quite appreciate, which a lot of other girls don't like but I do.'

'Oh please,' he said. 'Please. Tell me. Show me.'

THE EARL OF DILBERNE
LUNCHES WITH THE POWERFUL

1.00 p.m. Friday, 27th October 1899

On the Friday, Robert found himself, to his surprise, lunching at the House of Lords with not only the Prime Minister himself but the Unionist Leader of the House, Arthur Balfour, the Secretary of State for War, Lord Lansdowne, the Colonial Secretary, Joseph Chamberlain, and the President of the Board Of Trade, Charles Ritchie. Balfour had actually beckoned the Earl over as he entered the Peer's Dining Room, and had a chair fetched for him. Everyone moved up in a most welcoming way.

Robert wondered why. His interest in politics was fitful; he had no great influence in the land, other than that perhaps his friendship with the Prince of Wales, the Queen's son, might be seen as potentially useful to some. He attended the House of Lords because he liked the calm of the library and the company of civilized men.

Because there were no women around, it was a place free of troublesome emotion. A man could say what he pleased, not what it pleased a woman for him to say. There would, perhaps, be some friendly antler-locking, but little bitterness.

Robert had no great ambition to improve society. Experience had proved that intervention in any social plan merely ended up with shifting the boundaries of good and bad around. What advantaged some could only ever be to the detriment of others. Give workers a bath and they would keep coal in it. Raise taxes and the wealthy would save money by dismissing their servants. Mostly he kept his opinions to himself, voted for Salisbury, and left it at that. But he was no fool, and well aware that this sudden elevation to the grace of the grand panjandrums' table meant they wanted something from him. Which, considering his financial plight, could only be to the good.

In the first reading of the Exportation of Arms Bill that morning, a bill which 'sought to prohibit the export of certain classes of military equipment when it was necessary to prevent such equipment being used against British or allied citizens or military forces', Robert, though by birth and inclination a natural Tory, had voted with the

Liberal Unionists against the Bill. It had been passed by only three votes, not surprisingly because as a bill it had been hasty and ill-conceived, as Mr Baum had happened to point out during the course of breakfast, and had alarmed mining interests. Smokeless coal and its by-products could easily be converted into military equipment, and gold was often used in trade between nations, even when they were in a formal state of war. Mr Baum, for one, would certainly not want this badly constructed legislation to go through in its present state, nor would many of his friends whose prosperity depended upon the free international passage of trade. A vague patriotism must be weighed against loyalty to friends and national advantage against national pride.

As he had listened to the discussion of the Bill with Mr Baum's strictures in his ears, Robert had decided that for once the Liberal Unionists were in the right: the Bill should not pass. In joining the 'Noes' he had become a floating voter, and as a floating voter he must be wooed and won, which was why he now enjoyed the company of anyone who was anyone in the beleaguered Conservative party. The beef was excellent: the Yorkshire pudding light and golden, the gravy excellent, better than any Cook achieved. But she was something of a French cook. Not of the old-fashioned English variety. There was no fancy French cooking in the Lords. He liked it this way.

Conversation was at first light and cheerful: no pressure was put upon him, no reproach on his batting for the wrong side. He hoped they'd get round to suggesting some form of preference, an actual paid job in the administration — hardly a Secretaryship, that required unusual intelligence, let alone a President, which suggested unusual probity: but a junior Ministry, even if only of Fisheries — the trout fishing at Dilberne Court being famous — would claim a good salary, and a good salary at the moment would be more than useful. He wondered briefly how much he had realised that voting 'no' would be to his financial advantage and quickly dismissed this from his thoughts. He was a bumbling fellow up from the shires, no sort of wily politician.

He had listened to Baum's voice, that was all, and responded to it, as was his duty. Baum's was the voice of an experienced man of commerce. Robert wished he and his family had been more civil to the man. It was the behaviour of a rich man who thought himself unassailable. Now suddenly he was a poor man. It behoved him to change his ways.

'The war was inevitable,' observed Salisbury over apple pie and clotted cream, 'though most regrettable. The behaviour of the Boers gave us no choice. We have to protect our colonial citizens from their bullying and the natives from their cruelty. One could not countenance a Dutch South Africa with, what? German naval ships using its ports? The Boer would bring back slavery if they could, too. Yet jingoism, as one sees it in the press, is most distasteful. But one hardly wants to arm the enemy, does one, Robert? The inference taken from your vote this morning might be that you do.' Ah, finally, thought Robert, over cheese, to the point.

'Nor does one want to impoverish the nation, sir,' he said.

'In what way impoverish?' asked Ritchie of the Board of Trade. 'Why do you say that?'

'To quote a character in *Major Barbara,*' said Robert (by great good fortune Isobel had persuaded him to take her to the Shaw play at the Savoy, and he had woken from sleep to hear a few memorable lines), ' *"the worst of crimes is poverty"*, and what leads to poverty is damage to our great manufacturing industries through government interference. The Bill is both contrary to mining interests and too vaguely drafted to be safe.'

'Well well,' said Salisbury. 'Quite understand your position, Dilberne, but perhaps you should avoid the theatre in future. If Mr Shaw has his way we will all end up Whigs!' Robert relaxed. He'd got away with it. 'We must get to know you better, Dilberne. You're a good fellow, well liked, with quite an influence in high places.'

High places? The PM, Robert supposed, could only mean the Queen. But that was folly. He had met the old lady three times, true, but being a friend of the Prince was the opposite of a recommendation. The old lady thought her eldest son quite unfit for the throne, and was so confused by her daily dose of sedatives from the quacks that however he behaved she was not likely to change her mind in a hurry. Where the Prince had influence was round the gossipy dinner tables of London's high society, and surely Salisbury in his gravity, could not take what went on there seriously?

'I hope you trust in our Party's capacity to steer the great ship of State into smoother waters than we have lately encountered,' went on Salisbury. It seemed as much a plea as a statement.

'I do indeed, sir,' Robert replied, with the

formality which seemed suddenly to be required of him, 'given the accumulated sagacity gathered at this table, I could not do otherwise.' But he found he had crossed his fingers as his Irish nanny had taught him to, when obliged to tell a lie. Had Balfour caught the action and frowned? Robert uncrossed his fingers casually.

'Good,' said Salisbury. 'Good man. Stay with us.' His beard was whitening fast — along with the Queen he grew old — but his authority was undiminished.

'No harm done,' said Balfour. 'This time. The Bill goes to second reading.'

But his tone was very much that of the schoolmasterly 'Just don't let it happen again.'

Robert felt, as they left the dining room smiling, that he had passed whatever test it was and that he might get something even higher and better paid than Fisheries. He certainly hoped so.

Arthur Declines a Bride

5.30 p.m. Friday, 27th October 1899

It was late afternoon before Arthur returned home. His mother was waiting for him. When she said it was time to discuss his marriage he expressed surprise and told her if money was still a problem he had been making enquiries as to a possible sale of the Arnold Jehu. He had paid five hundred pounds for it new: second-hand it would fetch a mere three hundred pounds. It was true enough; he had certainly contemplated selling even before seeing Flora, but the real reason, to which he did not allude, had been his speculative interest in acquiring a Serpollet or a Stanley — the newest models of which arrived fitted with a condenser, thus greatly reducing the amount of water the car must carry. He could of course make his own, with time, and sufficient garage space.

His mother for her part ignored this talk

of automobiles and simply showed her son a list of the twelve most eligible young heiresses from abroad currently in London. There were photographs of a few, sketches of others in the *Illustrated London News, McCall's* and the *Royal Gazette.*

Arthur laughed.

'Leftovers from the Season, I suppose,' he said, leafing through the folder. And it was true, none were blessed with beauty, though a few looked kind and friendly enough. But as his mother was well aware, that is not what young men are looking for, especially if others are looking, and they are always looking.

What Arthur saw was what his friends would see: jaws that were too large, eyes too small, foreheads too low, teeth crooked, bosoms too big or too small, legs too short or hands too big. Girls with wealth and beauty were in short supply. Wealth will make up for a good deal, but not everything. Whoever was to be his wife would have to take her place in London's society if he was to have any fun at all, let alone the respect of his peers, as he had realized with a shock when Flora said yes to his mad and panicky proposal. And children — there had been enough animal breeding on the estate going on during his childhood to know just how important heredity was. If a bitch, a filly or a mare 'got out' the line never ran true even though the particular mating had no issue. The bloodline was sullied. One had to marry a virgin, and Flora was certainly not that.

The Duke of Anglesey's younger brother had married a very beautiful singer who was rumoured to have spent time in the Prince's bed, and was accepted in society, but it seemed Royalty was exempted from the rule, and left no taint.

'Mama,' he said now, 'not even to save the family fortune will I marry one of these. Do you really want a bearded woman to mother the Hedleigh grandchildren?'

'You are too cruel,' she said. She was looking at her most charming — plentiful light brown hair loosely piled on top of her small head, her bright, large blue eyes mischievous. He realized that in choosing Flora he had chosen someone very like his mother. The distasteful Dr Freud over in Vienna would have something to say about that. Something rather unpleasant, no doubt. Rosina would keep quoting the psychiatrist's views on 'sexuality' and 'neurosis' over the dinner table, even when there were guests. It was most embarrassing.

'May I remind you that your father married me for my money, and we have lived happily ever since?' Isobel now said to her son.

'But you were a beauty,' he said. 'You are,' he corrected himself.

'Then what are we to do?' she asked. 'Starve?'

'Pater can sell his stables and stop gambling,' he offered. 'Rosina can stop giving money away. Money is such a vulgar subject, anyway.'

'My dear boy,' said his mother, 'we are moving into a new century. The acceptance of vulgarity is the beginning of wisdom. I thought, of the two of you, you might be the one to live in the real world, but I see you do not. What is to become of us if you do not grow up and rather quickly? You are bright enough, just idle. Like your father, who is perfectly intelligent, but so easily diverted.'

'I'll go and see Baum if you like,' said Arthur. 'Perhaps he will lend Pater more. He's rich as Croesus.'

'Arthur,' asked his mother, 'do you even know the meaning of the word "interest", as it relates to money?'

'No,' said Arthur. His mother sighed.

'In order to lend,' she said, 'people have to be offered an inducement. It is normally money. The percentage of the original loan is known as simple interest. Compound interest is when interest is added to the principal, so that from that moment on, the interest that has been added also itself earns interest. And then of course favours can be asked on top of that. The Prince, for example, offers Mr Cassel honours in return for loans. This very year, and against the Queen's wishes, Cassel was made a Knight Commander of the British Empire.'

'Mother, that is a scandalous rumour. Her Majesty does only as her duty directs.'

'I daresay,' said his mother, 'but you are very ignorant of the ways of the world. We have little to offer Mr Baum other than to receiving his wife into my drawing room to meet others with whom she can ingratiate herself, and so enter Society. There is no end to the ambitions of the children of Abraham.'

A most dishonourable thought flashed through Arthur's mind, quickly to be dismissed. If his mother was to sacrifice her son to an unknown and plain heiress for the sake of money, perhaps she should consider sacrificing herself to Mr Baum? She was beautiful enough, though past her best years. It might work.

'Your young lady friend, whoever she is,'

said his mother, 'at least provides an honest service in return for her pay. Perhaps you could share her with a friend and halve the cost? No one will think less of you.'

Arthur was shaken. How on earth did his mother know about Flora? Of course: as ever, the servants' hall. One imagined as a lover that one was invisible, but it was not the case. Others saw, looked, noticed, talked. Arthur usually and prudently asked Reginald to drop him off 'somewhere in Mayfair', but occasionally, if it were raining hard, he asked to be taken to Flora's exact address. Reginald would take the news back to the servants' hall. Someone, probably Grace the go-between, must have told his mother.

'Mother,' he said, 'I don't think this is a suitable conversation for you to be having with your son. It's the kind of thing fathers are meant to talk about. Just don't worry about things so, old thing. Something will turn up. We won't starve. Pater wouldn't let us.'

He declined to look further at the list drawn up by Grace.

'Absurd,' he said, and left the room and took a bath.

SOMETHING TURNS UP

5.45 p.m. Friday, 27th October 1899

It was Minnie O'Brien who turned up, only daughter of Billy and Tessa O'Brien of the Chicago stockyards. She was twenty-five, a slight fine-featured girl, with strong eyebrows which lent her face character and intelligence. She was delicate in her habits — 'fussy' according to her mother — her chin a little pronounced perhaps and her neck a little long, but her arms the right length for her body. She had little white hands, a bosom neither too pronounced nor too slight, and with the plentiful brown hair and blue wide eyes Arthur so favoured. Better still, from a young man's point of view, she was without annoying ideas of social progress of the kind that made Rosina such difficult company: she liked to paint and draw and was interested in the history of the decorative arts. Her voice was soft and sweet, and her accent when she spoke was only slightly American, she had had the best elocution lessons money could buy in Chicago.

Even as Arthur left his mother's side that afternoon, Minnie was driving round Belgravia, perched next to her mother Tessa in an old-fashioned four-wheeled growler, noisy but comfortable, provided by Brown's hotel for visiting guests — Americans always asked for them; they were 'cute'.

Tessa was a large, red-faced, energetic woman who spoke her mind and spoke it loudly; how she had produced so refined and spiritual a girl as her daughter no one could understand. Though some of her cattier friends did murmur that on the occasion of the foundation of the Art Institute of Chicago — of which, as wife to a leading meat baron and philanthropist, Tessa was naturally a founder member — she had vanished for an hour or two behind the antiquities with a certain well-known English painter, Eyre Crowe, whose slave painting 'Slaves Waiting for Sale' had graced the walls of the Institute thereafter. The meaner would even search for likenesses and compare Minnie's wide-apart eyes and strong brows with a sketch of Eyre Crowe also held in the Institute. Some said yes, some said no. And rumour had it that Billy

O'Brien was not capable of producing a child. There had been some unfortunate accident in the stockyards when he was boy. Others said no, Billy had a gruff enough voice, didn't he?

Tessa O'Brien's husband Billy, broad, big-bellied, vigorous and ruddy-faced, had started in the stockyards at seventeen, was running a single abattoir at the early age of twenty-five, and five of them by the age of thirty. By the time he was forty, he was the capitalist conquistador of all Chicago, where the hogs, cows and sheep of the USA were gathered, slaughtered, packed and from thence dispatched. He was too busy to be jealous or possessive of his wife — either emotion would divert him from his main business of making money — but all knew that his daughter Minnie, so fragile and refined, was his darling. He kept her well away from the blood, splintered bone and occasional accidental human remain which went into the hamburgers for which the nation was now famous.

'Belgrave Square, honey,' Tessa was saying. 'And what d'ya know. There's the Mexican flag. Don't say the beaners actually have an embassy in a proper country? We want number seventeen, driver.'

'Mama, where are we going?' asked Minnie, alarmed. 'You can't call on people you don't know. Not here in London.'

'I am simply leaving my calling card,' said Tessa, 'as Mr Eddie that nice concierge suggested. It is all the done thing here. Then they'll be in touch with me. It's the Earl and Countess of Dilberne's place. Fancy us from the stockyards making it to Belgrave Square. When you do meet the son make sure you don't say anything clever.'

'Why ever not?' asked Minnie.

'Because it puts men off,' said Tessa. 'Don't you want to end up with a husband?'

'Not particularly, Mama,' said Minnie.

'Do try to be not so peculiar,' said Tessa. 'After all that's gone on you can't afford to be choosy.'

The growler drew up, and Tessa gathered her plentiful skirts and went up the broad steps of No. 17 Belgrave Square and pulled the front doorbell. Mr Neville came to answer it, took one look at who was waiting, and assuming it was someone calling about the vacancy for an assistant cook said, 'Down the steps to the servants' entrance, please.'

Tessa was not easy to put out. She thrust her calling card upon him. 'Don't go dropping it, honey,' said Tessa. 'It's not muck. Neither am I. Tell her Ladyship Mrs Billy

O'Brien and daughter are staying at Brown's and waiting her call.'

'What I do for you!' she said to her daughter, nevertheless, as she hoisted up her skirts and got back into the motor carriage. 'Even their servants are stuck-up snobs. But you can't live with your mother all your life. You won't be able to stand it and I certainly can't.'

'I don't mind that much,' said Minnie. 'And there's Father too. He'd like it.'

'Your father wants the past forgotten, you married off, out of his hair and with a title he can crow about. Surely you owe him that, after all he's done for you?'

His daughter had spent some weeks living in sin with a painter in his studio in the lively post-fire Burnt District in Chicago, and taking no care whatsoever to be discreet about it, until she discovered he was already married and had three children. After that Minnie had ceased to be a marriageable prospect at home, just an endless source of gossip. Now she was twenty-five and ageing fast.

'But does it have to be an Englishman?' begged Minnie, examining the perfect ovals of her pink fingernails, as the driver resumed his trip around the grander residential areas of London. 'I have met a few. All they do is hunt foxes, kill birds and eat meat. Couldn't it be a Frenchman? A Parisian artist, perhaps? How about Toulouse-Lautrec? He has a title.'

'How you do delight in teasing me,' said Tessa. 'He's a dwarf and a drunkard and the Good Lord knows what else.'

And she tightened her formidable jaw, and Minnie's sensitive mouth took on its six-year-old's sulky downturn, which only happened when she was in her mother's company, and they continued their sightseeing in silence. Tessa was glad enough to be in London, for the winters in Chicago were monstrously cold: their house at home was centrally steam-heated, pipes clanking and banging as if they had a life of their own — but set your nose outside the door and it froze off. Here icicles melted almost as soon as they formed. London houses were poorly heated but at least were quiet; servants moved about on tip-toe and spoke in hushed voices, at home everyone shouted as if they were out of doors in a high wind and herding cattle.

She missed Billy and his strong arms round her at night — he liked a cuddle and she liked a grope, and it was pleasurable enough even if it couldn't ever be quite the real thing — but the Brown's Hotel's box-spring mattresses were magnificently comfortable and she resigned herself to being apart from Billy. She must concentrate on getting Minnie settled. The sooner it was done, the sooner she, Tessa, could get home.

Tessa wondered if perhaps while in London she could leave a card at Eyre Crowe's residence. But perhaps better not to stir things up. He was an old man by now, successful and wealthy. It would be simple enough to find out where he lived. The Art Institute of Chicago had links with the Royal Academy. He might be pleased enough to see his daughter: but his wife, should he have one, and most men of wealth and position did — might not be pleased: word might get back to Billy, who would see it as disloyalty after all he had done for Minnie: and heaven knew how Minnie would react — it could be opening a Pandora's box of trouble. Besides which, she could not be 100 per cent sure — it was just that as Minnie got older she looked less and less like the other contender to her parentage, Billy's red-headed best mate Kevin Murphy, a man without noticeable sensitivities, and looked more and more like the English artist. Minnie belonged amongst the English titles, not the stockyards, and that was the truth of it.

HER LADYSHIP RECEIVES TESSA O'BRIEN'S CARD

10 a.m. Saturday, 29th October 1899

It was ten the next morning before her Ladyship was handed Mrs O'Brien's card. The butler had seen no need to hurry. He was a small bald man with a mild squint in gentle brown eyes, and half the size of his wife. 'But Mr Neville, why did this take a day to come to me?'

'I did not think your Ladyship would particularly care to receive it. She looked like trade to me, your Ladyship. Certainly she did not know how to behave. Calling cards are received and delivered in the mornings only.'

'You must learn, Mr Neville, that times are changing. The most significant in our society can often seem the most shabby. They are so busy making money they have no time for style. It is a pity but it is the case. Fetch me Grace.'

'Grace,' said her Ladyship, when the latter

appeared, 'why did Minnie O'Brien not appear on my list? She seems by far the most suitable contender.'

'I did not see her as at all suitable for the Hedleigh family, ma'am. According to the concierge at Brown's, Mrs O'Brien and her daughter Minnie were due in on the *Oceanic* — and it does seem the girl's single, has trust money and is heir to the father's fortune. But he's an Irish meat baron; nothing but a jumped-up butcher, and the girl has a reputation. She's soiled goods, ma'am, and doesn't try to hide it. She won't do.'

'And Viscount Arthur is not soiled goods?' asked Isobel.

'It's different for men, ma'am. The lady of the estate needs to be above reproach. Women need to set an example. I'm not putting myself up as an angel, but they say Minnie O'Brien lived for a time with a married man. It's like dogs or horses, the way I've heard his Lordship say. Once a bitch has got out, she never breeds true.'

'As a matter of interest how did this news get to you, Grace?'

'The concierge at Brown's got it from the *Oceanic*'s purser, who got it from the chef of the new Silversmith hotel in Chicago, who was a passenger, and he got it from an art dealer in New York — I can't exactly remember the details but news travels fast. I didn't think a cattle family, ma'am, would be what you wanted. Aren't they only one step up from gangsters? Hang their enemies from meat-hooks in their abattoirs?'

'Low gossip, this is, and rumour, Grace, and you are not to spread it beyond these walls. Speak to the Brown's concierge — and explain to him that this is a calumny, both pernicious and false. The girl is spot-less, and everyone must know it. There'll be a good tip for him next time I come by for tea.'

And no tip for me for telling lies, thought Grace. She was still hurt and angry. Where was the acknowledgement of the ingenuity, time, effort and skill required of her to come up with the list? She had even 'been nice' to Mr Eddie to get hold of it, though it was true she might well have done that anyway, and now her advice was simply ignored, swept away. You just couldn't trust the gentry. They would treat you as one of themselves when it suited them, and treat you like muck when it didn't.

Grace was feeling generally discontented. She was fond enough of the young Viscount and wished him well, but if he was going to marry for money, let him at least marry a girl fit to carry on the Hedleigh name. Well, she would see to it that he did.

EATING OUT: A DINNER PARTY AT PAGANI'S

8.30–11 p.m. Tuesday, 31st October 1899

So that was how it was that less than a week later Arthur and Minnie were seated next to one another at a dinner party in Pagani's in Great Portland Street, a restaurant favoured by American visitors, a place where Tessa was recognized and felt at home. The Countess had booked a private room but Tessa would have rather they'd sat in public to see and be seen, so that she could recount back home which famous world musicians and artists she had encountered. They compromised on an alcove where they could see but not easily be seen.

'My, oh my, I must say, I must say,' she kept repeating. 'Little Tessa sitting in London at Pagani's! If my friends could see me now!'

Mrs O'Brien, as Robert and Isobel agreed, when comparing notes later that night, was both outlandish and oddly attractive. She spoke too loudly as Americans were given to doing, and was alarmingly overdressed, more as though for a ball than a restaurant. Diamond necklaces were not for dinner, nor for too large an expanse of décolletage not in first youth. A clip, or ear-rings would have been right. She actually thanked the waiter when he brought the beetroot soup rather than pretended he didn't exist, which was the English way. Yet, both agreed, she was good-natured enough, while she didn't know quite how to conduct herself, who from the land of log cabins and cowboys ever did?

The girl had made a better impression: pretty enough, if a little quiet, although the mother made up for both of them, and aesthetically acceptable, wearing a triple string of pearls, and a simple uncorseted blue dress with modest neckline, which clearly came from one of the new, very fashionable and expensive French *couture* houses. What Arthur thought of her it was impossible to say. He'd yawned once or twice, but perhaps he was tired, though from what Isobel could not imagine, and had seemed distracted.

There were a mere eight in the party: his Lordship and herself, Tessa and Minnie, Arthur, the widowed Austrian Ambassador,

Francis, and his niece and nephew — Janika, nineteen, beetle-browed, stout and serious and the eighteen-year-old Jan — from next door, had joined them. Jan had the looks and style of a young god, broad-shouldered, bright-eyed and with a thatch of blond hair and clean-cut features, and very little to say. His Lordship took the head of the table. Isobel feared it would not be an easy occasion: 'eating out' was still something of a novelty, and rather exciting, a trusting to the fates of ambience, company, food and comfort. But as it was, everything went smoothly enough. Any awkward silences were quickly filled by Tessa, and they were far enough from the other tables not to draw too much attention when she whooped with excitement or dismay. Isobel found she was enjoying herself. So apparently was her husband: his presence was required but hardly his serious attention.

Asked politely about the journey over Tessa O'Brien talked at length, and volubly about the crossing in the *Oceanic*. No, she said, the O'Briens had not enjoyed the trip one bit: the boat was vastly overpraised. It had been built for speed rather than for comfort, and rattled. There being no deck for a healthy promenade in the salt air, one was obliged to walk about *inside* the ship. There had been nothing to do but eat and use the library. It was a very grand library with a glass dome on top, true, but left room for only two chimneys when all the other Blue Riband contenders had three or four.

'Wouldn't you agree, child? A dreadful trip. No need to be bashful. Speak up!' her mother demanded.

'The library was very well-stocked,' said Minnie, 'which makes a change for a sea voyage.' Her voice came at half the volume of her mother's, but was clear, pleasant and distinct, and only gently accented, unlike the mother's. 'But apart from the saloon there were no portholes on board, only electric bulbs where portholes would usually be, four thousand of them, I believe, all dimming when the generators ascended a large wave, brightening when it descended the other side. Since we were mid-Atlantic there were quite a lot of waves. Reading was not easy, but I managed.'

'That boat was designed by the finest architect in Europe and you are very lucky that your father has made enough money for you to travel on it,' said her mother.

'I am sure that is true, Mother,' Minnie said, patiently. 'But perhaps ships are meant to have builders not architects. It juddered

166

all the darned way from New York to Southampton.'

'Do not use that language, girl,' said her mother. 'And it was *Oceanic*'s maiden voyage. Small things can go wrong first time out, then they know what bits of the machinery they've got to tune up. They'll sort out the generators in no time.'

'The Admiralty paid to reinforce the bulkheads with iron plating,' observed Arthur, with a rare show of interest in what anyone was saying, 'so it could be used by the Navy should a war break out. That would account for the juddering.'

'Not of course that anyone expects war,' said his Lordship, rather hastily. But then he was sitting next to the Austrian Ambassador. Germany and Austria-Hungary were thick as two thieves when it came to naval matters.

'If it was good enough for J. Pierpont Morgan I'm sure it was good enough for us O'Briens, Minnie,' said Tessa.

His Lordship ordered dinner for everyone, as was his habit, consulting no one about their preferences. For generations Hedleighs had been told to eat up what was on their plate and not argue. It had worked well enough for him, why not for others? Discussing food was not in good taste in any

167

case, and why would he want his guests wasting their time doing so? He ordered *hors d'oeuvre variés, potage borscht, filets de sole Pagani, tournedos aux truffes, haricots verts sautés, pommes croquettes, perdreaux voisin and salade,* followed by *soufflé au Curaçao.*

Tessa, accustomed to choice as she was, almost cut up a little rough, insisted on being told what *borscht* was and finding out it was a beetroot soup said she didn't fancy it, and asked for soup of tomato instead. She asked the waiter what *perdreaux voisin and salade* was when it was at home, and when he hurried off to ask the maître d'hôtel, Tessa said, 'See, he's only pretending to be French. Minnie excels in French. You know what it means, don't you, Minnie!'

To which Minnie, with a hint of a smile, innocently replied, 'It's just a salad of lost neighbours, Mother,' which made Arthur look at her twice and smile back, which annoyed Tessa, who nudged Minnie and hissed, 'I told you not to get too smart, Minnie. I can't see what you think is funny about it.'

Isobel formed the opinion that Tessa was as anxious for Minnie to get together with Arthur as she herself was to get Arthur together with Minnie. It created a bond

168

between them of, if not quite friendship, at least of common interest. The woman did not know how to behave, true, but would soon enough be back in Chicago, where no doubt she flourished, and Isobel wished her well.

The Austrian Ambassador, Isobel realized rather too late, as he let slip the occasional reference to Jan's athletic skill and elaborate royal connections on his mother's side — the poor woman was deceased — had the same ambitions for his young relative as she did for hers. A rich wife.

But there was no danger, as it happened: Minnie was indulgent to Jan but saw him as a boastful boy. She got on famously with Janika, and they talked happily enough about the charms of the *Art Nouveau* — all around them in Pagani's — and how and why fine examples were so sadly lacking in the O'Briens' native land. She and Arthur exchanged but few words — Isobel hoped Arthur could remember to talk about something other than automobiles, shooting birds, his tailor or the weather, but feared he would not. He did not easily reveal himself to young women. Rosina had mocked him too often into silence when he was small.

Rosina had declined to join them: she had

to attend a reading of Havelock Ellis' new volume of essays on sex psychology and secondary sexual characteristics in males.

'Have to?' her mother had enquired.

'I could get out of it,' Rosina had said, grudgingly, but when she added that she hated dining out with her father because he always ordered for everyone and would try to make her eat meat, and there would be a row, Isobel had conceded it might be better if she stayed away.

'Besides, Mama,' said Rosina, 'it's going to be so embarrassing. It's just all so obvious. Minnie O'Brien! Even if she did marry Arthur what makes you think her father will part with a cent?'

'Your father and he will no doubt come to a gentlemanly agreement.'

'Gentlemanly?' shrieked Rosina. 'Do you know about Billy O'Brien? Do you know about the stockyards? They're a disgrace to modern civilization. He treats his workers like so much machinery. If they wear out he throws them away. They were better off in the cotton fields.'

'Your father and Mr O'Brien,' said Isobel, 'will come to an agreement because without a penny there will not be a wedding. She will be anxious to be married. The girl's not as young as she used to be.'

'Nor any better than she ought to be,' Rosina said and giggled. 'According to Grace. Second-hand goods, Mother. You're selling Arthur to buy soiled goods?'

'I am happy to tell everyone you have a landscape painting class,' was all her mother said to that. 'I don't want our guests subjected to a diatribe.'

Robert, the business of ordering briskly done, took little more interest in the women and children, and was now talking with Francis von Demy about naval exercises in the Pacific. He had to be prudent, since Austria and Germany tended to think and act as one, and it was common knowledge that the Prince did not get on with his cousin the Kaiser. The former had been overheard saying to the Count at last year's big Christmas ball at the d'Astis', 'Never trust a cripple. They hold too great a grudge against the world to wish the best for it.' The Prince knew how to put his worldly wisdom elegantly and concisely, which was why Robert thought, he managed to stay popular, in spite of scandal after scandal.

The Kaiser had a withered arm, a source of distress to his grandmother the Queen. The Prince's passing comment on his cousin had come back to Her Majesty and been the source of yet another royal row.

The Prince was often considered an excellent diplomat: it was just when Kaiser Bill was concerned his guard had been known to slip.

Robert's first impression of Minnie had been favourable, just as first sight of a mare or a bitch could tell a countryman as much as he needed to know. As a mother to the future Dilberne heir she was acceptable. Glossy coat, even teeth, regular features and a soft voice which made the American accent almost quite bearable. She looked genial and docile enough. She might even have an intellect, though he did not think that was what his son currently looked for in a woman. Compared to the Austrian girl, whom Isobel had brought along presumably in the interests of comparison, there was no contest. A pity for the Ambassador's family that though the boy had got looks, the daughter had not: plain girls were hard to marry off.

And then his Lordship concentrated on his dinner — he already rather regretted choosing the truffles; they tasted, if you could taste them at all, of something mildly rotten — and trying to extract such information from von Demy about the naval bases as the latter was willing to divulge. The diplomatic game being played in Europe and in the colonies, as the major powers vied for long-term influence and control in the world, was so much more interesting than Fisheries, where he feared he was destined. Remarkable how quickly one's area of interest changed when one's gold mine was sabotaged by enemy irregulars. On the other hand if he got Fisheries and a regular income the irritating problem of money would go away.

After those at the table had consumed the *hors d'oeuvre,* the sole, the *tournedos,* and the partridge, time came for the *soufflé Curaçao.* A hush descended upon the restaurant and even the waiters paused, trays poised above their heads for a second, as in a stop-motion film. Dame Nelly Melba, fresh from the Opera House and that evening's triumph in *La Traviata,* was entering Pagani's sumptuous arched lobby, unbooked and requiring an after-show supper with friends. Space was made for her party, chairs found, menus produced, the kitchens kept open: no trouble was too great. Her dress was elaborate, frilly, and emerald green, trimmed with fur. She bore herself theatrically, but with majesty.

'She'd not be a beauty back home,' said Tessa in far too loud a voice. 'What's all the great hoo-hah? Look at the size of her nose!'

'Do hush up, Mother,' said Minnie, gently, and Tessa did. 'You know you tell me yourself to mind how quiet everyone is over here.'

She's a nice girl, thought Isobel, not spiteful or condemning when others would be. Minnie would do very well for Arthur; she might be a little too clever for him but one can't have everything.

'Minnie can sing better than Melba,' Tessa was saying, 'she's been to all the finest teachers in Chicago. Not so loud of course but with far less crackling.'

No, upon enquiry, it turned out Tessa had not heard Melba live but on a phonograph. Therefore the 'crackling'. Everyone looked at her strangely. But then a little later Tessa came out with 'We're a Donegal family, sure, lots of labouring cousins back in the bogs of the old country, but Billy's cut them out of the will, the lot's going to Minnie,' which was obviously aimed at the Dilbernes, and not the Austrian party. Young Jan clearly had a bad head for wine — probably unused to it — and was looking flustered and altogether ineligible, the carved young lips floppy rather than strong, the eyes bleary not alert, and in general seeming not so much youthful as unformed.

Arthur, on the other hand, was looking

very well, strong and Byronic, his mother thought, mature and more than eligible. The high white collar of the shirt framed his face, the white set off his high colour, and his curly hair sprang with such energy from his head no barber could ever reduce it to ordinariness. The flavour of the aristocrat clung to him — a mildly petulant air softened by habitual courteousness, a heightened sensuousness kept coolly under control — yes, if Minnie was a catch for her wealth, so was Arthur for his birth and breeding. His silence, for he was hardly talkative tonight and his mother wondered why, could, she hoped, be mistaken for gravitas and strength of will.

The fact was, though Isobel was not to know this, for her back was to the entrance lobby, that during the *borscht* course, Flora had entered the restaurant in the company of the Honourable Anthony Robin, a slim, lordly fellow whom Arthur knew, having fagged for him at Eton, where he was familiarly known as Redbreast, and known him later at Oxford, where he had been, like Arthur, a member of the Bullingdon Club. Flora in Pagani's? This was just not right. With another man? With Anthony bloody Robin of all people? She had slipped off a white mink stole and handed it to a waiter.

When did she last have a fur stole? She was looking rosy and very happy, like a girl having a good time rather than a girl earning a living, her smile friendly enough and not calculated. Though perhaps — could one really tell? She was wearing a silky white dress, uncorseted, with leg of mutton sleeves and little white satin bows fastened everywhere. Her hair was piled up loosely as Arthur's own mother sometimes wore hers. Redbreast was looking unbearably proprietorial.

Flora caught Arthur's eye and gave him a little apologetic smile, which made him suspect her the more. The two of them were led to one of the more private booths where diners who did not want to attract too much attention were put. Now he could not see them but watched as champagne and lobsters went to their table.

He tried to pay attention to what was going on at his own table but it was difficult. Mother was unashamedly hurling the O'Brien girl at him. He'd hoped she'd forgotten all about the marrying money business, but apparently she was still bent on it. The O'Brien mother was a nightmare, a circus act, she hooted when she laughed and threw herself about all the time as though she had all the space in the world, which he supposed in her own country one did. The girl didn't seem, well, objectionable. She looked virginal enough but then so did Flora. He marvelled at how the worst kind of woman looked no different from the purest kind. Prostitution was meant to show in a woman's eyes, in the hardness of her glance, but in his experience this was by no means the rule. The effects of poverty would show, in tired skin, a mean look, hardness of expression, but not always the effects of disreputable character. He wondered briefly what the reality behind Minnie's gentle demeanour might be, but did not dwell on it. He was too taken up with outrage at thoughts of white-bosomed Flora and Redbreast conjoined that were too disgusting to face. He felt ill. Yet it was not as if he loved Flora. Men didn't love whores, they used them. No, the problem was that she was taking advantage of him. He was paying for exclusive rights, and she was failing in her side of the bargain. She was royally cheating him, taking him for a fool. Exclusive, my foot!

When, over coffee, his mother suggested he accompany Minnie to the Victoria and Albert Museum to view the oriental ceramics, Arthur did not have the emotional energy to wriggle out of the arrangement.

He found he had agreed to call for Minnie at two the next afternoon. Von Demy then suggested that Jan and Janika came along too, and Arthur agreed to this too though Mama was looking daggers. Better four of them than two; conversation would be easier. With any luck Jan would know about steam cars and leave the girls to look at old bits of heathen china to their hearts' content.

He thought it was strange that when their party was leaving his father caught sight of Flora and said, 'But isn't that — ?', and then broke off, and when Isobel quizzed him, said, 'Oh, nothing. Just the way that nowadays the strangest people get to the grandest places.'

Not that Pagani's was in the least grand, Arthur thought. Gold wallpaper and a sprinkling of famous people with greenery-yallery pretensions did not make a place grand. Give him Rules or the Savoy Grill any day. Though the food hadn't been too bad. The *perdreaux voisin* was just plump partridge slices on lettuce leaves with some kind of red sweet sauce. The meat baron's wife was like a rather plump partridge herself. The daughter was like the *sole Pagani,* delicate and fresh with chewy bits in the sauce, mussels and prawns.

But Flora, ah, Flora, she was the *soufflé Curaçao,* evil, frothy and aromatic, and infinitely desirable. He realized he too had drunk quite a lot, especially of the Saint-Estèphe, the better to blot out the infernal vision of Flora and Redbreast in each other's arms.

ANGRY PEOPLE

4.30 p.m. Friday, 27th October 1899

If Grace was angry with her Ladyship for ignoring her advice, and found it painful to realize just how lightly she, Grace, could be relegated from almost-friend to mere employee, Mr Eric Baum was incensed with the whole Dilberne family. They had mocked him and made light of him and worse, had failed to realize just how much consideration he offered them — running half the way from Lincoln's Inn to Belgrave Square, kept waiting first on the step and then for breakfast — or even to take seriously how much they owed him. Money came easily to them, but had not to him. But it was not just his pocket they had hurt, but his pride.

Grace had gone straight down to the servants' hall where they were having tea to let everyone know that Miss Minnie O'Brien, soon to be affianced to Master Arthur — not that the girl knew anything about it, but her Ladyship had set her mind on it and wouldn't stop until she had her way — was not just a fortune-hunter but a title-hunter too and no better than she ought to be. But all that happened was that the staff ganged up against her.

'Good for her,' said Elsie. 'You're just jealous because you're still sweet on Arthur. But he's a big boy now.'

'That's enough of that,' said Mr Neville. 'And I'm surprised at you, Grace. Tell-tale tit, your tongue shall be split, and all the little puppy dogs will have a little bit?'

'Pull the other one, Grace,' said Reginald. 'Master Arthur's lady friend in Mayfair wouldn't stand for it.'

'You're going to get done for pimping one day, Reggie,' Smithers said, 'and serve you right. The law's changed. Taking Master Arthur along the way you do.'

'Isn't against the law,' said Reginald. 'It isn't a brothel, just a nice little flat. It's only when one or two gather together it counts as a brothel. Now if Miss Rosina was to move in . . .' It had become known that Miss Rosina believed in free love; Reginald had driven her to a lecture by a Dr Havelock Ellis on sexual inversion. 'Only then they might get me for procurement.'

'That's enough of that,' said Cook. 'Smithers, there's gristle in the shepherd's pie. You should have gone through the meat before you put it in the pan. And the porridge this morning was lumpy.'

'Excuse me,' said Smithers, 'but I am the parlour maid not the cook. I occasionally help out, that's all.'

'Now now,' said Mrs Neville, 'see what you've done, Grace? Set them off!'

'Another thing,' said Grace, 'the reason we're still in this Belgrave hellhole and not in Hampshire is because his Lordship owes Pickfords so much they won't send the movers in until he's paid the bill.'

That made more of an impression. There was silence, broken by Reginald.

'Nah,' he said, 'that sort of thing doesn't happen to toffs.'

And Elsie said, 'If they're as broke as all that, how can Minnie O'Brien be a fortune-hunter?'

All reflected.

'She wants his title and he wants her money,' said Grace, 'just because you don't want to hear it doesn't mean it isn't so. We'll all be out of a job soon enough.'

Another silence.

'If they did go bust,' said Cook, 'I'd be all right. I'd go over to chef for the Countess d'Asti in Eton Place. She keeps two live-in kitchen maids, not one live-in and one agency, like here, and two afternoons a week off.'

'We'll join you, Cook.'

'You haven't been asked,' said Cook.

'Yes we have,' said Mr Neville. 'We've had the odd sign of interest. But she's nouveau, she doesn't know how to keep servants, the way Lady Isobel does. No one would guess her Ladyship's father was in trade.'

'Let's hope it doesn't come to it,' said Mrs Neville. 'It's true, old money's easier to work for than new. Old money looks after you, new money uses you.'

'Bad blood has to out,' said Smithers. 'See it in Master Arthur and his whore, see it in Miss Rosina and her bloody parrot. No consideration.'

'Always darkest before the dawn,' said Elsie. 'If we were all let go, Alan would have to marry me. I'd have no one else to turn to. I'd have a baby.'

'It won't come to it,' said Reginald. 'Toffs know how to look after themselves.'

And all agreed, over roly-poly pudding, a boiled suet pastry jam roll cut into slices and served with custard, and very comforting and filling, that this was probably the case, and their employment was secure.

'Speaking for myself, I like being in London. Nothing ever happens in the country,' said Smithers. 'I miss my mother but at least we have Royalty to dinner.'

'I don't have a mother,' said Lily, and snivelled a little. She had barely spoken before. All turned to look at her.

'You have us,' said Mrs Neville cheerily and decisively. 'Make yourself useful, girl. Clear the plates and bring in the cheese.'

Which Lily did. She was the flower girl from Whitehall his Lordship had stopped to give money to. She was so small and thin Reginald had taken pity on her, brought her in and fed her. Then Mrs Neville had warmed her and washed her so she didn't smell. Elsie had given her some old shoes. She was a street child, homeless. They'd made up a bed for her in the cupboard under the stairs. Smithers had argued against it: the child had impetigo, someone would have to pay for a doctor, someone was bound to start asking questions; but the next day Lily had scraped the parsnips for Elsie very efficiently (always a nasty job if the tubers are not fresh and firm) and somehow or other, like a stray kitten, the child had charmed her way in and here she still was.

'I can always start up a brothel,' said Reginald, watching her little hips squeeze behind a chair to get to the sink.

'No joking matter,' said Mrs Neville.

'Wasn't joking,' said Reginald.

MRS BAUM WAITS

7.50 a.m. Wednesday, 1st November 1899
'Still nothing interesting in the post, dearest,' said Naomi Baum to her husband Eric. She was expecting the invitation from Countess Dilberne which Eric had promised her was on its way. Every morning she looked, every morning there was nothing. She had a nice new wire cage for letters to fall into but all that fell into it was an amazing number of bills for Eric relating to the new house. It was a lovely house, and when the garden had had time to grow would be beautifully situated, and of course she was grateful to him: but here she was with no friends and no neighbours and where was her life? Gone, gone, along with her grandmother and all memories of the family past.

Eric Baum, with his wife Naomi and their little children Jonathan and Barbara, had recently moved, along with Naomi's eighty-year-old grandmother, from St John's Street in Islington, where he and his family had an adequate rental above a carpet shop, to a spot between the villages of Hampstead and Golders Green. Here he had had built a quite splendid eight-bedroom house, set in a garden which was still, on this the first day of November, no more than a large patch of mud, and was likely to stay so until the spring. The road was still unmade-up and waiting a name from the Council. But the land had been cheap and it was obvious that London must soon explode out of its containment in the Thames basin and creep up the hills to the north. The air would be cleaner and the fog might not reach so far. Also, rumour had it that the Charing Cross, Euston and Hampstead Railway Co. was to drive the tube northwards from The Regent's Park; in five years time what were now green fields would be prosperous suburbia and land prices extortionate.

The move had proved expensive, and tragic too. On the rough roads to North London, Pickfords had managed to shatter Naomi's grandmama's Russian tea-set, delicate porcelain cups and saucers. On opening the precious shoe-box, initially taken with her on the long trek out of Odessa when she was a child, finally in 1899 to be set on a mantelpiece in North London still wet with fresh paint, the old lady had discovered nothing inside but splintered shards of red and gold porcelain. Nothing would do for her but that it was an attack upon all Jewry by anti-Dreyfus forces.

Baum, irritated by her irrationality, harassed and tired, had mocked her. 'What, Pickfords' men, anti-Dreyfus?' It had seemed a small enough crime, in the circumstances, but the old lady, nervous of the move in the first place, becoming more and more agitated on the journey out of London, had fallen into a rage at this final blow, accused him of betraying his own people, flung up her arms, clutched her head and collapsed senseless there and then, in front of Edward and Barbara. A doctor had moved her, acutely ill, to the hospital at New End in Hampstead where she could at least receive emergency medical care, and there had died within hours, before more suitable arrangements could be made. It had not been the best start for Naomi. She had not wanted the old lady moved. But Eric and the doctor had insisted, knowing it was the only chance she had of living.

And *shiva* had to be sat as best it could be in an unfurnished house in a strange community, and Harris Price the rabbi had to travel all the way from the St John's Wood

Synagogue. Naomi was most upset and saw the death as a bad omen for the future.

Eric kept to himself his belief that actually it was a good omen, that the broken tea cups were a sign that a dismal past was behind him and his family: that his children would grow up into a new century, in an England where to be a Jew would be a matter of pride, and not to be a victim, hated, feared and despised.

He felt he owed everything to Naomi, clever, kind and pretty Naomi, who had met the middle-aged Maude Cassel, daughter of old Ernest Cassel the financier, when both were working for a Jewish children's charity in Spitalfields. Naomi was a struggling young chemistry student from the Royal College of Science, who still had time for charity work, and Maude did what she could to help and encourage her. Girls like Naomi would create the future. Naomi had recently become engaged to a brilliant fellow student, one Eric Baum. Maude had attended the wedding, and told her father Ernest about the boy's successful studies in gold cyanidation. Ernest asked to meet him, was impressed and linked him up with John Courtney, the international lawyer, suggested the boy acquire a background in law, and funded him to do so. Now Courtney,

Baum and Co. specialized in mining law in South Africa and handled a percentage of the many Cassel investments in Natal.

Maude had taken the Baums to a Christmas party at the d'Astis' place. Eric had set up an — well, 'acquaintance' was hardly the word: the social gap was too great — but at least a business association with the Earl of Dilberne. Courtney and Baum now acted as the Hedleigh family business management, replacing their former stick-in-the mud advisers, Stitch and Stitch. Viscount Arthur's Hedleigh cousins — plain masters and misses all, the children of his two uncles — Alfred and Edwin Hedleigh, had inherited small sums through their maternal grandmother, which Stitch and Stitch now also administered. The children had not lost, but neither had they gained, and money must be made to work, that was the way of the new world. Money could not be left alone just to lose value.

The deal with Cassel which had enabled Eric Baum to lend Dilberne money had gone somewhat awry, and Eric had actually lost money on it. Not much, but the subsequent personal debt, which had remained unpaid month after month had somewhat soured the relationship on both sides. What he'd mistakenly thought was a real friendship with the Earl of Dilberne, which would perhaps end up with a spot of shooting on the Dilberne estate and a new social life at a level appropriate to his own rising income, had not transpired. He had been kept waiting deliberately at his Lordship's front door. He had nevertheless ventured to push his luck, and hinted, perhaps rather strongly, that an invitation to his wife for one of the Countess's social events would be in order. But no invitation had ever arrived. He had led Naomi to expect one, and Eric hated to disappoint her.

The 'garden' was still a mound of builder's rubble. Naomi was often in tears as she tried to set up house so far from the East End, so far from the shops; buying from unfamiliar and on the whole unfriendly shopkeepers who did not understand bargaining, had not heard of feather quilts, and sold strange bland foods which her forbears would have spat out in disgust. There was no synagogue near Golders Green. With the arrival of the children her whole life had become circumscribed with domestic obligations. Enough to do as wife and mother and to keep the religion alive in this land where she was often made to feel a stranger. Her children were to be enrolled in the City of London School on the Embankment where their religion was tolerated, even encouraged. Until the Tube actually arrived at their doors — and no sooner was a transport company created, with great fanfare, than it seemed to go bust — the journey there and back would be time-consuming. If they'd only stayed where they were life would be easier.

'Not with an east London address,' Eric had said firmly. The NWs will very soon come into their own, mark my words. Friends and associates are buying round here. Now we've gone first they're following. Start a school in the garden room while the children are little. I promise you an invitation from the Countess of Dilberne will arrive soon. I will see to it. You will charm and delight society as you charm and delight me.'

He did not tell his wife the humiliation he had been exposed to on the steps of Belgrave Square. But he would show them. He would pay them back, squeeze a little harder. His Lordship had at least voted against the Exportation of Arms Bill. That must have gone against his landed gentry grain.

But the Countess of Dilberne had evidently not taken the hint about the invitation. She was nothing but a selfish snob. Attractive, yes, not thin-blooded and high-browed like so many of the real aristocracy, but looked as if she was capable of having a good time in bed. She had no reason to give herself the airs she did. Her father had started as a miner. She was living off borrowed money. Her good fortune was due to luck and looks, not hard work like his own. He would like to see her brought down a peg or two.

The bad news was that building the house had been far more expensive than he had anticipated. Land prices had shot up while he was mid-transaction. The building of the new Underground station, which had lured him to Golders Green in the first place, was to be delayed, perhaps for years, and he'd have to take the bus to Finchley Road, and thence to Chancery Lane, changing at Oxford Circus. He rose at six each morning and did not get home until eight, sometimes later.

They would be made to pay. He would tighten the pressure.

TESSA TELLS MINNIE HOW IT IS — OR TRIES TO

9.30 a.m. Thursday, 2nd November 1899

'He would make your life easy,' said Tessa to Minnie. 'And it would please your father very much. You could have a big society wedding in Westminster Abbey or St Paul's.'

'I don't know that I want an easy life, Mama. I would rather have an interesting one.'

'You had an interesting one with your Mr Stanton Turlock. And look where that ended.'

'It wouldn't have ended if you hadn't interfered.'

'He was a madman! Of course it would have.' They were breakfasting in their rooms at Brown's. The coffee was rich and strong, the rolls and the butter fresh. They were enjoying their stay. They bickered, but idly. Minnie was recovering from a broken heart and public humiliation. She had fallen in love with her art teacher, Stanton Turlock, a

194

handsome young painter of unfashionable subjects, mostly Red Indian chiefs, whom he painted in the same way that he made love to Minnie, with verve and ferocity. Alas, buyers preferred landscapes to put on their walls, rather than depictions of the mighty now brought low. Both Minnie and Stanton saw this rejection as a sure sign of his genius. In the name of free love and the power of the muse, and celebrating the event with a very public party, Minnie left home and moved into his studio in the romantic Burnt District. She later told Tessa that the heady fumes of turpentine and paint must have besotted her and drugged her senses. There was uproar at the Institute and of course at home. Tessa and Billy had had Stanton Turlock tailed by a private eye who came back with the information that the painter had a double life. He was already married, and had a wife and children in San Francisco: money from Minnie's bank account was already being filtered off for the wife.

Billy O'Brien had Turlock, never reckoned wholly sane, it transpired, beaten up and locked away in a lunatic asylum, and Minnie was obliged to return home. She was ashamed, chastened and stunned by the extremity and rapidity of dramatic events, but told herself she had recovered from Stanton's betrayal quickly enough. It was the idea of Stanton Turlock she loved, not Stanton himself. Fortunately she had not fallen pregnant. But her reputation was lost amongst the decent families of Chicago, and her beloved father even forbade her to go on painting.

She'd come home to Prairie Avenue with a sex-inspired Monet-style flower-subject canvas tucked under her arm and Billy had just torn it to bits in front of her eyes. That had offended and upset her more than losing her lover and her 'reputation', for both of which she discovered she cared very little.

'I'm a practical man,' Billy had said. 'I don't blame you. You take after your mother. A girl on heat's no different than a sow on heat. She takes it where she finds it. Just stop this art shenanigan. I don't mind it in a gallery but it has no place in a decent Catholic home. Your mother wants grandchildren, and no one in this town is going to marry you. You'd best go abroad and buy yourself some toff who doesn't know your history. Your mother would like an outing. And a title in the family is good for business.'

Tessa was indeed happy enough to go on a European tour, to stay just around the corner from the Royal Academy where so many of Eyre's paintings were exhibited. There could be no harm in just looking, in reminding herself of the past, when she had been the kind of buxom blonde girl painters liked around, as bed companion, model, cook and laundress, preferably all at once. She had heard that he was still unmarried, there was no Mrs Crowe. There would be nothing untoward in her visit, no risking her own marriage; so many and so much depended upon it, Billy himself, her standing at the Art Institute of Chicago, charities all over the land, and there could be no upsetting any of it all.

But still it would be interesting to see *The Dinner Hour, Wigan,* of which she had seen a copy, painted in 1874 when Eyre had returned to England, and see whether the girl in the foreground was as like her in the original as it had been in the reproduction. She'd worked in the packing factories in Chicago when first she met Billy — well, that was not quite accurate. She'd met him in the burlesque theatre where she worked of an evening. He liked to watch but couldn't do. It didn't stop him loving her or she him. He'd had a nasty accident in the yards when he was a lad and would never have children. All his energies went into

197

making money. But he was always good for a cuddle and had even let her know that if she wanted his friend Murphy to sire a child, he would look the other way on one occasion and one occasion only. The occasion had arrived and in the same week, as it happened, had an impulsive encounter at the rather drunken opening of the Art Institute of Chicago with Mr Eyre. Minnie had arrived, and if the baby didn't look in the least like Murphy, Billy wasn't to know a thing like that.

Life never turned out the way you expected it. One way and another, it was quite a marvel Minnie had turned out as steady as she had, and with any luck another marvel was in store for the bog-Irish O'Briens when the girl ended up as Lady Minnie Dilberne, society beauty, in quaint old England.

'Besides, I don't think they let commoners marry in Westminster Abbey,' Minnie said.

'You wouldn't be a "commoner", you'd be a viscountess.'

'Only on the way out, not on the way in.'

'But you've been thinking about it?'

'Oh sure,' said Minnie, casually, as if it was nothing to anyone.

'So you like him? Really like him?'

'Ma, I scarcely know him. We spent one hour in the Victoria and Albert museum. Which is so impressive — do you know the Queen herself, whom no one ever sees, actually came to the opening? It is all very glorious. I am so in love with England. As for its native sons . . . I daresay one is much like another, and this one is good-looking and pleasant enough. Though all he can talk about is the number of birds he's killed, and steam automobiles, and what a disgrace it is that electricity is taking over from steam — or maybe he thinks that's a good thing, I don't remember; I didn't listen all the time. But then Pa can talk about nothing but hogs, sows, cattle and refrigeration cars, and you and he get on happily enough. One has to take men with a pinch of salt.'

'But I haven't got a brain, Minnie, and you have. You will be easily bored.' She looked at her daughter with sudden alarm. 'It's all very well dressing up and playing at Lords and Ladies, but you'd be such a long way from home. Supposing you were lonely.'

One thing to persuade a daughter to marry when you think she will not, quite another when you think she is likely to do it. She said as much to Minnie. Minnie should think long and hard about the man she married. Some women, these days, even chose to stay spinsters rather than put up with a man.

'But I thought you wanted grandchildren, Mama. And Papa is right, I blotted my book so badly no one I'd accept would accept me, for all my money. Even if I had stayed a good girl, there'd always have been too many like me on the market, and it is a market: Papa certainly thinks so. All my friends had declarations of love before they were twenty and I never had a single one.'

'You will say these clever things that put men off.'

'No, it is worse than that. I am perfectly good-looking but there is something about me just not very attractive to men, and I must face it. I don't know why, it's just like that.'

'I do. You look at men as if you judge them.'

'But I do judge them. What can they expect? They are not gods; they are just male human beings. How can I pretend otherwise? Stanton was the only one who ever said he loved me, and he was mad. Or so Father says, not to mention a whole team of alienists. What am I to make of that? No, I will do without love and marry suitably and please everyone. This young man seems totally suitable.'

Tessa sat down heavily. She burst into tears at the shock of it all, indeed she howled, so noisily that the chamber maid knocked on the door and asked if everything was all right. Minnie assured her everything was, and sent her away. She went over to her mother and embraced her.

'You just cannot be upset, Ma. This was what you wanted. You tell me time is running out for me and I am not likely to do any better. Arthur and I talked it over as we walked round the Serpentine. He was so bored in the museum I took pity on him and we agreed to go for a walk. The young Austrians stayed behind, they are so accustomed to being stiff and formal the museum seemed a garden of earthly delights to them. Arthur and I spoke freely. I like that about him. He says what he thinks. Few men do: if they did most women would run from the room screaming.'

Tessa gaped at her daughter. Minnie in England seemed a different person than the one she knew at home. The one in the USA was withdrawn, discrete and diffident, and had indeed attracted few beaux — partly because her father suspected every young man who came along to be a fortune-hunter and drove them all away — and partly because if her father didn't do that, she did,

201

wilfully or no. How Stanton, who it transpired had already spent months in a lunatic asylum suffering from an ailment called manic-depression — had succeeded where many had failed, Tessa could not imagine. This English Minnie had gone to the museum wearing an uncorseted gown which showed her ankles above her little buttoned boots, and if you looked at her from behind you could see the actual movement of her hips as she walked. It was very daring, and so very much in advance of anything that was done at home.

'In suiting others we suit ourselves,' said her daughter now, more blithely. 'Arthur's parents want him to marry someone rich, and I turn up. My parents want me married and settled down before I do something else dreadful, and he turns up. We are obviously made for each other. Fate has decreed it. He is taking me to Rotten Row on Saturday but the style of horse riding over here is very different — he warned me. He's quite a jolly man, really.'

Tessa smiled, and looked her daughter up and down. She saw everything that she had made, and, behold, it was very good.

'Whadd'ya know, Melinda,' she said. 'Well — whadd'ya know!'

A Proposal at Second Sight

1 p.m. Saturday, 4th November 1899
The outing had been more than diverting. Minnie hadn't felt so cheerful since the blow of discovering Stanton's deception, and the depths of it. The man who defied convention, who despised marriage as a bourgeois fantasy, was already married, had two children, and a history of insanity. She had vowed never to trust a man again, let alone love one. But now, on the banks of the Serpentine Lake in Hyde Park — how she loved London! — Arthur had wound a twig around her wedding finger and said, 'There, we are officially engaged.' Then they had pecked each other on the cheek.

'Are you serious?' she had asked.

'I am completely serious,' he said. 'It is time I got married. One has to look after the succession, you know. My mother has decided you will do, not least because you are a wealthy woman and know how to behave. Your family has decided I will do because I am a viscount, eventually to be an earl, not as good as a duke but certainly better than a baron. You will not interfere with my steam cars: I will not interfere with your little artistic sketches. Once we have achieved two sons, one for the title and one spare in case of illness and accident, we will both be free to go our own ways.'

'I must have time to think about this,' she said.

'You disappoint me. You seemed a woman of quick decision.'

'Oh very well,' she said. 'Let's do it. One could go further and fare worse.'

The expression on his face did not alter. He just blinked a little.

'We will wait three months before we announce the engagement,' he then said, 'for the sake of Society's reaction, and for the sake of the household, which would otherwise have hysterics. We must show some sign of developing passion between us. The servants like a show of true love. It makes the crops grow, according to a Scottish wiseacre called Frazer, as reported by my sister Rosina, who is very learned and goes to lots of lectures. Rosina is anxious that I get married to save her the necessity, though you may not be quite what she has in mind.

The harvest has been poor lately and though I doubt that our marriage will put an end to the depredations of Free Trade, it will cheer the estate workers no end.'

'I can see that is important,' she said. 'My father maintains that happy hogs are profitable hogs.'

'So over the next months I will pretend to woo you, and you will pretend to be doubtful about accepting me. Then you will capitulate, and we will declare our true love. We will tell no one, except possibly my sister Rosina, who you have not yet met, and loves a secret. She is very tall and more like a man than a woman. I hope she doesn't put you off. She is very advanced, and I advise you to disapprove of her views in front of my parents, especially my mother, though I have no idea whether you'll disapprove of them or not.'

'You are putting a great deal of trust in me,' said Minnie. 'My mother is very good-natured and loves to buy clothes and tease my father, but she doesn't take formalities very seriously. I imagine I will have to take many things very seriously if I am to be an adequate Lady of the Manor at Dilberne Court.'

'I will drive you down there soon so you can inspect it. We may have to take a chaperone. Perhaps we could find someone quieter than your mother? Though I have nothing against her; she seems a very jolly woman.'

'She is,' said Minnie, 'and as for a chaperone, please realize I am an American. In the new world, young women manage very well without being watched all the time.'

'I can see it would be more fun without one, though I am not sure that I approve. But there will be staff waiting for us at the other end. The place is Jacobean with all kinds of pompous bits added on through the centuries, but still really quite pretty, even quaint in a large kind of way — there are forty-five bedrooms — but not very comfortable. In becoming a viscountess you will sacrifice a great deal of comfort, and will have to live with a great many dreary family portraits. It will be hard work.'

If indeed Arthur did as he said, and drove her down to Dilberne Court, Minnie would know that he was serious. As it was she could not be completely sure. His voice had a slightly jeering quality, as if he were mocking her. American men spoke from the heart when they spoke to women. English men spoke as if through some emotional filter made of flannel: it was hard to know what they were really about.

'*I wish to preach, not the doctrine of ignoble ease,*' she quoted, '*but the doctrine of the strenuous life.* Theodore Roosevelt said that earlier this year. I met him at a reception after he spoke in Chicago. It was a wonderful speech, about the feminization of America. My father said it might be true in New York but it couldn't be said of Chicago.'

'Was he wearing yellow gloves?'

'I don't think so,' Minnie said, confused.

'We were guests at his wedding in St George's Hanover Square ten years or so ago. He was wearing yellow gloves. It was such a foggy day it was just as well. Mr Roosevelt's gloves were about all you could see in the church at all. I thought perhaps it was what all Americans wore to their weddings. But maybe it was just a safety measure because of the fog.'

'Oh you are dreadfully sharp,' she said, 'and cynical, and not at all what I'd thought Englishmen to be, but I like that. And so — we have friends in common in the person of Teddie Roosevelt.'

'And we have not had a single fog since you came to the country,' said Arthur. 'You must bring good cheer. I hope you paint bright cheerful scenes?'

'Landscapes, mostly,' she said. 'Wide plains and large skies. I daresay I will have to bring them down to English haystack level — your galleries are full of such paintings — when I become a proper English lady.'

'So long as you are not an impressionist,' he said, 'or you will make our fogs worse. In Oscar Wilde's estimation, it is art that created them in the first place, in particular the works of impressionist painters.'

'I know,' said Minnie. 'I think we will get on very well. Wilde talks about the wonderful brown fogs that come creeping down the streets, blurring the gas-lamps and changing the houses into monstrous shadows. The current climate of London can only be entirely due to this particular school of art.'

'Don't be deceived, Minnie. May I call you Minnie, not Miss O'Brien? You don't seem at all like a Miss O'Brien. I must warn you I am primarily an engines man. I only know about Wilde because Rosina made me come to a talk at the Slade where they were discussing a book called *Imitations of Art*. I yawned all the way through to make her angry, which she was.'

'But *Imitations of Art* was part of my course at the Institute too,' she said. She knew now was the moment to mention Stanton Turlock, but she did not. Time enough later.

'Obviously we were meant for each other,' he said. It was a pity that his voice still had its slightly facetious note. 'Here, let me try to kiss you, and you will pull away and I will look most upset, and so we will continue until it is time to declare our most practical and convenient troth.'

He bent to kiss her — her head came up to his shoulder — but she did not pull away. For his part he did not object or look upset but kissed her on the lips. His lips felt soft in the middle but quite hard and firm round the edges. Stanton Turlock's lips had been the other way round. She preferred Arthur's, which quite startled her. She had thought she would never fancy another man again. Not that Stanton had done much kissing or wooing. He proceeded straight to the point but with such conviction it had been impossible to resist. A gentle suitor would make a change.

'I quite look forward to marrying you,' she said. Were they joking, were they not?

'We might even fall in love,' he said. 'That would be most convenient. I do not deny that it would be better if you were one of us, obviously, but the ones of us available at the end of the season are quite unbearable to look at, and mostly rather poor. All the rich ones have been snapped up.'

'My father sent me to Europe to buy a husband and a title,' said Minnie, 'and he will pay generously. We get on very well, on the whole. His settlement will certainly be more than enough to pay off all your family debts. My mother can persuade my father to do anything. He worships the ground she walks upon. She wants grandchildren and would love them to have titles. They mean a lot in America. This is the kind of talk that is usually left to lawyers but shall we simply get on with it ourselves?'

'We already are,' he said, 'I appreciate it.' So since she was declaring her assets, she added that she also had a few hundred thousand dollars in a bank account in London, it suiting her father's tax arrangements to have her keep it there. 'I could always "borrow" from that if I had to, though I would rather not.'

She also suggested that since she was the only child, the sole heir to the O'Brien Meat Company, to have her as his wife would open up lines of credit for anyone who had the great name Dilberne — enough to buy new harvesting machinery to put their acres back into profit again, not to mention purchasing any number of steam cars, or electric, or even cars with internal combustion engines. She hoped that would compensate for the vulgar absurdity of the nature of her father's business.

He did not deny any of that, but merely remarked, 'There is no future in the combustion engine, unless we can figure out some better way of compressing the fuel — air mixture it requires. Even if it can be done, water is free and all around us: petroleum has to be refined and is expensive and there must be an end to digging it out of the earth.'

Then he observed that his mother might find having the O'Brien Meat Company in the family something to hide rather than celebrate, but he did not think his father would be anything other than heartily relieved.

'My father is very good at acquiring and spending money, just very bad at paying it back. I must admit I take after him. You will be quite horrified to hear about my tailor's bills.'

Then he took her hands in his — he had traces of black engine oil beneath his nails, just as Stanton always had green oil paint — and said that even if her father refused them a penny he might very well still marry her. Better an entertaining life than a dull one. 'Don't you agree?'

Minnie had found herself blushing. At the

beginning she had been vastly entertained by Stanton; in the end unkind people had forced her to look at the truth. He was a liar, a cheat and a betrayer, even a male nymphomaniac, and, according to her mother's doctor, suffered from a manic-depressive psychosis. Until he became violent she hadn't even noticed. She thought it better not to bring the subject up with Arthur. Young men could be very high-minded. They liked their wives to be virgins, and she liked Arthur.

'Oh yes, yes,' she said fervently. 'I have to confess that my real name is Melinda, but nobody calls me that.'

'I like it,' he said.

'Now, Mama,' Minnie said to her mother over the next morning's breakfast. 'I didn't mean to tell you all this and you are to keep it to yourself. People can be very strange. Tell no one yet that Arthur and I have already reached an agreement. Look how upset you were yesterday, for no real reason at all, other than that we were being practical, when it would have been nice if we were being romantic.'

Tessa said she wasn't one for keeping secrets; they seemed to speak themselves when she was around, but she could see the sense of it. She would keep mum. She asked how they had parted yesterday and Minnie said that Arthur had delivered her in a cab back to the hotel, and they had been careful to give the concierge, Mr Eddie, the impression that as a romance this was in its very early, merely friendly stage. She had offered Arthur a limp hand and he had touched it with his lips, through her gloves, in the most formal way.

'And did he suggest you meet up again?' asked Minnie's mother.

'We are to go riding together in Hyde Park in a week or so,' said Minnie, 'but he has to do some work on his automobile first.'

'Typical male,' said her mother. 'But I suppose that's better than nothing.'

A MATTER OF REPUTATION

5.15 p.m. Saturday, 4th November 1899
'Butter wouldn't melt in her mouth,' Mr Eddie had said in the lobby to the under-manager, gazing after Minnie's retreating back when she arrived back from her walk in the Park with Arthur. She'd been wearing an uncorseted red velvet gown from Liberty which followed the lines of her body, an unusual sight in a smart hotel like Brown's. More such dresses were to be seen in the Ritz, which catered for a younger crowd. 'Someone ought to warn that poor young man.'

To the outside world, Mr Eddie, red-faced and smiling and getting on for fifty, seemed the soul of good nature but was in truth a weary and resentful man, sending guests off as he did to shows he would never see, restaurants where he would never eat, delivering hot water bottles in the middle of the night to chilly maiden ladies, and expensive lady bed-companions for men who travelled alone. He passed on information about guests, mostly for money but occasionally on moral grounds. Mr Eddie had not yet had word from Grace to the effect that the O'Brien girl was to have her reputation protected.

Mr Eddie often thought how sensible it would be if only the chilly maidens and the rampant men could get together, but that was not how the world worked. Also, it would be very hard on his pocket. A hot water bottle went on the bill at two shillings with usually a sixpenny tip for him: a lady companion of really high quality could cost as much as twenty-five pounds for a short visit, fifty pounds for the night, and a fiver for him. Once he had been given a tenner, but the lady in question was indeed a lady, and did it for fun, not because it was her vulgar profession.

He liked Grace, whom he saw when she was about her Ladyship's various errands, delivering letters, presenting her card, welcoming her guests, collecting packages from abroad. They could share their discontent with so many of the inequitable ways of the modern world — the class system, the oppression of the proletariat and so on. He thought that one day he might ask her to marry him, though perhaps he was too old to change his ways. They could join their nest eggs together, buy a little house, and start their own household. But then they might start complaining about each other, instead of she about the other servants, or he the hotel guests. Best to leave things as they were. Occasionally he could persuade her to join him on the sofa in his office for the odd half-hour. She would take no money from him: she said she saw these sessions as fair exchange: it was not only men who had desires which must be satisfied. She was a strange one, too clever for him, but always welcome on his sofa.

When Grace called by, breathless, with a message for him to the effect that Minnie O'Brien's reputation was to be protected, he agreed to spread the news that she was pure as the driven snow, a virgin, but an enemy had spread rumours about her in Chicago, later discovered to be wholly untrue. These things were easily done. Grace was grateful and showed her gratitude in the usual way.

Arthur is Moved to Visit Flora

5.30 p.m. Saturday, 4th November 1899

Arthur had been well satisfied with his conversation with Minnie in the Park. They were two of a kind. She did not whinny and moan and flutter fans as girls were inclined to do when meeting a well set-up and eligible young man. She liked him well enough, as most girls did. She was probably fertile. With the Irish blood came many children. She was no prude, and almost eager when he kissed her. What a stroke of good luck. He had told his mother something would turn up and it had. They would marry, his tailor's bill would be paid, his parents would be pleased, and he would be able to pay Flora's rent without worrying whether his funds would suddenly dry up. The wretch Baum would be put in his place, his father freed from financial pressure. A pity about the Meat Company but it was not too high a price to pay to save the

217

family's face and fortune. He and Minnie would make their home in London, somewhere better than Belgrave Square, with more mews garaging.

The kiss had been interesting. He'd meant it just as a bit of acting but it had set off a spark between them before he had even touched her lips. Recalling it put him in mind of Flora. He would go and visit her, become part of her, drown in her. It was how a man relaxed. He was entitled. Sex set off a kind of creative energy in him; vaguely to do with the tightening of screws, the driving of pistons, the grinding of cog wheels; when it was finished with, new ideas were left in the detritus of experience. Get rid of the feminine and the masculine was set free to act.

He had not of course mentioned Flora's existence to Minnie. It really did not concern her now, and even after the marriage, if all went well, it still would not. 'Thou shalt not commit adultery' applied to other men's wives, not bad girls off the peg. That surely was what Moses meant, when he handed down the Commandments; sex with slave girls did not count as adultery for Abraham in the Bible, and Flora was to all intents and purposes a slave girl. One woman all your life, otherwise burn in hell?

It just did not make sense.

Nevertheless Arthur instructed Reginald to drop him off on the corner of Half Moon Place instead of at Flora's door. He was glad he had. There was a growler there already, its light off, and the driver waiting, trying to read a newspaper in the gloom of the gas lamp. Why? Flora had strict instructions to keep herself available from six to eight every evening: no visitors. Worse, monstrously worse, the yellow silk curtains of her bedroom on the top floor were closed and he could see the silhouette of a man and a woman. The man he had no doubt was Redbreast, and the girl was Flora, her hair down around her shoulders. They were not doing anything alarming, just standing talking, but that made him angrier still. What had they got to talk about? Yet Redbreast leaned towards her as if she fully engaged his attention.

'Little hussy,' said Reginald, sympathetically. 'Pretty little place this too, compared with many round here. Must cost a pretty penny. I hope you're not the one paying the rent if you're sharing. The police can get you for that these days. You'd be keeping a disorderly house. I blame Mr Gladstone. Shifty old bugger.'

'I am well aware of the law, Reginald,' said

Arthur stiffly, though this was the first he'd heard of it. It was not the kind of conversation one enjoyed having with a servant, no matter how useful and worldly wise that servant was. It was Reginald who had found him Flora in the first place, pointed out that the Half Moon Street flat was to rent.

'Sorry, sir,' said Reginald. 'It's just you have to be careful with the better girls like Flora, and your Flora's one of those. They promise things but you can't trust them out of your sight. Do you have a key?'

'I do, of course.'

'Then why don't you just go in, sir. Two can play at sharing.'

Arthur felt quite shocked when he worked out what Reginald was suggesting.

Though had not Flora suggested something more unusual than the missionary sex they had so far indulged in? If he paid for it? Knew how it worked? Well, he was already paying.

'I imagine the other gentleman is Mr Anthony Robin of the Foreign Office, sir. I recognize the growler.'

Arthur was hesitant. There was so much he knew he did not know. He had read *My Secret Life* at Oxford, but it was so long and densely written, grubby and vaguely disgusting, it quite put him off sex for a time. You had to work out the positions to make any sense of what was going on and there seemed no point. There had been Grace the housemaid when he was fourteen but she was hardly experimental, and Flora had never so far offered anything fancy. He felt both aggrieved and excited.

'If you ask me, she deserves what she gets,' said Reginald, so Arthur let himself in the front door, and ran up the narrow stairs he had paid for and found Redbreast standing by the bed he, Arthur, had paid for, and Flora whom he, Arthur, had paid for, naked upon it, wriggling on her white mink wrap, rosy legs stretched wide apart with wanton lack of modesty, and a length of pink silk between his rival's hands. It seemed he was about to tie one of her wrists to the brass bedstead. He had removed his jacket, but was otherwise fully clothed. His waistcoat was a sober-patterned damask.

Arthur was glad he had been to a proper school, as had Redbreast. Gentlemen knew how to deal with any social situation they happened to find themselves in, and how to surmount embarrassment. One kept one's cool and made a joke.

'I think this is my property, Redbreast,' he said. 'Perhaps there is some misunderstanding here?'

'Oh my dear good man!' said Robin. 'If it isn't Dillybutt! Of all people!' Arthur winced at the use of his nickname. He hadn't heard it for a good ten years.

'Don't tell me this lass has been misbehaving? Flora, have you?' Redbreast bent over her, the end of his old school tie tickling her breasts, so she wriggled and giggled the more.

'He promised to marry me and he let me down,' said Flora. 'I owe him nuffink.' She usually managed a proper 'nothing', but in what could only be a surfeit of guilt her pronunciation had reverted to its original.

She tried to slip off the bed but Redbreast caught her wrist and tied the silk scarf or whatever it was to the shiny brass rail so tightly she fell back on it, gave a little cry of alarm and quickly put her legs together.

'You promised, Dillybutt? Had you been drinking?'

'Indeed I had,' said Arthur. 'I would hardly have asked her sober. But since I pay well over the odds for exclusivity, old fellow, I can't quite work out what you're doing in my house?'

'Then you are not entitled, Flora,' said Redbreast, 'and must keep your side of the bargain. I too have paid over the odds.' Redbreast tied her other wrist to the bed, and though she tried now to keep them together, parted her legs forcibly.

'See to her ankles,' said Redbreast, speaking with the authority of a fag master, so Arthur felt he had no choice but to obey. He found what he thought must be the white silk belt Flora had been wearing at Pagani's and used it to grab the left ankle and tie it to the bedpost — she tried to kick out at him, but he got the leg caught soon enough — and used Redbreast's now discarded old school tie, black silk with blue diagonals, to secure the other ankle.

Flora did not seem too aggrieved by the process. She kept talking and imploring for mercy and occasionally giggling. 'A silent woman is above rubies,' said Redbreast. 'Be quiet.' And, surprisingly, she was — if briefly.

Life was very curious, thought Arthur. There was Minnie, with her discreet body, her quick mind, her formality, with whom one could have one kind of intimacy and this one, a plump rosy shape full of exits and entrances, which offered quite another.

The matter was settled amicably enough and to both their advantage. Redbreast had first happened upon Flora weeping in the park, claiming to be an unfortunate virgin abducted from school by the man she claimed had now 'let her down'. She needed funds to sue for breach of promise: then she took him home, explaining that the expensive flat had been borrowed from an actress friend until she had raised the necessary money. It wasn't as if she was a whore. She wasn't used goods, she claimed, on the contrary, she was good as new.

'She has quite a way with words,' Redbreast said. 'That almost put me off. One doesn't want to think of a brain working too hard behind that pretty face.'

Redbreast had agreed to pay Flora's rent, and ten pounds the hour on top of that. She brushed up well, he'd even taken her to Pagani's, and risked meeting anyone he knew. You'd never know from the look of her what kind of girl she was.

Neither of them wanted to lose her. They would simply share her, as she had tried to share them. She had started it. They agreed Redbreast would pay half the rent, from now on. Arthur would continue with the keep. Arthur must have the lion's share, for was he not paying more? Granted, from each according to his ability, to each according to his need, but it was still 70/30 in Arthur's favour. Things Arthur had thought not possible, Redbreast assured him, were.

'Oh no, no, please,' Flora moaned as

Redbreast delineated exactly where and how they would attend to her. Arthur remembered the word from *My Secret Life:* 'doodles', faintly ridiculous, were always going stiff, stiffer, failing, growing stiff again — as his was doing now — a source of anxiety as well as satisfaction, rubbing here, rubbing there, explosions and squirtings of juices and so on, mucky stuff, ridiculous and disgusting. But looking at Flora, he began to see the charm of it. Something, whatever it was, had to *happen.* Redbreast had his clothes off. His 'doodle' was magnificent, surprising for so lank and academic-looking a man. Flora seemed to regard it with admiration, even fear, but then so she had honoured Arthur's 'doodle' when first she saw it. Mind you, Arthur's was not bad, better than almost anyone in his House at Eton for his height.

While Flora cried for mercy and regularly moaned 'Ow, it hurts, have mercy, sirs, please don't,' and so on, and even managed a tear or two, she continued to offer herself, he noticed, by no means averse to sharing any of her attributes to amplify her pleasure. Really, these women were corrupt; they made beasts of men: he would only marry a virgin and make sure she knew nothing and never got to find out anything.

Why did one do this, he wondered, why was one driven to these slippery, mucky endeavours: the instinctive jerking and pumping, in and out, in and out, as if seeking out some vital centre that was so frustratingly elusive, and when you found it, ceased to be of any importance at all? It was an appetite like hunger, he supposed, that had to be satisfied if you were to live, and the same sort of unreasonable drive, just that this could only be honoured when it was employed to keep the race alive. Unlike food, which had dignity, elevated you, honoured you — a good *tournedos,* a delicate *soufflé Curaçao* — desire was designed to humiliate you by making you as low as the filthiest rutting beast; it made Flora mock the squealing of the sow as she was serviced, he and Robin mimic the stupid grunting of the boar as it did its business; yellow satin, pink gauze, white mink, scarlet damask, but still underlying it the sour black mud of the pigsty.

And why was he so glad to see that Redbreast's doodle, though stouter than his own, if not necessarily longer when fully extended, did not have such excellent staying power? Why did that make him want to crow like some cock? It was beyond all sense.

When the pair left, some three hours later, Reginald and Redbreast's driver were not only still patiently waiting, but, Arthur was sorry to see, in conversation; no doubt comparing the habits of their masters and betters. Well, it couldn't be helped. Boys would be boys, everyone knew.

Reginald was unnecessarily inquisitive and asked Arthur 'How it had gone', and Arthur said he thought the girl had learned her lesson — though in truth when he left he had the distinct impression Flora was laughing at him, and when he told her he and Mr Robin would be coming round for her attentions together every Saturday afternoon to get what they had paid for, and separately whenever they felt inclined, she seemed not too vexed at all. Girls were difficult to impress.

'I've known some of these girls take on six or seven at a time,' said Reginald, 'and not turn a hair. You say she was out with Mr Robin last night?'

'They turned up at Pagani's.'

'Did she, sir!' said Reginald.

'She can't possibly have known I'd be there,' said Arthur.

'Very few secrets in this town,' said Reginald. 'I reckon Grace and Mr Eddie have something going on. What's the betting your little friend was wearing a white mink stole? If she was, it's the one the girls pass round. Nothing like a jealous man to part with cash. She knew you'd turn up. How much more did she get out of you tonight?'

Arthur deliberately failed to answer. She'd got ten pounds more because he'd felt bad. He'd been a mug, that was the truth of it. Now he saw himself, not Flora, as the one who had been used and abused. Reginald, seeing the set of Arthur's jaw, prudently fell silent.

Arthur took a hot bath when he got home, and spent a long time in it. His father had recently installed copper pipes for running hot water and Arthur was glad of it. Otherwise Mrs Neville would have made a fuss having to fetch hot water from the kitchen while the staff was doing dinner, and been curious. He was not proud of what had happened. He wished it had not. But he looked forward to the next time he saw Flora, with or without Redbreast, and also of course to riding with Minnie O'Brien on Rotten Row. But he had the Arnold Jehu to see to first. He had missed dinner but Cook might find him some bread and cheese and then he might spend a little time in the garages with his real darling.

THE GIFT OF EQUAL STATUS

11.10 a.m. Tuesday, 7th November 1899
Tessa had arranged that she and Minnie
should go first to Belgrave Square to collect
Lady Isobel, and accompany her to her
dressmaker in Kensington. One way and
another things were progressing nicely.
Greater love hath no woman than to share
her dressmaker with another. Lady Isobel
was granting Tessa the gift of equal status.

'It's all very well, Mama,' said Minnie,
'but a whole day shopping! Perhaps I could
slip away after lunch and go to the National
Gallery! So many paintings I long to see.'

'I'm sure we have far better ones at home
in Chicago,' said Tessa. 'And no, there'll be
no slipping away. You just concentrate on
turning yourself into a future countess. See
how it's done.'

And Tessa tapped her rather plump foot
in its little, heeled crocodile shoe, rang for

the carriage, and without further discussion she and Minnie went shopping.

The Earl of Dilberne Contemplates the Future

11 a.m. Tuesday, 7th November 1899

It was a remarkably boring morning in the Lords, thought Robert. Dreary bills about electric power, dull debates about the various principles of inheritance in the Colonies. Lunch, though, was livelier. There was much animation about Ladysmith: it seemed things were not going too well, horse fever was rampant, the hills around the town were awash with fleeing refugees. Reports came escaped by heliograph and messenger — the Boers had cut the telegraph — that grown men, delicate ladies, children alike, were being herded into carts and shipped out of the area with little water and less food, carrying what pitiful possessions they had with them. Many Boers in all probability travelled with them, making their escape with the genuine refugees, to link up with their friends. Underground tunnels were being built where families

231

could shelter from weaponry, but they were dusty, dangerous and vermin-infested.

Rumour had it that the northern firm Armstrong Whitworth was selling the Maxim machine gun to both Boers and British forces — a claim Robert was able to dismiss. One thing to sell arms to both sides in the American Civil War, as had indeed occurred, but surely Armstrong was a fiercely patriotic man, and would never do anything to harm British citizens or their interests. The Maxims were coming from Sweden via Germany; Robert had it on good authority. That is to say, the Austrian Ambassador had let it slip.

News of the Modder Kloof mine disaster had spread through the House. There was much sympathy for Robert — 'just the kind of thing we're fighting these Dutch to prevent. To save the diamond and gold mines — our boys will get it back, don't worry.' The kind of thing the irritatingly bumptious young Winston Churchill had been saying the other month: no wonder he'd lost his election at Oldham to the Liberals — too brash, too moody, too warlike for the North, but determined not to give in and to stand again.

But something else Churchill had said in that conversation came back to him now, a sudden shaft of light cutting through into the sepulchre of a subdued House. Churchill, wide-eyed and excitable, animated rather than cast down by obstacles, had declared: 'The only way to make money is to spend money.'

'But you must have some, to spend it in the first place,' Robert had pointed out.

'Borrow it,' said the young man. 'Borrow more, make more. My late father's good friend Ernest Cassel could be helpful. You should meet him.'

'As it happens we are acquainted,' his Lordship observed, and added that his affairs were with Courtney and Baum. To which Winston had said, 'Then you're on the right road. My father was a great man for diamonds. Did him no harm. But in my view diamonds and gold are too risky: they *cause* wars. Best to choose something less sparkly, something that gets less attention. Manganese? Dull stuff, but mix it in with iron and mine flooding ceases to be a serious problem. The supports won't rust. If you can drain a mine you can save a mine.' He himself was sailing straight away for Capetown to report the new war for some newspaper. The new ease of communications — telegraph, telephone — was a boon to journalists. Imagination could flourish, feeding on immediate news and extremity of event. He would be back in time to take on Oldham again.

At lunch the Earl was nodded over to the powerful table for port and brandy, and discovered to his surprise that he was considered as an expert on the troubles in Natal. News travelled almost as fast in the House as it did at home. His voting against the Exportation of Arms Bill had marked him out as someone who at least had opinions on the matter. Having a view on Armstrong and Maxim guns had added to the general perception of Dilberne as a fount of knowledge.

Robert feared for his country if he was considered thus. Salisbury was an old man: his hands trembled as he took his glass. He forgot what he had just been told. His cabinet was still stuffed with lords, earls, viscounts, the odd marquess — most of them set in their ways, unable even to bring themselves to equip the army with Mausers or Maxims because they were repeater weapons and somehow ungentlemanly. One shot at a time was fair; more was too reliant on vulgar machinery, not valour. If one was to believe Churchill, the fight to crush the Boer was apparently more to protect the diamond and gold mines of the Natal than because the Boers were so unpleasant to the natives, which was the construction given to the public.

Well, the old chaps hadn't done much of a job protecting his mine.

The need was for a steady hand at a steady wicket, one that didn't tremble with age, as did Salisbury and his cronies, old tremblers all. Perhaps in a coming upheaval something in the War Office might come his way, or in the Colonial Office; bugger Fisheries. He must aim higher. He needed to. The rewards were more attractive. Times were hard when a man must pay more attention to his prospects than his integrity.

Young Miss Melinda O'Brien could have a very benign influence on his prospects. She was Irish, fine-featured and good-looking enough but with a name like hers presumably a Papist. The Irish Catholics were never renowned for intellect. Too many potatoes. Probably best, if Isobel's efforts with the O'Brien mother continued to bear fruit, and the O'Brien fortune ended up with Arthur, that Minnie could be persuaded to convert to Church of England. He wondered what his grandchildren would look like? Be like? Could a child inherit republican fervour? Young Churchill's brashness certainly seemed to have something to do with his American descent on his mother's side. Hadn't something gone wrong there — the expected dowry not come through: her father had reneged on the deal — had there been a bankruptcy?

If Isobel had her way, and Arthur did indeed marry Minnie, there was no absolute guarantee that the father would come up with the goods. Then what? Because Isobel's father had been generous when she married did not mean that Minnie O'Brien's fortune was certain. All the coal money had gone. Isobel was convinced he had lost it all gambling and horse racing, but the vast majority had been swallowed up by the estate, what with an outrageous tax at five pence in the pound, the price of land catastrophically descending, the impossibility of raising rent from tenants without ruining, starving them — forget profit from grain or livestock, so much was now imported from abroad. Gambling was a drop in the ocean; a necessary, useful relaxation.

There must be a way out. It was unfair to put pressure on young Arthur to marry where he didn't want to. Isobel could be ruthless. He would have a word with her.

The young whippersnapper Winston Churchill had said 'borrow the better to spend': probably that was the way forward.

He would call at Courtney and Baum's and spread oil on the waters: he had perhaps been rather peremptory with Baum — but who would not be, dragged from their bed so early in the morning? He hoped Isobel had sent an invitation to Mrs Baum. It was a regrettable reality that social acceptance could be used as a tactic to win friends and subvert enemies. Also, to calm those to whom one owed money. The bill for the first round of the copper central heating pipes was in — whole-house heating was not really an extravagance. One had a reputation to keep up. Freddie, Countess d'Asti had had her house in Eaton Place centrally heated: even the attics for the servants. Isobel would fidget until she had the same.

'Why so silent, Dilberne?' someone asked, startling him. 'Sorry to hear about your mine.'

Robert smiled. 'Couldn't get a word in edgeways,' he'd been thinking to himself; he was going over the conversation last month with the thick-skinned young Churchill. How he'd had the nerve to plonk himself down a table of the great and the good, and started entertaining perhaps not everyone, but those he cared about, with his war stories from India and Cuba: wherever there was blood and gore, there he seemed to have popped by. Now he moved on to the Battle of Omdurman in ninety-eight. A force of eight thousand of Kitchener's cavalry had been responsible for defeating a rabble of fifty thousand natives. Magnificent, as Churchill described it. Kitchener lost only forty-odd men, with less than four hundred other casualties, leaving ten thousand enemy dead and thirteen thousand wounded. It showed what well-trained cavalry could still do in a place like Africa, even when grossly outnumbered. All fine and good, Robert considered, except that now the cavalry horses in Ladysmith had been decimated by fever.

He was relieved when his bookmaker Fred had him called out of the House. Fred had some other tips for him for the St Anthony's Cup, the steeplechase at Newbury. Was his Lordship interested? Fred also mentioned that his Lordship's bill was running a little high, and perhaps he could see his way to meeting it in the near future, and his Lordship said of course, of course. The future was beginning to look clear, and altogether rosier. The day had turned from unlucky to lucky. He could feel it in his water.

THE FITTING OF THE DRESSES

12 noon Tuesday, 7th November 1899

It was two day after Arthur's visit to Flora, and the morning of his Lordship's sudden visit to Mr Baum, that her Ladyship and the O'Briens went touring the smartest dressmakers and milliners of London, spending money the former did not have, and the latter had in plenty.

'I'm sure we have just as good in Chicago, and far more becoming styles,' Tessa observed in Madame Pearl's, thus causing her daughter some embarrassment. Tessa had a bad habit of comparing her own city to London, always to the latter's disadvantage. 'Our trams don't rattle so, I'll swear,' she'd say. 'Our streets are cleaner, our horses are bigger, our buildings higher, and everything is so much newer and smarter.' It was a habit born of insecurity, Minnie could see, the kind of brashness that gave the Americans abroad such a bad reputation. Minnie had tried to warn Ma not to do it, and she did try and try, but kept forgetting. On this occasion she even apologized, saying, 'Oopsadaisy, sorry! It's just your hats are so big one could take off at the nearest puff of wind.'

'I dare say you have good reason to fear wind,' observed the Countess of Dilberne kindly. 'You come from the "Windy City", I believe.' She liked to show off her knowledge of transatlantic life.

The new Paris fashions were already in, and dominated the coming spring's styles: wide-brimmed and piled up with crushed velvet roses in glowing true-life colours. They were charming, and Minnie, generally bored by hats, was persuaded to try one on. Tucked away amongst the velvet extravaganza was a glittering cluster, of jewelled cabochons in malachite and turquoise. It was not Minnie's usual style: she preferred simplicity in the way she dressed, but when Tessa said 'My, Minnie, your young man would go for that, any man would,' Minnie actually blushed and said she'd have it. It cost twenty-five pounds, simply because of the jewels, and it was coyly half hidden amongst folds of lush fabric. That was just a single hat, and Tessa bought a couple of crimson grosgrain turbans for herself and

Minnie in case the wind caught up.

Isobel caught the blush and was glad. Arthur had been remarkably reticent about his walk in the park with Minnie, almost offhand, but had acknowledged 'She was all right,' he supposed, 'for an American', and he might take her riding in Hyde Park when he had time, as soon as he had fixed the Jehu so it was fit for a long drive. He forbade further questioning, and fixed his jaw in a way very reminiscent of his father, so she desisted. She was not displeased, but wished he would get on with it. Someone else might come along and snap the girl up.

Her Ladyship assured Tessa and Minnie that they simply must have new ball gowns — leg o' mutton sleeves were going out of fashion, bustles were simply not worn any more, the interest having moved up to above the waist, and tiny waists were vital if the curved silhouette was to be achieved. There would be balls between now and Christmas to dress for. Fredericka's Christmas party was famous for its showiness, though its guest list was not necessarily as exclusive as Isobel thought right. Writers and musicians were asked along: too many did not have a title and journalists from the society columns were in attendance. Freddie even held a kind of artistic salon every three months, for which she could obtain an invitation if Tessa cared to go along. Dress was remarkably free and easy: Tessa should perhaps have some tea gowns made up; she'd had her dressmaker create a very fetching one indeed for herself in a fine white lawn and pale pink lace, though she wouldn't herself wear such a thing outside her own home.

It was at Freddie's Christmas party three years ago that Robert had first met Mr Baum. That had not endeared the event to Isobel, on the contrary. Indeed, she had failed to add Mrs Baum to her guest list for her next 'At Home', as Robert had lately insisted, having got a glimpse of the address. Golders Green? Whoever had heard of the place? Some patch of ground outside central London proper, where once green fields had been, now muddy squalor as the property developers got hold of it? It did not augur well for an acquaintance! She supposed the new century was coming along and one couldn't cling too much to the old ways, but Mrs Baum was going rather far, and too fast.

She was not looking forward to her own charity dinner in the presence of the Prince of Wales, only just over a month away. It would put the whole household into turmoil. Royal guests always created tension.

Guests tried to impress or went too far the other way, and were aggressively nonchalant. It was at Robert's insistence that she had invited the Prince and Princess, reciprocating a previous invitation to dine at Marlborough House which they had taken up. To her dismay the Prince had accepted, though the Princess declined on the grounds that she was representing Her Majesty at the opening of a shipyard on the Tyne that very day. As an excuse it could scarcely be argued with, and at least gave Isobel more freedom when it came to the guest list, which was yet to be made final. She need exercise less tact, less care not to offend or provide a source of gossip.

What she would need to provide was a sprinkling of pretty girls around the table. They were easy enough to find in the Season but in November they were in shorter supply; so far Isobel had only been able to rally plain and dumpy ones.

Should she invite the O'Briens? The Prince would be delighted with Minnie, as he was with any pretty, cheerful, cultured girl, but he would find the mother loud and coarse — the kind of person one might expect to meet at the d'Astis', but hardly at the Dilberne's. Isobel resolved, nonetheless, to invite both mother and daughter. She liked Tessa. She was tired of obeying the proprieties. Doing the right thing, running the estate, living up to the Dilberne name, setting an example, giving royal dinner parties and balls, had done her no good in the end. She had been reared frugally, but at least without financial anxiety. These days, she could not help noticing, the bills that Mr Neville brought in on their silver tray for his Lordship to open, tended to stay unopened. Robert was like Arthur, with his general over-trust in providence, his Micawberish confidence that 'something would turn up'. As men got older their initial propensities and prejudices hardened: experience did not bring new insights, but merely reinforced the conclusions they had come to, sometimes misguidedly, when young.

Or could it be the case that it was the Prince's influence leading Robert astray? Relying on horses to win races or cards to be lucky, as the Prince did, in the words of her father Silas, buttered no parsnips. Where would it all end? Bankruptcy? It could happen, did happen. The humiliation would be unbearable.

But in the meanwhile she needed a new dinner gown for the seventeenth. She had almost nothing to wear that had not been seen at least once: Christmas and its festivities had not yet arrived, the spring fashions were in. She supposed she should economize, but what was the point? She would never outspend Robert. Or perhaps it would be prudent just to buy a new fan and be satisfied by that? God knew they were large and spectacular enough this season to dwarf any gown.

The three women went by appointment to a Court dressmaker in Bond Street, where sherry and petits fours were proffered as they chose fabrics and patterns, and made purchases.

'Moderation is the fatal thing: nothing succeeds like lavishness,' said the Countess of Dilberne, as Tessa ordered three dresses at eighty-five pounds each. Even she felt slightly awed at the meat baron's wife's lavish tastes. Isobel looked at some fans but found them unexciting in spite of their size, and ordered a dress with a decidedly Gibson Girl silhouette for the royal dinner. She was tired of looking established and staid.

'Never had your education, your Ladyship,' said Tessa O'Brien. She had been swigging rather than sipping the sherry. 'So take me as I am, just a bloody bogtrotter, left school at eleven, but not doing half bad for a girl who started half-naked in a burlesque show. Mind you, there was rather less of me then, but Billy doesn't seem to mind a bit, he likes me as I am.'

' "Nothing succeeds like excess",' said Minnie, rather quickly, for her Ladyship was looking quite startled. 'It's a quote from Oscar Wilde, Mama. A very smart but not very savoury Irishman, a writer who'd been in prison. We don't quote from him much in Chicago, as people do here.'

'I'm sorry for the poor man,' said her Ladyship. 'His plays did make me laugh, and we should not hold an artist's life against his work.' Which quite surprised and impressed Minnie.

The ball gowns once seen to, laced stays to keep the waist in then had to be bought from a shop devoted only to lingerie. Minnie thought the frankness of the window display rather remarkable, the length of bare leg displayed, though she said nothing out loud. Well, why not? A body was merely a body: she could not see it as a source of sin, though Puritans as well as Catholics saw it as such. For her part, Tessa, happily buying what was described as a lattice ribbon corset said she hadn't seen anything so indecent since her days in burlesque. Then there was the Italian, Fortuny, to visit for tea gowns; Minnie said she'd rather go for one of the new fluted and ruffled blouses with a plain skirt. As she had a naturally small waist she would try and do without the swan-bill corsets that the style normally required, and be able to move more comfortably and freely in her day-to-day life.

'She's quite the Gibson Girl is Minnie,' said Tessa. 'Quite the new woman, she thinks herself an equal of any man. Will your Arthur put up with it?'

'Really, Mother,' said Minnie, 'I think that after a single walk in the park, it is rather soon for me to understand what Arthur puts or does not put up with, or indeed to care.'

'I think my son will have a little trouble moving into the new century,' said her Ladyship, cautiously. 'His sister Rosina is a new woman and quite a powerful personality. But I fear Arthur prefers young women to be tractable rather than argumentative.'

Tessa said she had always found Minnie perfectly biddable, and chose a floating, flowing tea gown of finest printed silk with a tiny little pattern of gold and pink, held together at neck and wrist with strings of tiny shells.

'Very fancy, but when do I wear it?' Tessa moaned. 'What is a tea gown when it's at home? Is it for the bedroom? Holy Mary, it seems made for a man to get into, rather than for a decent woman to put on. All these pesky buttons and bows. And Minnie will never have the patience for them.'

'I must lend you Grace then,' said her Ladyship, 'to "unpesky" your dressing. Grace is my most excellent lady's maid. I will have her take a servant's room in Brown's, and attend to both your needs while you become accustomed to our ways. You can trust her to know what to wear and when to wear it. She will see to your hair, cope with the hotel staff, remind you of your appointments and make sure you get there on time. I shall manage very well without her for a day or two.'

Tessa, who had lived all her life without a lady's maid, was pleased enough to accept the offer, and further thrilled to receive Lady Isobel's invitation when they'd returned laden to Brown's — dinner with the Earl and the Countess of Dilberne in Belgrave Square in the presence of the Prince of Wales himself on Tuesday, December 17th.

'Oh, Minnie,' Tessa shrieked. 'Now it's dinner with Royalty. Play your cards nicely and this could always be your life. All this and a swanky London lady's maid too. If my friends could see me now!'

In the Servants' Hall

6 p.m. Tuesday, 7th November 1899

'The nerve of it,' said Grace. 'And they're neither of them any better than they ought to be, mother or daughter. Sending me off to Brown's like a paper parcel.'

'I thought you was a good friend of Mr Eddie's,' said Mr Neville.

'That's as may be,' said Grace, 'but it's not the point. I should at least have been given warning. I don't know what's got into her lately.'

'And I don't know what you've got against her Ladyship suddenly,' said Mrs Neville. 'One moment you're thick as thieves, the next you're all moans.'

'I've nothing whatsoever against her Ladyship, but I don't like to be taken for granted. And I don't want to see some wild American girl ending up as the Countess of Dilberne just because she's got money,' said Grace. 'If you give respect, you deserve respect.

249

But these days it's go here and go there, do this and then the other, without so much as a please or a thank you, and no respect at all.'

'Keep your hair on, Grace,' said Mrs Neville. 'If Miss Minnie is as bad as you say, Master Arthur will soon enough see through her.'

Reginald snorted and said Master Arthur had as much sense as a wire brush. Flora wasn't half giving him the runaround.

'Flora?' asked Smithers. 'Not that same Flora that was his Lordship's fancy piece a while back?'

'That's the one,' said Reginald, 'not that Master Arthur knows that, and not that he needs to know. Or her Ladyship for that matter. So obvious but she never noticed.'

'Nobody needs to know,' agreed Mr Neville sharply. 'We'll have no more talk like that.'

'Flora's doing nicely then,' said Elsie, 'for someone not quite so young as she used to be.'

'She is, but she's keeping nicely,' said Reginald. 'Bathes in asses' milk, I daresay.'

'Perhaps someone ought to tell the American girl,' said Elsie.

'I may,' said Grace. 'Or I may not. I'll think about it.'

'She ought to be grateful if there's another interest,' said Reginald. 'Otherwise Miss America will be worn out as an old rabbit within the week. I'm telling you. The things our Master Arthur gets up to . . .'

'Not in front of Lily, if you please, young man,' said Mr Neville.

It had taken only days and already the flower girl was plimming up and plumping out and beginning to look more half alive than half dead. Her nails were scrubbed, her scabs and rashes had vanished, and she now relished the daily baths that had at first made her shrink with fear of pneumonia. She managed a sweet and grateful smile as she swept up ashes and scrubbed pans. The staff regarded her with pride. She was their project and doing well. What would become of her they had no idea. They would keep her until either the mistress discovered she was feeding more staff than she knew about, and either then took her on as staff or ejected her, or Lily worked out some way of looking after herself. In the meanwhile she was happy enough with a mattress in the cupboard under the stairs next to the big black central heating boiler.

'She could always go to Miss Flora,' suggested Reginald. 'She'll be looking for a maid soon, the way things are going.'

But Mrs Neville said no girl once under her roof would be allowed to go to the bad in such a way.

HIS LORDSHIP STARTS A COMPANY

4 p.m. Tuesday, 7th November 1899

After his conversation with his bookmaker Robert took a cab down the Victoria Embankment and walked through to Lincoln's Inn. His journey was not wasted. Baum happened to be at his desk, in his rather small and pokey offices when his Lordship turned up without warning at the door. Baum welcomed Robert in, but without the somewhat fulsome obsequiousness he had come to expect. In putting himself out so obviously as to call in person, rather than summon the lawyer back to Belgrave Square, Robert feared he had perhaps made a mistake. If one showed the slightest sign of weakness people got above themselves.

Not for the first time his Lordship wondered how he had happened to get so involved with Baum, this no doubt clever but unpredictable person, who wrung his hands like a character out of Dickens, lent you large sums of money at the drop of a hat, and yet made you feel you were to blame for his misfortunes, when actually it was the other way round.

Baum, in spite of his protestations to the contrary, had scarcely made the risk involved in the Syndicate's Modder Kloof mine clear. The relationship between General Kruger of the Transvaal and the Boers of Natal was close, but no one had expected an outbreak of actual hostilities, let alone the possibility of actual sabotage. The might of the British Army had seemed so assured: the Boers by comparison a mere captious rabble. No doubt Baum had got a fair commission out of the deal: more than fair, no doubt. Well, there was no point in beating about the bush. An attack was always the best policy. He got straight to the point.

'Thought I'd drop by and see you, Baum,' he said. 'I'm not denying I owe you money, quite a lot of money. All the same I don't take it kindly when you threaten me with foreclosure in front of my family and on my own front steps. Gentlemen do not behave like that.'

Baum seemed taken aback at such plain speaking. He visibly quailed. The Earl of Dilberne took the view that Baum couldn't decide which way to jump. As it turned out, he apologized.

'If I spoke too peremptorily, sir, please excuse me,' Eric Baum said, with considerable dignity. 'Whatever may have been said was in the heat of the moment. Now, how can I help you today?' His Lordship adjusted himself to this development, and took his time; he gazed around the office with an affectation of purpose that was fairly convincing. Mr Baum had a female secretary, of which Robert vaguely disapproved, feeling that the presence of a woman in an office could not be conducive to efficient business, but she did bring tea and biscuits, and was a pretty enough lass.

'I have a strategy, Baum,' he said. 'Gold and diamonds are all very well, but they attract trouble. They speak of easy riches. There are other less spectacular valuables to be found underground, as, with your background, you will know very well.' And he waxed lyrical on the theme of the rich seams of coal to be found further North in the Limpopo. He had recently read reports in the House of Lords library as to the promise of these deposits. He knew the sort of thing to say: his father-in-law had been much involved setting up the Newcastle industry. 'That is most interesting,' said Mr Baum, 'but coal mines, like gold mines can get flooded, either by accident or design. It is too risky.'

'But mines can be drained,' said Robert. 'Time was when two weeks was the longest any mine could remain under water without being abandoned; wooden props disintegrate and weaken quickly under pressure; iron props corrode and rust. The mine, be it coal, diamonds or gold, collapses. But add manganese to iron and iron survives both water and pressure. So now let us mine for manganese as well as the rest. Then a flooding becomes not disaster, but inconvenience. The structure, once drained, remains sound. We have lost the Modder Kloof mine, but let it be the last one in all South Africa to go.'

Baum stared and said nothing for a while.

'I'd very much like you to join with me in this venture, Mr Baum,' said Robert. 'My name will carry weight with investors. We cannot be seen to run scared just because a few Dutch hotheads run wild. It is not patriotic.'

'Baum and Dilberne,' said Baum, speculatively.

'Dilberne and Baum,' said his Lordship. 'Rare earths, manganese, chromium. And copper. Progress is progress. A small local war will not stop the exploitation of the mineral wealth of the colonies. If our coal mines are also producing manganese others will be slow to notice. Others will need what we can sell them. Mr Baum, there are more uses for rare minerals in heaven and earth than are dreamt of in your philosophy.'

'I too saw Sarah Bernhardt play the Prince of Denmark earlier in the year. My wife insists on taking me to the theatre. She is very literary. That bit was near the beginning, before I nodded off.'

'Then we have something in common, Mr Baum. I too fell asleep.'

'We have just moved our address,' observed Mr Baum casually, though Robert detected a slight undercurrent of threat. 'Perhaps her Ladyship's invitation, which my wife expects, may have gone astray?'

'I will ask my wife to be sure that another one goes out at once, Mr Baum. She has been very busy. The Prince is coming to dinner in a week or so, but I have no doubt the numbers can be stretched.'

'Please thank the Countess indeed on my wife's behalf, sir. Thank you.' He paused. His Lordship nodded, and waited. 'You are suggesting I go in with you on this business deal? You assume I will lend you yet more money in order that I, with you, can develop a plethora of mines across South Africa?'

'I couldn't put it more clearly myself,' said Robert, blithely.

'I should, I think, put the matter to Sir Ernest Cassel. There is a lot of money involved.'

'I would be thoroughly obliged,' said Robert, unsure as to whether Baum was referring more to the projected venture, or to his own existing debt.

'My wife,' said Mr Baum, 'would be charmed to meet the Prince.'

It was a pity, thought Robert, that his new partner had no idea at all how to behave. But there you were: the new century was coming in a very few weeks. It would bring any number of horrors with it. Arthur would in time have to deal with the new world. He trusted that the boy was better armed to face it than he, who had been formed by the old world, could hope to be.

'But naturally, she must meet him!' said Robert. 'His Highness too loves a visit to the theatre. They can talk about *Hamlet*.'

'I don't think that is necessary,' said Mr Baum. 'It would be enough for her to be in the same room.'

And they left the subject, while Robert wondered how on earth he could save the Prince from Mr and Mrs Baum, who probably had had to shave her head upon marriage and wear a wig. Isobel was always slightly reluctant to host a dinner for the Prince of Wales in any case: she claimed royalty bought with it a great deal of nervous exhaustion, extra staff, and extreme care in seating. Robert knew the Prince preferred a good shoot, or a day at the races to a ball or a dinner, and when in London he'd just as soon go to a club in the company of a few friends until the early hours, and thence depart on his own for more clandestine adventures. But he was not averse to a good dinner and had been known to summon Cook and congratulate her on her culinary skill; no wonder he was so popular with the people. The common touch, it was described. He noticed detail. His energy was formidable: his friends, including Robert, were for the most part always glad to get home to their wives and their own beds. He gazed at the mottled bark of a leafless plane tree outside the window. It looked leprous in the fading light. To be a Prince, or the friend of a Prince in any century was always a tricky business. These days the violence of hostility was metaphorical rather than literal, delivered by newspapers or angry husbands, not hard steel, red-hot pokers up the posterior, or butts of Malmsey wine, but it was always there, waiting. Human nature did not change, and the mob was always in the wings, ready to slit your throat or flood your mine.

'Thank you for your visit, my Lord,' said Mr Baum, and went on to say that there was a great deal of paperwork to be done, capital to be raised, others would need to be involved, but that he thought it quite possible that Sir Ernest Cassel would take a positive view. 'Your initial debt could well be, shall we say, *subsumed,* into this future project of ours. It would not, however, be proper for me to represent both our interests so I will ask Mr Courtney to look after yours.'

The enigmatic Mr Courtney of Courtney and Baum proved to be a respectable-looking City gentleman in his mid-sixties, with a splendid moustache and an unnerving resemblance to the late Mr Gladstone, which Robert held mildly against him — Mr Gladstone having been a Liberal: but he could see the irrationality of damning a man simply on the grounds of his facial 'brush'. Mr Courtney asked whether the Countess would want to be involved in the scheme and his Lordship said very much so, at which Baum said, 'Her Ladyship to my knowledge has a very good business head. By no means always the case with women.

260

You are most fortunate, sir, in your wife.'
Robert found this to be rather impertinent,
but then so much about Mr Baum was, that
one more offence scarcely mattered.

The setting sun emerged from a cloud and
its rays made the dull mahogany of Baum's
desk gleam. The sense of a weight being
lifted, which Robert had only known with
half his mind to be there, caught him by
surprise.

Mr Courtney left, and Eric Baum and the
Earl talked casually about the St Anthony's
Cup at Newbury, about which Mr Baum
was surprisingly knowledgeable. Robert had
not seen Baum as a racing man, but at least,
if as now seemed inevitable, he would have
to be introduced to the Prince, they could
talk about horses. Heaven knew what Mrs
Baum would have to say to anyone. Mr
Baum wished his Lordship well in his flutter.

'By the way,' said Mr Baum, 'I had notification from Coutts that the rent you're paying for the Half Moon Street flat has been
increased.'

His Lordship looked blank.

'Viscount Arthur's tenancy,' Mr Baum
said.

'Flora!' exclaimed his Lordship. 'Good
God, is that still going on? I don't think

Tessa O'Brien is going to appreciate that.'

Tessa O'Brien, his Lordship explained, was an American, and the mother of a very pleasant young lady, and there was some hope that she and his son would have a future together.

' "Stockyard" O'Brien from Chicago?' asked Mr Baum.

'The very one,' said his Lordship.

'Well done,' said Mr Baum. 'I certainly have to hand it to you, my Lord, one way and another.'

GRACE AT BROWN'S

Wednesday 8th November onwards, 1899
Grace, at her Ladyship's pleasure, had been
loaned — 'as if I was some slave' — to the
O'Briens, with instructions to help the pair
with the intricate niceties of dress and
custom in London's high society. She had
been installed, at Tessa's insistence, not in
the servants' quarters of Brown's, in the attic rooms, but in a real, if smallish, guest's
room down the corridor from the O'Brien's
suite, complete with fruit, flowers, choco-
late, cleaned twice daily by the chamber
maid and supplied with unlimited fresh dry
towels.

In the beginning Grace had gone down to
meals in the hotel staff dining room, where
the servants' food was a lot worse than it
was in Belgrave Square. Within a couple of
days she felt bolder, and dared to ring for
room service. She loved the Club Sandwiches, a new invention from the United

States, a whole seven course meal pressed between two pieces of bread — chicken, beef, ham, turkey, tomatoes, salad and fruit chutney — taking up only one plate.

This luxurious living, instead of impressing her, made her restless and annoyed. A box spring mattress could only be so soft, linen so crisp and white, apricot jam so delectable. There must be an end to indulgence? And how did it happen that the idle rich managed to live so well and do so little except spend? She had become accustomed to escorting Rosina to the many meetings where political and social indignations of one kind or another were expressed, and when Mr Eddie asked if she would join him in an outing to the International Working-men's Association — which now accepted women — she had no hesitation in accepting. She found herself soothed by the thought of the inevitability of revolution amongst the masses, the certain victory of the working man and woman. But she could see that though hotel staff could well be organized into strike action to hasten the day when the proletariat could take over the means of production, there would be a difficulty in getting domestic staff to revolt. At No. 17 they were too well-fed, and too busy bickering and gossiping to worry about long working hours and low pay.

In the meantime, Grace did what she was employed to do as perfectly as she could. She would teach Tessa and Minnie how to dress and behave. Barnardo's children's home had instilled in her long ago the need to fulfil her obligations and live each day as if her last.

'To sweep a room as for Thy cause makes that and th'action fine', she had sung at least once a week for all her young life, and the message had sunk in. There was virtue in servitude. God dealt you cards at birth — your looks, your wealth, your status — and it was your duty to play them as best you could.

For a week there was no sign of the rumoured invitation from Master Arthur. Grace was both relieved and not surprised. Minnie was so unlike the girls Master Arthur normally favoured, neat and refined, rather than full of body, lips and bosom (as she, Grace had been fifteen years ago; no longer now, alas, thanks to late nights, early mornings, cold attics and the passage of time) that he would see no more of the girl than civility required. He would stand out against his mother's wishes easily enough. He was not one to woo where he was not inclined. And very possibly he had been told about Minnie's past, and realized she was not a fit branch for the Hedleigh family tree.

Her task as lady's maid to Mrs O'Brien ('just call me Tessa, dear') and Miss Minnie ('do drop the "Miss", Grace. I'm just Minnie') was not onerous: they preferred to do their own dressing and coiffing: Miss Minnie would go off unchaperoned about London, spending time at the art exhibitions at the Foundling Hospital and the Victoria and Albert Museum while her mother had fittings at the dressmakers, beauty treatments in Bond Street and spent money, which she clearly liked to do. Offered a choice between the most expensive and the not so expensive, Mrs O'Brien unthinkingly chose the former. Miss Minnie used more discretion. She was beginning to be quite attached to Miss Minnie. A pity about her past.

Minnie's Odd Ideas

11.30 a.m. Saturday, 11th November 1899

'You know,' Minnie said to her mother, a week to the day since her walk in the park with Arthur, 'it is all very well and very enjoyable to spend one's life having one's clothes fitted and spending money on them while others wear rags but I fear it will merely draw the revolution nearer.' They had left their hotel room to scour the stores for yet more filmy chiffon tea gowns Tessa could take home as gifts for her friends. Elegant home gowns from Marshall Field's back home and even occasionally from Sears Roebuck were all very well, but even Tessa had to admit they lacked the fanciful quality of what could be found in London.

'Just you keep your wicked radical ideas to yourself,' said Tessa. 'Grace wore the prettiest little hat yesterday. Quite cheap and plain but it kept out the rain which was more than mine did, and quite a few men glanced after her.'

'You mean she could always sell herself if she had to.'

'I suppose so dear, yes.'

'Conspicuous consumption is the mark of the unfree servant,' said Minnie and her mother groaned and asked her not to start.

'You read too many books,' she complained. Minnie said it was her mother's fault because she had booked them on the *Oceanic* on the trip over and there had been nothing to do but use the library. You couldn't look out of portholes; there were just big round, modern electric lights where they were meant to be.

'The sooner you're married and settled the better,' said Tessa. 'Before you turn into some cranky old maid. Aren't you looking forward to going shopping? Have they found something wrong with it? All you thinking young women are such goshdarned wet blankets.'

'The *Oceanic*'s library had all the latest books, naturally. I was reading Veblen's *Theory of the Leisure Class.* But the library was only for first class passengers. Four hundred of us. The thousand in steerage were not allowed in. Doesn't it seem strange to you that those who need to read most are not allowed to read?'

'Not in the least,' said Tessa. 'The poor things would only dirty the pages with their grubby fingers.'

'Mr Veblen talks about women's dress as a burden placed upon them by men, to bring order to the confused and transient social structure of a highly organized industrial community.'

'Spare me,' said her mother. But Minnie would not.

'It has never occurred to me before,' she said, 'that women wear corsets and white gloves to show the world that they need not scrub floors,' she said. 'But it's true. Fashion renders you helpless. High heels and hobble skirts stop you running, corsets stop you breathing, and hats stop you seeing. The more fashionable you are the more helpless you are. A man hangs you with jewellery to show you off as a possession. In the modern civilized scheme of life the woman is still the economic dependant of the man.'

'Cuss that boring library and Mr Vabberlin too,' said Tessa. 'All he wants is for everyone to have nothing and look miserable. Don't let your young Arthur get a whiff of these fine new opinions or he'll be off like a shot. A man likes a girl to dress well.'

'I'm afraid my young Arthur is already off

like a shot,' said Minnie. 'A full week and I haven't heard a word.'

'Oh, that's why you're so darned cranky,' said her mother. 'Don't you worry. He'll be back when he thinks you've missed him enough. Any time now, I'd say.'

'Anyway,' said Minnie, 'a woman can't be forever wondering what a man thinks or doesn't think.'

'Oh yes she can,' said Tessa firmly. 'What else is there to do? I'd best wire your father for more money. Things are so dear over here. Back home a girl gets proper value for what she spends.'

When they got back to the hotel, there was a card from Arthur asking Minnie if she'd go riding with him on Saturday.

MINNIE PREPARES TO GO RIDING

In the Morning, Saturday, 18th November 1899

Minnie was in such a good humour the next morning that Grace, who had been thinking it might be as good a plan to tell Miss Minnie about Master Arthur's carry-on with Flora, as to tell Master Arthur about Miss Minnie's scandalous carry-on with a married madman, did not have the heart to do it. A ride in Rotten Row, she told herself, was as likely to put them off each other as put them on. Minnie looked too delicate to be much of a rider and would have no idea how to conduct herself with the formality required on the Row.

Her practical concern now was that Minnie had neglected to pack her riding habit, and there was no time to purchase a new one, let alone fit and alter it by Saturday. So Grace walked all the way over to Belgrave Square in the hope of borrowing one from

Miss Rosina.

Rosina rarely rode, seeing riding as demeaning to dumb animals, though she looked extremely handsome in her habit. It would be a good enough fit for Minnie. When laced, Rosina had the same twenty-two-inch waist as Minnie, though unlaced Rosina's was a good three inches more. The habit consisted of a very nice tailored jacket in grey twill with a flared skirt, silk-lined, smart waistcoat, gaiters which made the most of dainty feet and a jaunty and very modern bowler hat.

Rosina was happy enough to lend the costume out. Grace presumed upon the almost-friendship she managed at times with Rosina to ask her what she thought Master Arthur's motives were in relation to the O'Brien girl.

'Viscount Arthur's motives? Arthur has no motives. He has no brain. Not even enough to successfully marry for money,' Rosina snapped. She was in a hurry, as so often, on her way to a meeting of the Fabian Society in Essex Hall just off the Strand, and not interested in pursuing the line of conversation. She was having to go without Grace as an escort, and that put her out. Grace tried, in passing, to persuade Miss Rosina to wear a corseted dress if she was going out alone in the crowds, but failed.

'They're only Fabians,' Rosina said. 'They wear sandals and socks and never trim their beards. They talk a lot about the Life Force and Free Love but are far too nervous to do anything about it. I will be perfectly safe. Far safer than you will ever be amongst your revolutionaries, properly done up and corseted though you are, and with not an inch of flesh showing.'

'I have an escort in Mr Eddie,' said Grace, proudly, and was pleased when Rosina darted an almost friendly smile at her in response.

Miss Rosina was not so bad. At least lately she had taken to feeding Pappagallo on Brazil nuts and not oily pine nuts, so that the peevish creature left a less messy trail behind it as it half-flew, half-hopped with its clipped wings about Miss Rosina's rooms. When both Miss Rosina and her Ladyship were safely out of the house Lily would be sent to clean up after the creature. She was proving really useful.

It seemed to Rosina unfair on first principles that, of the two of them, Arthur would succeed to the title and the estates. She was the elder child, but the younger male took precedence and would inherit the lot, whereas she was obviously the more competent. One day she would raise the matter at a meeting of the Fabians. They fought for social justice, and surely the equality of the sexes should be amongst their aims; they shouldn't only be interested in the betterment of the poor. It took courage to stand up and speak in public — one's voice squeaked and rose in pitch when one was nervous — but one day she would manage.

Mind you, her voice could be no squeakier than that of Mr H.G. Wells of whom everyone took an inordinate amount of notice, but whom she found rather disappointing to meet, he being rather smaller than one had supposed. He had an interesting gift for stirring up trouble, she'd observed. She'd been to a talk by him about his novel *The War of the Worlds.* He'd suggested that the cruel Martians with their invincible fighting machines were perhaps the human beings of the future, when human brains had outstripped all of their other organs, and that technology was the path to victory. It seemed reasonable enough to her, but various religious groups, both the Quakers, who were pacifists and the Catholics, who were anti-evolutionists, had been loud in protest. Blows were exchanged. Grace had had to hurry her out before things grew nasty, and Rosina, annoyed by her persistence, had failed to give her the usual five-shilling tip. She quite liked Grace and sometimes she had stimulating things to say; she liked to think that she, Rosina, had helped educate her, but Grace had to remember she was a servant.

WARM TOES IN GOLDERS GREEN

7.50 a.m. Thursday, 16th November 1899

The smart new bronze-plated letterbox made its customary clack and Naomi ran in her stockinged feet to see what the postman had brought. The carpet — newly fitted, three-ply Australian wool, a beautiful dark red with a light olive scroll decoration, was thick and soft beneath her toes. The whole house was warmed by the best and slimmest grey iron radiators available. Eric had spared no cost. There was no invitation amongst the letters but Naomi now had the feeling that one day soon it would come.

She was suddenly feeling more cheerful, at last, she imagined, recovering from the death of her mother, becoming accustomed to the peace and quiet of the suburbs. The children's noses no longer ran. The necks of their shirts were not grimed with dirt after a couple of hours' wear. Their faces had smoothed out and their cheeks glowed. The carpets were in and the builders almost gone. She had a lovely home. The streets outside were being paved and the mud would soon be under control. The street even had a name. The plates had just gone up. Hampstead Way. A few more Jewish families were known to be moving in. The local butcher had agreed to sell kosher meat, and she didn't have to schlep the children all the way to St John's Wood to buy it. Eric was generous with the house-keeping: if she wanted something she asked for it and the money to do it would be there.

Her beautiful built-in wardrobes were filling up with dresses; she had a beaver coat. She had a very pleasant *shiksa* girl to live-in, so that on Saturdays the life of the household need not stop. Her husband loved her. She knew she was lucky. So her student life was behind her, and her dreams of being a famous scientist, another Marie Curie, were at an end. But how else could it have gone? A woman had to choose between children and a scientific calling. And what kind of woman would she be if she denied Eric a family?

It troubled her that Eric now so seldom went to the synagogue with her on Saturdays. Change the rituals and you weakened the faith that had kept the Jews together through the centuries. The argument, which you heard mostly from men, not women, that the rules could be relaxed, that some of the customs and rituals that went with desert life could be altered to fit in with an age of automobiles and machinery did not impress her. Sometimes she felt Eric was quite capable of denying his faith altogether, allowing himself to be subsumed into gentile society altogether. Well, she would not let that happen.

If only she had an *entrée* into High Society she need not lament the past, but could be part of a brighter life. It had to be faced that nothing about Golders Green glittered. What was the point of a beaver coat if there was nowhere to be seen wearing it? By lunchtime Naomi was feeling discontented again; she wanted to be free of the feeling that the centrifuge of life had whisked her up and flung her round and landed her abandoned on the outskirts of existence and there she would remain for ever.

When he came home that night, she waxed quite lyrical to Eric, who looked at her with his gentle eyes and said he was doing his best. She wanted her invitation to Belgrave Square, to the charity dinner on December 17th where the Prince of Wales himself would be present. She had seen it announced in *The Times.* Eric had told her it was on its way. But he had told her the same, as she reminded him, about an invitation to a glamorous charity function that had been and gone and no invitation. Until this next invitation turned up she would not keep Eric out of her bed, which would be failing in her wifely duty, but she would take care not to enjoy it when he was.

Minnie Asserts her Rights

2 p.m. Thursday, 16th November 1899

Minnie, presented with Rosina's riding habit, borrowed by Grace for the occasion, expressed her admiration, for it was indeed splendid, both jaunty and exquisite, but refused to wear the skirt, and demanded jodhpurs.

'I hope you don't mean to sit astride,' said Grace, aghast.

'I most surely do,' said Minnie. 'Side-saddle at a gallop isn't safe. Do you want me to break my neck and die?' Minnie sometimes thought Grace might want exactly that. It wasn't that she said anything at all out of turn, but the *way* Grace spoke left Minnie in no doubt but that she disapproved of her. She hoped the secrets of her past had not travelled with her. It was not impossible. 'No, Miss Minnie,' said Grace. 'I want you to sit side-saddle, take the air at no more than a gentle trot, and not bring mockery down on the house of Hedleigh.'

'Oh very well then,' said Minnie kindly, respecting her judgement. 'If you insist. But why are you all so frightened of bodies over here? Everybody has one!'

Grace thought, and said that when she was small a kindly family had taken her in and that when she had taken her weekly bath she'd had to do so in a sort of tent so as not to get sight of her own body, and once she had been caught peeking, and been beaten so hard she had never forgotten it. Minnie said she had been sent to a convent and the same thing had happened to her but she could never think about bodies as the nuns thought of them, or of not using them as nature suggested.

'When I was fifteen,' said Minnie, 'and on one of my father's ranches, I stayed on a bucking steer for four whole seconds before I fell off.'

Grace looked horrified. But Minnie seized her by the hands and whirled the maid around the room, crying 'Oh Grace, Grace, Grace, forgive me for being me. Really you know I can't help it.' Which did actually evoke a little smile of sympathy in Grace. However irritating the 'Yankee' girl was, she had the gift of saying what she felt, a rare thing in Grace's experience. Upstairs was too refined: in the basement, the wrong side of the green baize door, all was a peculiar blend of prudery and rudery. She suffered from it too, she knew. She wasn't like Rosina: she couldn't loosen herself from her own background.

But Grace blenched when Minnie then told her to unpick the seams and draw out the whalebones with which the riding jacket made a mono-bosom of her chest. Grace stopped smiling. The girl seemed determined to exhibit her body as nature made it, not as garments rendered it decent. It was as though she had the instincts of a whore, but without the excuse of needing money to survive.

RIDING IN ROTTEN ROW

11 a.m. Saturday, 18th November 1899

Rotten Row was not the morass of deliquescing mud Minnie had somehow expected, but a handsome, broad, sanded thoroughfare, like an avenued racecourse, along the Knightsbridge side of Hyde Park. There had been a violent gale the night before and any last leaves had finally left the trees.

Arthur went riding in a top hat, which Minnie found rather strange. At home people used horses for getting about rather than for showing off their best clothes. They just wore flat caps to keep their heads warm or wide brimmed hats to keep the sun off. But Arthur looked good, she granted, in a top hat: the formality suited him, for on occasion he could look too boyish, spontaneous and floppy-haired for his own good. This afternoon he certainly looked like a man. For the first time she was slightly in awe of him, and when he laid an elegant grey-gloved hand on her arm and smiled, she felt gratified and flattered. Last time she'd been with him there had been engine oil beneath his nails: there probably still was, but what you didn't see you needn't dwell on.

Her father's broad, reddened hands were often ingrained with dirt, no matter how her mother nagged him and oiled them. He was a cattleman and proud of it, wealthy beyond his own belief, but changed in any way because of it? No sir, not at all. Or so he presented himself. He shook hands with presidents, but wouldn't think of wearing gloves to do so. Her mother's hands too were broad and big, and these days puffy as well: she thanked her own good fortune that this particular inheritance had passed her by, so that the hand that now Arthur pressed to his lips in greeting, was small, long-fingered and in all manner elegant. Minnie did not wear gloves — how could you get the feel of reins, let alone your mount, through gloves? Arthur's were grey suede, fashionable no doubt, but would be the devil to keep clean.

Minnie felt of a sudden at a loss to know what to say to him. She had no brothers, her father was mostly too busy to be anything but remote, and she had been well chaperoned, until her sudden wild flight with Stanton. His discourse could be strange and sometimes irrational, but certainly did not amount to small talk. And in this country, she had quickly learned, polite small talk was valued. Few addressed subjects head on, from the weather to fashion, to the difference between country and town, or one country and another. Only yesterday conversation with Arthur had flowed so well: today, as it became self conscious, it faltered.

'If you don't know what to say to a man,' Tessa had told Minnie often enough, 'ask him a question. Then they can feel less of an eejit than you because they know the answer. Just don't ask him something he doesn't know. He'll hate you for it.' Minnie took the risk.

'Why is it called Rotten Row,' she asked. 'What's the matter with it?'

Arthur raised his eyebrows and complained that she was a stranger from a strange land — which in this country seemed something of an insult — and she replied that from where she sat in her saddle his land was a lot stranger than hers. It's just older, he said, a lot older. Rotten Row had been named *Route du Roi* two hundred

285

years ago when William of Orange had it cleared and lit as a safe route for him to get to Whitehall, and vulgar tongues had reduced it to a crude phonetic parody in the intervening years.

'That was back when your land was still inhabited only by buffaloes and Red Indians,' he remarked, and she didn't bother to deny it, wondering why he seemed so set on condescending to her about her supposedly 'colonial' character. She had an intuition that perhaps something had happened since she last saw him to change his mind about her desirability. What, though? Or perhaps he was just tired.

Arthur was in truth feeling a little exhausted. He had been staying up late in the garage seeing to the Jehu's new condenser, which was to his own design. This had involved borrowing a set of blacksmith's tools from the stables — forge, anvil, grinding machine, drills, ratchets, files and so on. He had only stopped for outings to Flora, sometimes accompanied by Redbreast, sometimes not. Today he was still slightly dazed by last night's encounter, but on the other hand invigorated by a world full of new possibilities, new excitements. Marriage to Minnie was still desirable, but only if it did not mean giving up Flora. His bride, for her part, would have to come to accept the unspoken mores and imperatives of the well-born English. He would behave honourably towards Minnie, of course he would; she would provide the Hedleighs not just with a new heir to carry on their name and create a new Dilberne, and fresh generations of children out of new breeding stock, but the life of his senses would remain his own. Intimacy with Minnie would be to do with the procreation of children, as the Church decreed, and a higher and better thing set apart.

Arthur could see that he should perhaps bring the subject up — as the Prince of Wales, to all accounts, had brought it up with Princess Alexandra before their marriage — out of simple respect for Minnie's intelligence, but now was hardly the time. He had too recently been in Flora's bed to think clearly, let alone to work out how best to introduce the subject tactfully. Perhaps a mention of the Princess's acceptance, indeed friendship, with some of her husband's mistresses, would work well? He had an idea that the Americans, for all their apparent frankness and vulgarity, were more Mrs Grundyish, more prone to moral disapproval, than was reasonable. But there was plenty of time before he had to deal with that.

He gasped a little as the silk of his shirt caught his shoulders where Flora's nails had torn the skin. The pain was pleasure as well. These were worlds far beyond Minnie's comprehension. He thought perhaps he could go back and see Flora in the evening. On the other hand a short sleep would be extremely restorative.

'You must understand that you are perfectly at liberty to change your mind about our getting married,' she was saying. 'I found our conversation the other day most exhilarating, and very un-American, and I will never forget it, but we may not have been in our right minds.'

He liked the way she spoke to him in this direct manner. He said he was as sane today as he had been two weeks ago, or was ever likely to be, and they would carry on the courtship as planned, and then announce it in a month or two. And he was pleased when she dimpled and looked happy. Flora had all kind of expressions, but a straight-forward look of happiness did not seem to be amongst them. When you offered her money the look of lasciviousness would increase and the aggrieved air decrease, and her limbs arrange themselves perhaps in a more accessible way, but it was not happiness for its own sake.

Minnie was looking very neat and chaste, he thought, in her perky little bowler, and perfectly suitable for a Dilberne wife. He would have to settle down one day and good wife material was hard to come by. She seemed efficient, competent and clear-headed, qualities which were necessary for her part in running the estate. He was rather vague as to what his mother actually contributed to the running of the estate, other than she paid visits to villagers, kept an eye on the sick and afflicted, and had started a school. Another reason, he suspected, why Isobel preferred life in Belgrave Square to that at Dilberne Court. Country life could be quite tedious for a woman, especially if she were not keen on horses, as his mother was not, and did not hunt. He was glad to see that Minnie was good on a horse. He had arranged a quiet mount for her.

As for Minnie, she realized that away from the constraints of everyday life, it seemed a girl could develop a great recklessness. What was she doing? This was not how most respectable courtships proceeded, slowly and cautiously. But she certainly did not want to go back to Chicago where Stanton lived with his wife, and she, Minnie, was an object of scandal. Even her new art teacher at the Chicago Institute, who had encouraged her, and talked so much of free love and the life force, had begun to look her up and down in a most speculative way, and wanted to paint her in the nude, so she had felt obliged to stop attending. She might as well have had a scarlet letter 'A' painted on her forehead.

The art schools in London actually encouraged women to paint and make it their profession; best to choose this perfectly amiable young man, whom she really rather liked, and her mother approved, and her father would if her mother told him to, and be done with it. She would end up with a title and no doubt a big wedding, even if not in Westminster Abbey — where she'd heard only royalty could marry — and have better-trained servants than they ever had in Chicago, and the fashions in London were so much better than at home. And the food over here — the Brown's breakfast was a joy, and the dinner at Pagani's had a *finesse* she'd never encountered anywhere: even in the new Silversmith's in Chicago the steaks were thick and bloody and the size of a plate, with sauerkraut on the side. And here in England there was culture. Everything had its history; even a riding track called Rotten Row was once a king's back yard. Her children would be part of all this, not of the mean, lace-curtain culture of the Irish in America. And she could study at the Royal Academy, or at the Slade. The Dilbernes would hardly object to that. And Paris would not be so far away.

Arthur's mount was a very elegant, nervy racehorse with a Russian name which his father didn't know he had borrowed. Arthur's father had been at the House of Lords deciding the fate of the nation, so apparently had not been around to ask. Otherwise of course Arthur would have sought permission.

It was decidedly a cut above all the other mounts on the Row this afternoon, they ranging from the scraggy and starving to the fat and waddling, it not apparently being 'the season'.

'Pater's been at the House a great deal this season.'

Pater. The upper classes all knew Latin as much as English, especially the men. And 'season' was a word that came up a lot.

'What season?' asked Minnie. 'I thought that was for the debutantes, when they are presented to the Queen. The one I just missed. There was a lovely sketch in the *Graphic.* So much flowing white silk, so many diamonds. It was one of the reasons I wanted to come, even though they said all the most marriageable bachelors had been snapped up.'

'The shooting season, silly,' said Arthur, and pointed out that most of the guns were currently in the country shooting birds, and most of the smart people were out of town. By rights he too should be in Hampshire at this time of year, but he had more than enough to occupy him in town at the moment. What was occupying him, she wondered? It was not as if he seemed to 'do' anything. In America men had jobs. They thought it was normal to work and earn. Here it seemed enough to be 'a gentleman'.

But Minnie hoped he was referring to her, and the suspicion that he wasn't caused a sudden unexpected pain in her heart, which unsettled her. If she was to marry this young man, she had thought yesterday, it would be simply as a sort of refined trade — coldly: his title and way of life in return for her money — the idea that she might suffer emotionally, as she had when she parted with Stanton the artist quite frightened her. But it was rather too late to worry. She *wanted* to marry him, stranger in a strange land though she realized she was.

She was being foolish, no doubt about it. She had stayed awake all the precious night

292

in a romantic haze, dreaming about living in a stately home with the Earl of Dilberne, one day to be the Countess, and in the dream coolness had ended up as passionate love. The detail of their lovemaking, visualized when half asleep, was much like the lovemaking she had engaged in with Stanton Turlock. Indeed, in her half sleep he and Arthur merged into one. She'd sat up in bed, wide awake and shocked at herself.

She could see her mother's point: if girls remained virgins their judgement would stay unclouded as to whom, and when they should marry. Of course it was a serious decision. Your husband decided your social milieu, your income and your friends, not to mention your children, so you had better get it right. No use envisaging divorce. To get divorced in the States you could at least claim mental cruelty: not here. Here if you weren't a good wife in the eyes of the law not even his adultery would get you out of it — and here if you left him he kept the children. Perhaps she would never ever be able to see things clearly again.

If just wondering what he did when he was not with her caused her pain she was a pretty contemptible case. If thinking about him made her think of Stanton naked in bed with her, her cause was lost. In her dream there were all kinds of things a man and woman could get to do with each other, if only you found a man prepared to experiment. But how, if you did not sleep with him in advance would you know what it was like? The cult of virginity was a nonsense. Again, she shocked herself. This young man with the floppy hair and the top hat could not possibly be, as it were, approached before marriage. 'Bad girl, bad girl,' she found herself saying to herself under her breath, in much the same way as she said to her little dog back home, 'Good boy, good boy'. If so many people in Chicago saw her as a bad girl and she didn't much care, it suggested they were right. That was what she was. Not that 'badness' was anything which necessarily barred you from joining the English aristocracy so far as Minnie could see.

All the same they wouldn't want their noses rubbed in it. She hoped gossip from Chicago didn't follow her. Her father had paid enough to try and ensure it didn't. Yet Grace seemed in her attitude to know something: did 'bad-girl-ness' show in the face? Could it so?

Minnie was seated side-saddle, in her skirts, in obedience to Grace and on a rather placid, slow beast with too thin a neck, and going at a gentle trot. Arthur bobbed up and down beside her on Agripin, a handsome bay. He told her all about the horse's ancestry and that his father had won him from the Prince of Wales in a wager, as if she should be impressed. Minnie was used to riding a Morgan, and bareback if necessary. It was not so great a skill. If you could stay on an unbroken ranch horse for half a minute you could do pretty much anything on a horse. Here on Rotten Row she and Arthur rode sedately together. Conversation remained a little stiff. Dull, dull, dull.

She asked Arthur what his pater did in the Lords. Arthur said he was not sure, but he had of late become exercised about Ladysmith where a gold mine in which he had interests had been flooded. Apparently there was a war going on in South Africa, which Minnie knew nothing about. Arthur enlightened her. But then there was a war going on between America and the Spanish in the Philippines which Arthur knew nothing about, so Minnie enlightened him on that.

'I don't think girls should bother themselves about wars and politics,' he said. He seemed put out that she should know something he didn't. Had not her mother warned her — better she'd stayed quiet or just talked about fashion plates and dia-monds?

Minnie could bear the sense of formality no longer. She reined in her horse, dis-mounted, unstrapped the saddle with ac-customed hands and tossed it to the ground, where it sank and all but disappeared into drifts of old leaves. She leapt back on the horse, and sitting astride, kicked in her heels and galloped off all the way to the Serpen-tine Road. It was most unladylike, and caused quite a stir amongst the onlookers. One or two riders had found energy and space to break into canter, but a full gallop had seemed impossible. Arthur found him-self quite stirred at the sight; wild girl on a wild horse. By the time she returned it was raining and the fabric of her riding jacket clung closely to her figure and showed it to advantage. Half the size of Flora's, true, but more elegantly shaped.

GRACE AND TESSA GO SHOPPING

2.30 p.m. Saturday, 18th November 1899
'I never was a quitter,' said Tessa to Grace.
'A little rain ain't goin' to scare me off.'

No matter how adroitly Grace held the umbrella Tessa's head bobbed about so that its spokes threatened to catch the feathers of her new hat. It was a very beautiful hat, wide-brimmed in a deep brown felt, an orange velvet band round the crown and a green bird of paradise curling around it, rather spoiled by the freckly and plump double-chinned face beneath, it would have looked better on the finer-featured daughter. Grace's own black bonnet was getting drenched and would need re-blocking when they got back to the hotel. It had a fetching simplicity, and quite suited her: she had had a few admiring glances herself from young male passers-by.

Grace felt quite skittish. She had stopped by Mr Eddie's office for half an hour early that morning, and had quite enjoyed it. There being nothing to gain from the encounter — she was for once not after lists for Lady Isobel or the Countess d'Asti, who had daughters to marry off — Grace felt less whore-like and more like a decent woman, and able to laugh quite genuinely at Mr Eddie's jokes. Ah, the uses of leisure!

Now she and Tessa were 'doing the shops', as Tessa put it, up and down Bond Street, charging through the grand emporia in a determined and exhaustive way. Reginald, on loan from her Ladyship, was following them in the cabriolet, to receive the plunder when the stores brought out their packages and samples. Grace would have been perfectly willing to lug them round the corner to Brown's herself, but Mrs O'Brien would have none of that. She insisted on treating Grace as her equal and Grace found it extremely bothersome, to use Tessa's own word.

Grace privately thought Tessa must be a little mad. The more she saw of her the more it was clear that the English aristocracy would be better off without any influx of bog-Irish blood. Mrs O'Brien's feet swelled with the heat, and she took insufficient care to conceal them when she lifted her skirt hem away from the mud and horse droppings. Or else she forgot to lift them at all. When they got back to the hotel Grace would have a fine time brushing the hems to make them fit to be worn. When the Countess returned from an excursion there was seldom any brushing to be done. Her Ladyship was fastidious, Mrs O'Brien was simply not.

'I beg your pardon?' asked Grace. 'Quidder?'

'I guess that means you don't understand what I'm saying, and want me to say it again, though why you ask my pardon for it I'm sure I don't know. I wish you'd all just speak the King's English and we'd get on better. A quitter is someone who gives up too easily.'

Grace murmured something to the effect that she hoped Mrs O'Brien had remembered about the d'Asti salon the next day.

'Lawks a mussy,' Tessa said. 'I forgot all about it.'

'Her Ladyship very kindly obtained an invitation for you,' said Grace, 'and it would be quite impolite for you not to be there. I fear it will be a rather mixed group of guests. I hear the Prince of Wales may deign to call by, though I'd have thought it was a little louche even for his tastes.'

'All I ever hear is the Prince of Wales here

and the Prince of Wales there,' complained Tessa. 'Back home they call him Dirty Bertie.'

'If I might make so bold as to mention it,' said Grace, irked at this description of the Prince by an outsider, ' "Lawks a mussy" is not an expression in common usage in Society.'

'You mean it's servants' speech?'

'Scullery maids, perhaps. Not parlour maids.'

'I heard it at the music hall over here,' said Tessa, 'and I'll use it when I goldarned choose. It's short for "Lord have mercy" and I sure do hope he will. Put that in your pipe and smoke it, Miss Prim and Proper.'

Grace lapsed into silence, until Tessa took it into her head to poke her in her ribs, and say,

'I forgive you, thousands wouldn't. So you can darn well forgive me.'

Grace actually managed a smile, and said Mrs O'Brien would need to decide on a tea gown; she would lay out a selection for her to choose from in the morning, and no, it was not the kind of occasion one needed to wear a tiara.

'One does not wear tiaras in the daytime,' Grace explained.

'Not even in the presence of royalty?'

Tessa sounded disappointed.

'No,' said Grace firmly. 'One might go as far as an unobtrusive silver band for the head, I dare say, flat, and very much fili-greed, with a diamond or two inset. Asprey's have some very pretty ones, just in from the Orient.'

Grace had an understanding with Asprey's, the Bond Street jewellers, as indeed did Mr Eddie: a small financial consideration for every customer they intro-duced.

'Minnie could wear something like that,' said Tessa.

'Unmarried women only wear diamonds if they are inherited,' said Grace, alarmed. 'Otherwise people will think the worst.'

'Let them think what they like,' said Tessa, going stomping off in the direction of Asprey's, followed by Grace with the um-brella. Mrs O'Brien's energy was phenom-enal. No doubt she ate a good deal of meat, considering her husband's business. Grace imagined, and certainly hoped, that the young people's Rotten Row outing had been rained off; forget the girl's fortune, the O'Brien name could only sully that of the Hedleighs. No amount of money, surely, was worth that!

But it was the timepieces in the window

of Asprey's that now attracted Tessa's attention. She seemed bent on buying one of their jewel-encrusted gold pocket watches and chains for Billy, to replace the plain but useful railway watch he swore by, but then changed her mind, turned on her heel and hailed Reginald.

'Thank the heavens above,' murmured Grace to Reginald, 'she's seen sense. We're going to go back to the hotel. She'll need a mustard bath for those feet. Her ankles are like balloons.'

But Mrs O'Brien had not seen sense. On the contrary. She demanded they be taken to the Royal Academy in Burlington House at Piccadilly. She and Grace were to go in; Reginald was to wait.

'It'll be closed, ma'am,' protested Grace. Sadly, it was not.

Tessa presented herself to the Curator, who had been about to go home, and who seemed shocked by the sudden presence of this large noisy woman from Chicago with a spectacular hat who insisted that she must be taken to see a painting by a friend of hers, Eyre Crowe.

The curator knew Crowe as a quiet, rather reclusive man with whom he occasionally dined informally at his studio in Charlotte Street. They moved in the same artistic circles. In the Curator's opinion Crowe was in, as it were, the First Eleven of painters, but his work was popular with the public, who much appreciated a large canvas when it told a story. Mr Crowe was unmarried, was looked after by a very homely house-keeper, and had certainly never made mention of any 'friend' of the kind who now presented herself. The Curator could see that, take away the florid colour, the stout waist, the plump cheeks and the over-elaborate hat, Mrs O'Brien would once have been a startlingly attractive woman of the fleshy kind. She wasn't demanding to meet Eyre Crowe, merely to look at a painting of his. But why? It was possible she was an art lover, but it seemed unlikely.

'The Academy is just closing for the day, madam,' he said. 'My assistant will be pleased to welcome you tomorrow. I, alas, will be in Brighton.'

'You won't get rid of me as easily as all that,' she said, 'not Tessa O'Brien from Chicago. I've surely come a long way for this. Thought I would, thought I wouldn't, plumped in the end for hold-your-nose-and-jump. I was looking at these timepieces, and I thought life's short and Billy O'Brien won't mind. It's only a blamed picture! *The Dinner Hour, Wigan,* please, mister, and I won't keep you too long.'

Tessa O'Brien? O'Brien? Where had he heard and marvelled at that name on official paper? Of course, one of the founders of the Art Institute of Chicago, that rather vulgar symptom of America's compulsion to establish some kind of cultural background for itself: and full of fakes, he had heard. This was what was thrown up, the crude ostentation of the new as it faced the artistic emptiness of its past. The curator considered that he had perhaps misjudged the circumstance. This was not what he had at first feared. Stockyard O'Brien's wife could indeed be more interested in the painting than the painter. Mr Crowe might yet be saved from the monstrous hat with the green and yellow bird of paradise curled around the crown, little pink beak poking out from amongst its poor dead feathers. The painting could suffer its attendance unaffected.

Then the thirtyish person who accompanied Mrs O'Brien, and seemed an altogether different and more demure type, wearing a pretty plain black bonnet under which wet hair showed interjected, 'Madam is from the United States of America, sir.'

To which Mrs O'Brien said, 'Lord save us, Grace! He knows that. This nice gentleman is delighted to take us where we want to go.'

Which, indeed, he did. Mrs O'Brien, he could see, was not accustomed to impediment to her will. Though the younger woman, who turned out to be her servant and companion, chafed and fretted about the need to get back to the hotel and 'get on'.

They made their way up the great staircase with its broad flat steps, then to the top floor of what started out as Lord Burlington's town palace, where some of the silk that had lined the walls for a couple of hundred years or so was now faded and even split in places, Mrs O'Brien remarked:

'But why do you dear English like everything so darned old and faded? Everything about my Institute that can be is new. And every bit as big as yours, and I guess bigger. That silk needs replacing.'

Grace winced. The curator said nothing, until they passed James Whistler's portrait of Eyre Crowe, which the Curator found a rather murky piece of work, almost ghostly, as if poor Crowe's very existence was in doubt. The curator preferred sharper lines and more convincing colours, and had spent many years fighting against hanging Mr Whistler's work at all: there was a meretricious quality to the work he had disliked. Whistler remained un-English, intrinsically foreign: he had spent too much time in Paris, let alone other places abroad no one had ever heard of, picking up a louche amorality.

It was against his better judgement that the Curator drew Mrs O'Brien's attention to the painting as they passed, and the noisiness of her response exceeded his fears — it echoed through the vaulted ceilings and drew a caretaker who was waiting to switch off the lights to see what was going on.

'Holy Mary Mother of God,' Mrs O'Brien cried. 'I didn't know about this one. And by Mr Whistler too. Eyre's right up in the world! Grace, would you say there was a little of Minnie in those eyes? Just look at the eyebrows — look at the shape of them!'

Then she clutched the younger woman's arm and said, 'Golly, what have I said! I didn't say a word. You didn't hear a thing, Grace,' but she neither seemed unduly upset, nor came back to the subject. She was too determined to get to see *The Dinner Hour, Wigan.* Her little plump feet went faster and faster up the stairs, the imposing Whistler portrait of Crowe left behind. The curator sighed, forbearing to point out that the Eyre Crowe in the portrait was a different Eyre Crowe, the diplomat, not the painter. People saw what they wanted to see.

But why *The Dinner Hour, Wigan* anyway? Was this not a very curious request? It was an unattractive subject, as various critics had remarked: a group of young women, Lancashire mill girls, gathered together eating in the street. But Eyre was always attracted by misfortune for a subject, a painter moved by moral as well as artistic principle, which was why the Academy, quite reasonably, housed so many of his works, in spite of the critics.

Mrs O'Brien plonked herself down in front of the painting and stared.

'A masterpiece,' she said. 'No doubt about it. Sure as eggs is eggs. It's as my friend Eleanor said. She saw it when she was over last fall. And she's right: that's me.' And she pointed to one of the tall figures in the foreground, a tall blonde girl with ample bosom, in a white cotton dress and her hair in a net, basket in hand, bending to the left with her girl companion, as though about to fall, but resting on a stone bench. There could be a certain lack of care in Crowe's paintings: he was often better at brickwork than the human figure. It was quite possible, the Curator could see, that Crowe had done a portrait of the young Mrs O'Brien, working perhaps from a photograph.

'He remembered me,' she said, simply. 'He didn't forget.' The curator suddenly liked her. He admired her tenacity, the immediacy of her folly. She was not to blame for her nationality, her breeding, or her lack of it. If it wasn't for the energy of people like Stockyard Billy and his good wife, America would never find any culture. For all one knew, the flow of art across the Atlantic might eventually be in the other direction. It could certainly make up in size for what it lacked in sensibility.

'All nicely cleaned up,' observed Tessa. 'In my experience working girls are a lot muckier than that. But then he always was a romantic, was Mr Crowe. I reckon we Yanks are a good deal better than you folk at keeping our feet on the ground.'

Mrs O'Brien was certainly not stupid, he thought. He was quite coming round to her. He liked a woman who could take in a painting at a glance and not feel obliged to stand for ever and admire. Perhaps he would encounter her again. She was turning to go when she hesitated, and then asked if he could kindly give her an address for Eyre.

It seemed to the Curator that colour drained from the maid's face. Or perhaps it was just the caretaker, turning off lights

308

other than the ones immediately near them, anxious to leave and get home to his tea, as who was not?

'Dear lady, I could not formally divulge such information about an Academician without consulting him first,' said the Curator, and beamed at her in a way that he hoped was disarming.

He wondered whether he should tell Eyre of this sudden visitation or not, deciding on balance against it. The woman could dispense patronage, but Eyre guarded his privacy, and the woman was at best a lionizer. And he himself wanted no sudden disruption to the quiet dinners *á deux* at the Charlotte Street studio. She might never leave his friend alone.

'Have it your own way,' said Tessa, 'probably just as well,' and she walked off without so much as a by-your-leave, head held high, footsteps echoing firmly and bleakly down the long high galleries, and then down the central staircase, pausing for a second again at the Whistler portrait, and then out of view. The maid followed meekly. She seemed defeated. He hoped for their sakes the rain had stopped.

Some Things, Once Said . . .

4 p.m. Sunday, 19th November 1899

'She is a nice girl, much more amiable than Rosina, and I don't mind the mother so very much,' said Isobel. 'I think dear Arthur is quite taken with little Minnie, and she with him. He came back from Rotten Row quite pink and glowing, not in the least sullen. It might almost become a love match.' She and Robert were sipping sherry. They had taken themselves early to bed, though feeling well enough. For once there was no lady's maid to observe them, which they saw as freedom, and no rags in her Ladyship's hair to make her sleeping uncomfortable, Grace having been temporarily exiled to Brown's to 'do' for Mrs O'Brien and her girl. Grace had made it clear that she had taken offence, as she did often enough, though seldom letting the exact cause of her displeasure be known. The lower classes were woefully prone to taking offence, as those with the obligations that went with a privileged background were not. Perhaps Rosina would raise the matter at one of her Socialist meetings, thinking she was doing society a favour. 'Sulking staff as a weapon of class oppression.'

'She's a lively shopper and keeps us all laughing with her quaint ways,' continued Isobel, of Mrs O'Brien. 'She is certainly no lady, but why should one expect someone from Chicago who lets one know she started in "burlesque" know how to behave? What exactly does "burlesque" involve, Robert? She spoke of it with a certain pride.'

Robert explained that it was a kind of vulgar theatre, when girls kicked their legs in the air, sang rather raucous songs, and married the best they could and Isobel observed that for a Dilberne wife to have such a mother was probably worse than to have a father who started life as coal miner, as hers had been.

'Very much worse,' said Robert. 'Trade has quite lost its stigma.' And he remarked that to have a cowboy in the bloodline at least gave Minnie O'Brien a certain transatlantic glamour.

'Grace tells me Mr O'Brien was no cowboy, but started out slaving in a Chicago slaughter house, up to his elbows in blood and bone,' said Isobel. According to Grace's perception, she said, the land of the free and home of the brave was a myth, the continent was peopled by tinkers from the bogs fleeing from famine, prepared to blow you up with dynamite as soon as look at you. Grace for one was very much against an American wife at Dilberne Court, according to her principles.

'We must bear in mind,' said Isobel, 'how important it is that servants respect their betters who employ them, if the anarchists are not to sweep away all order and its supporting tradition. It is our responsibility. Remember what happened at Greenwich.'

'The bomb was intended for France,' said Robert, uneasily. But no one could be sure of that. In 1894, an anarchist had blown himself up at the Greenwich Observatory for reasons no one could quite fathom, other than that he was part of an anarchist cell in London, and terrorist attacks in France and Russia had become almost common occurrences. That such a thing should happen in pacific London was almost beyond belief. France was another matter. The Paris Commune was less than thirty years ago.

'The girl looks fine textured enough,' said Robert. 'The triumph of nurture over nature, I suppose. Good nutrition and a few elocution lessons can make all the difference.'

'That is certainly one's hope,' said Isobel. 'Just add some good Christian values and even Africa will soon catch up.'

Robert frowned. It was the kind of casual remark she made from time to time which he wished she wouldn't, and so did many of her friends, taking their lead from the Marlborough set, where power and Society sat round the same table, and affected a kind of callous frivolity. Women were at their best and most charming if they reserved their comments for what they knew about.

Now, knowing that differing from Robert in her opinions often led to trouble, Isobel feared she had gone too far. Financial difficulties preyed on his mind and made him prone to outbursts of anger. To give voice to a political opinion which diverged from your husband's was hardly conducive to domestic tranquility, especially when they involved sexual matters. She quickly brought the subject back to the family.

'I really think we have the beginnings of a love match between Arthur and Minnie,' Isobel said. 'He says he wants to take her down to Dilberne Court and show her the estate. And I thought he only cared for machinery.'

'It doesn't sound like the Arthur I know,' said his Lordship. 'Perhaps he is trying to make Flora jealous.'

'Flora?' said Isobel, sitting upright in the bed as if to be better prepared for something worse to come. Robert always had someone or something up his sleeve. 'So I am right?'

'Oh, Arthur most certainly has a Flora. He is a young man and the sap rises. This particular Flora has aspirations to being a courtesan, but I fear she is little better than a common trollop. Though she dresses very agreeably. She was the one at Pagani's the other night with a contemporary of Arthur's. It quite put the poor boy out. He was hardly paying attention.'

'I was not aware that anything was wrong,' said Isobel.

'A boy has to do something while he waits for marriage.'

'Whatever it is, it can't go on after the marriage,' said Isobel. 'I won't have that. I hope Arthur realizes that. You must speak to him.'

Robert felt fortified by this sudden and definite response from Isobel. What sane man wants his wife to be too much of a free thinker? Having Rosina in his household was penance enough. If his wife and his

314

daughter did not get on too smoothly together, it sometimes troubled him that it might be because they were too alike. But really the generations were very different. Girls these days aspired to be little intellectuals: Isobel's generation, especially in the North where the population was more dyed in the wool, still assumed that too much thinking was actually harmful for the female mind. Mental exhaustion could lead to brain fever. Bluestockings were pitied: they would never be content with their female lot in life. Isobel had been moulded to devote her intelligence to running a household, choosing clothes and selecting menus. Errant thoughts might break through, but at least she did not go to meetings and try to change the world, as Rosina did.

'So like what Her Majesty is forever saying to the Prince,' Robert remarked. 'To his eternal irritation. "It can't go on after marriage". I haven't noticed His Royal Highness taking much notice, and poor Alexandra simply looks the other way or makes friends with her rivals. Where the Queen herself fails, can we poor Dilbernes do better? Let us just get the boy married, so we may get on with the important things in life, and worry about the Floras of this world later.'

He took the glass from his wife's hand, and ruffled her hair a little.

'It is rather pleasant when Grace is not about, don't you think?' he asked. 'It makes a change to be unobserved. Sometimes I envy our tenants the sheer privacy of their lives.'

'I certainly don't,' said Isobel. 'If I try to do my own hair my arms start to ache at once. But you have changed the subject very effectively. I suppose we must let Arthur get on with his life in his own way, Floras and all.'

'And I so seldom see you with your hair down. It is most attractive. Shall I eschew my dressing room for the night?'

'Yes,' said his wife, agreeably. So far as she was concerned sharing the marital bed was the point of the marriage. She had married for love, and the satisfaction of desire, and though she could see money had been a factor for him, and that love and desire had come later, at least it had quickly followed. Isobel felt the familiar surge of rosy pleasure through her limbs, and felt grateful to her Maker.

'One thing,' said Robert, 'about Mrs Baum.'

'Mrs Baum? Oh.' Isobel could see things were not going to be as simple as she had hoped. Something was to be required of her. 'I was going to invite her, was I not, at your request? I didn't exactly forget, Robert, but one rather resists this sort of thing. Since Melinda and Arthur are getting on so well, the reason to appease Mr and Mrs Baum seems to have rather gone. It is never such a good idea to mix business with one's social life, you know, if it is not absolutely required.'

'The urgency is still there, my dear,' said her husband. 'I would have informed you if it were not. Indeed, it is rather more necessary than before. The idea now is not so much escaping penury as acquiring wealth. It is an excellent aim. Our children may then make a free choice in their marriages. If Arthur decides Minnie O'Brien is not for him, we need not despair. If Rosina prefers never to marry, she need not.'

'The price of this is asking Mrs Baum to a Charity Tea? Very well, if you insist. I dare say she is a perfectly pleasant woman. She is welcome to sip my sherry and donate to a good cause.'

'No. More than that, my dear. She and Mr Baum must be invited to a dinner at which the Prince is present.'

The rosy warmth drained rather from Lady Isobel's limbs. She even shivered a little.

'Oh dear,' she said. 'Just to think of the royal dinner is exhausting. The O'Briens are bad enough. But the Baums? Why? They will hardly be socially at ease. I feel for them, as much as for my guests. The Jews don't eat shellfish. I will not be able to serve lobster, which is such a favourite with so many, or scalloped oysters, which is usually done at this time of year. And I believe pork too. So even roast suckling pig, which is the Prince's favourite, is out of the question.'

'The Prince dines frequently with the Rothschilds, and I have never heard him complain about the menu,' said her husband. 'More, Ernest Cassel is his good friend, and decorated by her Majesty —'

'You mean Cassel lends the Prince money, which he then gambles away, and the Prince has worn down the poor Queen, so this vulgar financier, who may be very clever but comes from nowhere, and has no loyalty whatsoever to this country, from some wandering tribe, receives a KCMG from her in return? You are in unholy waters, my dear. You're too simple. Mr Kruger of the Boers, according to *The Times,* would have it that the Rothschilds were behind the

Jamestown Raid, from whence our own personal losses at Ladysmith originated. They care nothing for patriotism, only for personal gain. Whatever you are doing, be careful.'

'It is bad for a lady's looks to read the newspapers so closely,' said Robert. He had not expected quite so much opposition to a simple request.

'Besides,' said her Ladyship, rather feebly, so he knew he was winning the argument, and her arguments more to do with the dinner menu than any serious principle, 'I have seldom seen Cassel at Princess Alexandra's table.'

'Because poor Alexandra is deaf,' said Robert, 'and became so within three years of the marriage, to the Prince's very great distress.'

'Ernest Cassel is a Catholic,' said his wife. 'Don't they owe more loyalty to the Pope in Rome than to their own country? And one tries not to have Catholics to dinner on a Friday, because of the lack of a meat course. All one can do for them is serve stewed pigeons, which unaccountably are treated as fish, but are never Cook's forte. Freddie's cook manages pigeon well enough, but her beef is never right. I am sure dear Freddie is trying to poach her. Well, well, then I will do what I can. We will ask them for the seventeenth, and the Prince will have to put up with both the Baums and the O'Briens. I really hope Rosina consents to be present and doesn't find a meeting she has to go to. The Prince likes Rosina.'

She had capitulated. Isobel too, Robert had no doubt, could see the benefit in any plan which would increase the family's future prosperity. She was her father's daughter. He moved his hand round her back beneath the silk wrap and felt her body move into his.

TESSA TOO LETS A CAT OUT OF THE BAG

7 p.m. Saturday, 18th November 1899

When Minnie returned to the hotel from her horse riding jaunt with Arthur she found Grace bathing her mother's feet in a most elegant blue and white footbath.

'Epsom salts,' said her mother. 'What they use over here for feet. My, what a day we had. Poor Grace got quite soaked. We went shopping down Bond Street.'

'Did you get a present for Father?' asked Minnie. 'He'll be missing us.'

'He'll be making do on his own, I don't doubt,' said Tessa. 'I wouldn't worry about him. I nearly bought him a nice pocket watch but he'll never give up his old railroad watch. How was your day?'

'I had a good gallop,' said Minnie, 'and Arthur forgave me for it, though he still thinks it is unladylike.'

'You are very bad, Minnie. You only do it to annoy. I thought you quite liked this young man.'

'Oh I do,' said Minnie, 'I do declare I am almost in love with him. I took good care not to make jokes or say anything sensible. That must mean something.'

'While your mother's feet soak, Miss Minnie,' said Grace, 'may I run you a bath?' Her tone had quite changed. It was friendly, even concerned. Minnie wondered why.

'Grace has forgiven us,' her mother said, unasked. 'She now sees you're natural born gentry, even if I'm not, and a fit wife for the Earl of Dilberne, so she's prepared to be nice to us.'

Grace gasped and scarcely knew where to look.

'Isn't that a fact, Grace?' persisted Tessa. 'See, I can read your mind.'

'I am no different this evening than I was this morning,' observed Minnie, 'whatever happened during your day.'

'But she is, isn't she?' said her mother to Grace, and then, turning to Minnie, said, 'We visited the Royal Academy of Arts and saw a portrait of your real father, Mr Eyre Crowe. Holy Mary Mother of God, Minnie, you're the spitting image of him, same eyes, same nose, I'd put my life on it. Isn't that a fact, Grace? You saw it for yourself.'

'Oh please, Mrs O'Brien,' said Grace, in a voice more high-pitched than usual. 'I saw nothing of the kind, Miss Minnie. Believe me. Just a blotchy portrait of a bearded man. I don't know nothing about art. I'm just the lady's maid. Mrs O'Brien, I'd be obliged if you'd just let Miss Minnie get out of these dirty clothes and on with her bath. We want her to look nice for dinner tonight. It is only an hotel dinner but even so.'

Minnie went quietly with Grace into the bathroom and took her bath. Grace helped Minnie out of her riding clothes. Minnie, accustomed to black servants, was disconcerted to find herself standing nude in front of a white woman, but thought she had better get used to it, though in truth her early experiences in a convent had marked her more than she would acknowledge. She felt a little stunned and dizzy, as if her mother had hurled a baseball at her head and she hadn't got out of the way in time. What had Tessa just said? Her 'real father'?

Tessa had made hints through Minnie's childhood, especially when Billy failed to use a spittoon or sneezed into his soup, and annoyed her, that Minnie was not her father's child and thanked the Lord for it, but since Billy had always laughed it off, and given Tessa a cuddle, and told his wife

323

to cut out giving herself airs, Minnie had assumed the claim to be just another of Tessa's passing follies. She knew the name Eyre Crowe. She had seen his painting in the Institute of Arts back home often enough. His name was engraved on the little brass plate beneath a painting of a group of clean and healthy girls waiting on a bench for the slave auction. All that slavery was over now, though freedom hadn't seemed to do the Negroes much good. She couldn't see that the squalor, filth and cold of the cattle yards was much of an improvement on the cotton fields. It didn't bear thinking about too much, any more than that she wasn't her father's daughter, which, frankly, if true, and she would not be surprised if it were, was rather a relief.

Billy was a good-hearted, jovial, generous, noisy, tolerant man, who did good in the community, ate enormously, broke wind frequently, was kind to cattle while they waited for slaughter, and never flaunted any mistresses in front of his wife. Billy and Tessa were two of a kind and, however fond she was of them, not her kind. No, she could accept her illegitimacy, or whatever it was, well enough. She'd just had to readjust her vision of herself rather quickly: Miss Melinda O'Brien — affianced, if secretly, to

Arthur, Earl-in-waiting of Dilberne. Billy was, she could see, not the best father-in-law for Arthur, but probably preferable to have in his life than a mother-in-law who had borne his wife outside the marriage bed. She must persuade her mother to stay quiet about Eyre Crowe, simply forget him, as she herself would. Was he still alive? It was possible, although one always assumed those who had paintings in gold frames in State museums were of the past. If so, it might complicate matters. She could live very well as Viscountess Hedleigh, the O'Brien girl. But Viscountess Hedleigh the Eyre Crowe girl? She did not want to lose Arthur. She was reeling him in as a fisherman does a salmon. He was tugging away at the line at the moment; the last thing she wanted was to have it snagged and snapped on unexpected rocks before she could pull him in. Arthur must get no hint of this development. Her mother must simply forget she had ever set eyes on a portrait of Eyre Crowe. So must Grace. Then everything would be as it had been. She stepped out of the bath clean, warm, rosy and composed.

Fortunately Grace had come to the same conclusion. 'I brought out the brown creased-silk with the low neck for Miss

Minnie,' said Grace to Tessa, tenderly drying her new mistress's feet. The swelling had gone down; the gold kid shoes would fit by the time she was ready for dinner. The shoes had cost as much as she, Grace, earned in a year. There must be some other way of living in which the harder you worked, the more money you earned. *From each according to his ability, to each according to his need.* It was a fine sentiment, but more a statement of hope than a declaration of intent. 'Miss Minnie can wear it with the pearls. Very simple and nice, suitable for a young girl.'

'Snakes alive, Grace,' said Tessa O'Brien, 'are you trying to turn my girl into a frump? That dress does nothing for her at all.'

'It's discreet and ladylike, Mrs O'Brien, and that's what we want for her at the moment. May I offer you a word of advice?'

'Advise away, Grace,' said Tessa. 'There's no stopping you anyway.'

'Silence is the best policy,' said Grace. 'Truth is too dangerous. Miss Minnie is as pure as the driven snow, born in wedlock, and legal heir to your husband's fortune.'

'You're a good woman, Grace,' said Tessa. 'But what a world of lies this is!'

'It's how we all survive,' observed Grace.

Rosina Spills the Beans to Minnie

10.30 a.m. Sunday, 19th November 1899

Rosina had arranged to meet her friend Diana at Essex Hall in the Strand. Rosina did not make friends easily, and was pleased when Diana had responded to her invitation to join her. Diana had studied the natural sciences at Girton, one of the few grudged Cambridge colleges for women, and though students received their lectures in a room above a baker's shop, at least they were allowed to study, if not to graduate. Girl students were not welcome at Cambridge, especially now they had taken to hitching up their skirts and cycling through the streets to lectures. Indeed, the effigy of a girl cyclist had been hung and burned in the Cambridge Town Square in Diana's second year. But Diana continued to cycle bravely on, though many other girls stopped.

Diana turned up to the meeting in the Strand on a bicycle, to the cheers of those gathering there to hear Sidney and Beatrice Webb talk on the nationalization of land. Rosina felt at ease in Diana's company. She was a handsome, vigorous girl, almost as tall as Rosina. Like Rosina, she had not done the Season out of principle, much to the alarm of her family. She was Anthony Robin's younger sister. Tonight she seemed troubled, and confided in Rosina, promising her to secrecy.

Her brother Anthony, she said, who was engaged to be married to a charming girl, one of her pals, was apparently a frequent visitor to a woman of bad repute in Half Moon Street. A cab driver had told her maid, who had told her. What should she do: tell his fiancée, her friend, or say nothing and let the marriage go ahead?

'Say nothing,' Rosina advised. 'Young men do that sort of thing. He will stop when he's married. Good heavens, if marriages didn't go ahead because the groom was not a virgin, there would be remarkably few marriages in the land.'

Diana said that was not all that was worrying her. She was sorry if this was news to Rosina but her brother Arthur was joining him in these seedy escapades. She had asked Tony and it seemed Arthur paid the rent. Under the definition of the new Amendment to the Vagrancy Act this made the dwelling a brothel, and though Arthur could probably not be convicted as a pimp, the press might get hold of it and there could be a nasty scandal, which would harm both her brother's career in the Bank and Rosina's father's political career. Particularly as the Earl had in his time paid rent on the same premises.

'How on earth do you know all this?' asked Rosina. Arthur, that did not surprise her. But her father — could it be true?

'Tony told me all,' said Diana. 'Flora — that's her name — told him that your father was her original protector. She asked him not to tell Arthur because Arthur thought he was her first, and she didn't want him seeing her as used goods. Of course, she may be inventing this sorry tale to justify herself in some way, but it all makes sense. My brother says I am being obsessive about the dangers and has no intention of stopping his visits. Men tend to be so innocent about what happens next. I thought perhaps your brother should be warned.'

And then the bell rang and it was time for everyone to troop back into the hall, though a few had left because it was a rather boring talk, in which Sidney had spent an hour explaining what he meant by saying that rents collected by landowners were un-earned, for surely the ground we walked upon was ours? The second half was equally dull, which was as well because Rosina was in a state of shock and had a great deal to think about. Her father, unfaithful to her mother to the extent of setting up a mis-tress? It could only be the Prince's influ-ence. And her mother? One's father's past infidelity was not something one mentioned to one's mother. Should she be presented with the truth, if it was really true? No, hardly; it was of the question. No matter how one's mother irritated one, one did not want to destroy her. Better to let the matter lie.

Arthur was another matter. He should be ashamed of himself. Diana's brother, and her brother, each wooing proper girls while keeping a whore behind their backs. Ar-thur's Minnie, mind you, was not exactly innocent according to Grace. Nor did Ro-sina believe for one moment that Arthur loved Minnie, or Minnie, Arthur — he wanted money and she wanted rank. The falsity of his smile was evident when he spoke to his parents, and to her, Rosina, of what a topping girl Minnie was. Not that an engagement had been announced, but Ar-thur had told so many people he was going to drive Minnie down to Dilberne Court in the Jehu to show the place off to her, it could only suggest to all that he saw her as a future bride and chatelaine of Dilberne. And all the time he was sneaking off (twice a week Diana had said) to this Flora-trollop's den of vice to meet up with Tony Robin, there to have his cake and to eat it too. Five years before she had thought Tony might be one man she could possibly marry: at least he was clever and serious, and one could sometimes have a decent conversation with him. But he'd quickly formed an attachment to another girl, a diminutive and very silly beauty, a Duke's daughter. A mere earl's daughter like Rosina was obviously not quite good enough for him, especially when she was three inches taller than he.

Reginald was there in the cab to pick Rosina up when the meeting ended. Diana cycled off on her bicycle, hair flying in the wind, wearing a crimson high-necked and red-corded tailored jacket, with cross-braiding down the bodice and a vaguely military air, a pair of divided skirts gathered at the ankles, and high-laced button boots. Rosina, who usually attracted attention in some loose and flowing modern gown, felt positively old-fashioned; not to mention cross, embarrassed, and ashamed that Diana knew so much about her family and to its discredit.

Rosina had not been best pleased when Isobel sent Grace off to work for Mrs O'Brien. She could hardly complain, having once told her mother that she had no use for a lady's maid, that she was perfectly able to draw her own bath, do her own hair, look after her own clothes and it was ridiculous for a perfectly healthy woman to ask another woman to do these things for her. But then she had been eighteen, and had not realized how much of adult life was spent seeing to appearance. Even the maids would change their clothes three or four times a day, if only adding or removing a starched and pleated cap or a frilled apron. On Mondays when the agency laundresses came in the rooms were foggy with steam which came up from the laundry, and the smell of burnt fabric as over-heated irons dashed to and fro over lace and muslin too fragile to endure them. It was amazing how much work two women of the leisured classes required.

She had managed to persuade her mother to send the laundry out. And though her father demurred, asking how she thought the laundresses were going to live if her mother didn't employ them, Rosina replied,

'Why, in professional laundries where they will be properly trained and worth the money they get.'

Meanwhile, as a governess she once had used to say, 'The miners in Africa starve.' Methodist Miss Penny would not have approved at all of the Dilberne's involvement with gold mining. If the Modder Kloof gold mine subsided and took down the family fortune with it, Rosina, hot from Essex Hall in the Strand, could see it was no more than they deserved. Bad enough to profit from the labour of workers on the land — for them to exploit the labour of those poor beneath it was doubly disgraceful. She wanted no part of it.

She was angry with her father for having made a mockery of his marriage: she was angry with her mother for letting him do it. Her brother was a hypocrite and a liar. She was angry with herself for her complacency in the past. She could see herself now as one of the oppressed of the world. She would earn her own living. Medical school would not accept her — she had fewer educational qualifications even than Grace — so she would go to Mr Pitman's secretarial college, learn shorthand typing and earn her own living: perhaps she could work in the offices of a Trades Union Congress or for the Fabian Society itself. She would move away from home and live in some romantic little room down by the river and be a bohemian. Or perhaps she could learn to paint, and be an artist? The world was full of opportunities!

By the time she got home to Belgrave Square, in time to change for the d'Astis' salon, she had decided what her response would be to the Arthur dilemma. She would ask Minnie out shopping, before any engagement was announced, and warn her about the kind of man she was marrying.

She had to dress without Grace's help. That did not help her temper. She flung a dozen outfits to the ground before she chose what she thought was appropriate to the event. A plain blue velvet dress and a small grey-brimmed hat with a wide leopardskin band round its crown worn at a rakish angle. It made her look modern and intelligent; if she was not to be valued for her looks she would be valued for her mind.

It was an enjoyable evening at the salon. Mr H.G. Wells was there, bouncing and squeaking away, and the Countess d'Asti gushed and squawked, her shelf of a bosom draped in layers of flimsy lace, very much mutton dressed as lamb. Rosina could never work out why her mother took the woman so seriously. The writers and artists who clustered round 'dear Freddie', as they loved to call her, were after her free food and drink and the occasional hand-out. At least her mother kept her dignity.

The lion of the evening was Henry James himself, haughty and dignified, up from Sussex. There was a most extraordinary story going the rounds that he remained unmarried because he had deliberately sat on a white-hot stove to scald himself and thus make himself unfit to be a husband. It was the kind of thing one heard at the d'Astis'.

H.G. Wells affected not to recognize Henry James, rather unkindly asking who the hippopotamus was. Mr James for his part seemed to rather admire H.G. as one who cultivated the common touch, of which Mr James was incapable, seeming to have been born stately and incapable of a short sentence. Rosina noted how, while her mother liked to invite guests who 'got on', the Countess deliberately chose those whom she hoped would not. Rosina's parents had declared themselves indisposed, which Rosina knew to be a lie. Arthur had simply not turned up. Rosina supposed he was off with his whore.

But Mrs O'Brien and her daughter Minnie

were present. Rosina introduced herself and was studiously pleasant and polite. The mother was just very Irish, with a loud voice, a red face and the cheerful air of the unthinking. She was nicely dressed, looking as good as her stout figure could allow, which presumably was because of Grace. Rosina herself was feeling rather under-dressed: none of the other women present seemed to want in the least to be valued for their minds. Minnie was smaller than Rosina had imagined, nice-featured, and a little frumpish in a dull bronze silk dress which did not particularly become her — perhaps Grace hated her. Nor was Minnie forthcoming on the subject of Arthur, beyond saying his mount had been the pride of Rotten Row, as hers was certainly not, and they had had to take shelter from the rain.

But the girl was not fit to be a Hedleigh and bring the mother's genes into the family, and heaven knew what the father was like. A meat baron, a stockyard king! A gangster! And — worse — Minnie proved she was just too intolerably American: she picked at Rosina's velvet gown, and said what a beautiful colour and texture the fabric was. English ladies avoided touching one another if it could be avoided. Minnie was just hopelessly *foreign.*

But her behaviour did give Rosina the opportunity of saying 'It's a Liberty's fabric. I would be more than happy to show you their little shop. We could have lunch or tea together there perhaps, and get to know each other better.'

And Minnie had said she would be delighted, she surely would.

A Dinner in Preparation

5 p.m. Wednesday, 22nd November 1899
The Countess of Dilberne had resigned herself to proper consideration of the Prince of Wales dinner and now discussed it with her husband. The menu had been decided, she told him, the invitations sent out: it was to be for twenty-eight. The number of guests was dictated by the size of the table. She began to feel she needed a larger dining table, perhaps one in a paler wood. Maple, perhaps? Mahogany was beginning to look heavy and old-fashioned. The cost of the dinner? Only sixty pounds, perhaps, when the need to hire liveried footmen and a silver butler was counted in.

'More like seventy-five,' said her husband.

'How did you know?' she asked, surprised.

'Whenever you say "only", I know you have underestimated by a quarter or thereabouts, so as not to alarm me. It is the normal habit of the female.'

338

'It is because men always say "outrageous" if one speaks the truth about expense,' observed her Ladyship. Rosina, she added, had taken the opportunity to point out that this was twice what Grace earned in a year; Isobel had remarked that it was also a third of Rosina's allowance for the year, at which Rosina drifted off, no doubt to feed her pet parrot its very expensive Brazil nuts.

'I told the girl it really was an unkindness to keep a flying bird cooped up in a living room with its wings clipped, and horribly unhealthy,' said Isobel. 'And more, the servants have to waste time cleaning up after it.'

Rosina had not bothered to reply, just raised her eyebrows. Goodness gracious, Isobel suddenly realized, the girl is jealous. She feels neglected because Grace is dressing Minnie O'Brien. Because she fears she is not attractive to men, and is too tall to be anyone's instant choice, and too proud to admit it to anyone. She would rather drive men off than risk rebuff. And she blames me because I am her mother and have failed to bring her into a perfect world.

She applied her mind to the dinner again. There were to be twelve courses: pheasant soup, caviar, tartlets of crayfish in a cream sauce, turbot with tartar sauce, grouse sautéed in sherry, ducklings *foie gras* with brandy and truffles, baron of lamb, a liqueur sorbet, salad, cheeses, fruit, and a *gelée marbrée.*

Robert complained that twelve courses were perhaps not lavish enough for a royal dinner, but Isobel held firm, saying it was more than enough for a private dinner. Isobel murmured about the price but Robert said she should leave the worrying to him, inasmuch as after the next cabinet shuffle she might well find herself wife to a Minister of the Crown; and whoever had heard of a bankrupt Minister? This so relieved and pleased Isobel that she offered to add another course, of roast beef, Yorkshire pudding and horseradish sauce, between the duck and the lamb, but Robert blenched and said she was probably right, twelve was more than enough. It was nearly the twentieth century, and probably by the end of it, the way things were going, and fewer courses becoming fashionable, just a tartlet, or salad and cheese with a College Pudding would satisfy even the grandest. Isobel went up on her toes and kissed Robert's cheek, saying she was the luckiest and happiest woman alive, and truly feeling it.

A Reconciliation Below Stairs

7 p.m. Wednesday, 22nd November 1899

Smithers reported the display of affection back to the servants' hall, and a warm glow ran through the whole household. Cook stopped worrying about the cream sauce for the crayfish tartlet: she had tried and it was no easy matter keeping the pastry crisp when doused with a hot sauce. But no doubt on the night she would manage. Elsie received a letter from Alan her beau, saying he had taken the pledge, and now he could say with confidence 'no hand that touches liquor shall ever touch mine,' because he was a changed man and saving hard. She had to get Mrs Neville to read it to her, because she could not read. She had never let Alan know that this was the case. Mr Neville undertook to teach her.

All agreed to forgive Minnie for the vulgarity of her mother, and for not being English; Master Arthur, they noted, had been very cheerful of late ('Not surprised,' remarked Reginald, and then quickly said 'Sorry, Cook,' so for once she decided to take no offence), so much generosity of spirit was attributed to Minnie. It must have been love at first sight, all agreed: things had moved so fast. What Dilberne Court needed was children to run around the garden again and cheer the place up. Miss Rosina was evidently not going to provide them, so the sooner the young Viscount's wedding bells were announced, and an heir produced, the better. Cook said she had never tried her hand at a wedding cake; there would be a shortage of eggs until the hens started laying again, but she had heard that grated carrot made an adequate substitute, volume for volume with eggs. The other secret was twice the sherry that the recipes said.

ROSINA AND MINNIE SHOP AT LIBERTY & CO

2.15 p.m. Tuesday, 28th November 1899

Minnie was delighted when Rosina invited her on a shopping trip to Liberty & Co. It was a good sign; she was to be welcomed to the family. Rosina had never seemed particularly friendly, but she had learned from Stanton that people did not necessarily look as they felt. Rosina's mouth would start twitching if she were feeling nervous, as Stanton Turlock's had, and she had the same habit of looking not at you, but slightly away from you. But she understood that: it came from an excess of intelligence and anxiety mixed, which ebbed and flowed like the tide. Arthur trusted Rosina, so she would also. She wanted to be friends.

Besides she needed a motoring hat, which meant a big scarf tied over the hat and under the chin, and Liberty's, though she had never been to the store, was known to have the best fabrics in London. Tana lawn, named after Lake Tana in Ethiopia, was the finest, softest cotton available anywhere.

Arthur was to drive her down to Hampshire in the Arnold Jehu steam car. She both looked forward to the journey and dreaded it. She had inspected the automobile in Arthur's garage, and it was certainly a graceful thing, and with its two large headlights like two bright eyes, had an almost human quality. She could understand his affection for it, though she feared it would be worse than a bony nag to sit upon for any length of time, while the large wheels rumbled on their thin white tyres, and the engine puffed and boiled behind them. A bolting horse seemed a lesser danger. But Arthur loved it, so she would learn to.

Arthur had said, 'She's fine going uphill, but used to be a little heavy going down: so now I've put in condenser in and fitted a different flash boiler which should really improve matters. She'll manage the Devil's Punchbowl now with no trouble. I'll just make sure that by the time we're on the top of the hill we're low on water to reduce weight. She'll still pick up a good head of speed but you won't mind that. I've seen you on horseback. We'll be grand.'

She loved him so she did not even demur. She must try not to tell Arthur she loved him. Nothing frightened men more than a declaration of true love; Tessa had told her so, and her friends lamented that it was true. Yet she had told Stanton Turlock she loved him, and it had not put him off, rather it had spurred him on. But then he was an artist and perhaps she hadn't really loved him. The initial sexual excitement which had carried her away and led her to 'give up all for love of a genius', a deed which she now regarded with embarrassment and horror, had faded quickly, even as Stanton's had, to be replaced by his low moods and bad temper. His professions of undying love had stopped; next thing he shrank from her touch. Then he had been seized by the Devil's own energy, ceaseless sex had replaced the hurtful indifference, and he'd start shouting, waving an old sabre, and threatening to slash the works of his rivals, convinced that Minnie was in league with them. 'I warned you,' Tessa had told her. 'These artists are just plain pesky.'

'Pesky ain't the word for it,' Billy had said. 'He's loco. A pig with a demon inside, trampling pearls. Go off and find yourself some better breeding material. And don't come back until you have.'

At least Arthur was not crazy. Madcap, but not gloomy, hurtful crazy.

Liberty's, a little shop off the sweep of Regent Street, was even smaller than she expected, but inside was all beauty. Everything seemed to glow. Fabrics hung gracefully, delicate flimsy furniture — little pieces placed here and there, suitable for the smaller town houses of London, Rosina explained, not like the ponderous family pieces she herself had been brought up with. Strange dull copper and brass pieces from Asia and Arabia whose use you couldn't even imagine, fabrics designed by William Morris himself, smocked dresses in smoky velvets which showed rather a lot of leg but had high, cluttered necklines, the kind of thing Rosina herself favoured. It was all enchanting, and had a special smell rather like the incense they used at mass, which she supposed was designed to drug you in some way, so you didn't notice how high the prices were. And they certainly were.

Yet it all seemed to Minnie slightly decadent, on its way out, a shrine to the past, an altar to the gods of greenery-yallery as the old century died. She had a sudden pang for the wide open spaces, the prairie and the lakes and the sweep of sky above, and the lowing of cattle as they were herded and the crack of the cowboy's whip, and the coyote's yelp and her father's kindly, if brutish, common sense. He funded an Art Institute but left the art to his wife, who valiantly aspired to discrimination but could never quite get there.

Minnie did not want to be the child of some effete English painter, though she accepted that she might well be. She wanted to be Billy's daughter. Surely a child belonged to whoever brought her up? She had no wish to seek out her natural father. Supposing it occurred to her mother to leave her husband and take up with Eyre Crowe? She was quite capable of it. If she, Minnie, had run off with Stanton Turlock, a rather inferior painter, might not her mother run off with a better one?

'A penny for your thoughts,' said Rosina.

Not on your Nellie, thought Minnie. She longed to tell someone, but it was for her mother to tell, not for her. Her mother had already been indiscreet. The news of her illegitimacy would probably be with the Dilbernes already. But they were like her father, interested in breeding and the inheritance of characteristics, and would probably prefer the blood of an English gentleman to run through the Dilberne veins, to that of a crude Irish peasant whose only merit was that he had managed to grow rich.

'You're very silent. Mama says your

mother is the opposite.'

Tact was clearly not Rosina's strong point, but at least she was honest and straight-forward. Minnie decided she liked her.

'She is very noisy but she has a good heart, and I love her very much,' said Minnie. 'I may be noisy too, but I'm struck dumb by the beauty of this store. Also by the prices.'

'I am surprised that you are troubled by the cost,' said Rosina. 'I thought the whole point of you is that you are rich.' She is so like Stanton, thought Minnie. She can't help but speak the truth as it occurs to her.

'I am rich enough,' said Minnie, 'but I'm just remembering that the workers who make these things probably get paid inde-cently little.' She guessed this was an opin-ion which would endear her to Rosina, and found that she had read the girl rightly. Ro-sina beamed and in the gentle light of the shop, looked almost lovely. If only she could learn to stand proudly upright and not stoop, and look others in the eye, she could be almost a beauty.

Minnie went in search of a Tana lawn scarf and found a very pleasant one, all peacock tails, in (the label troubled to say, and the store seemed very proud of it, whatever it was) Mr Arthur Silver's recent Hera design, all greens and blues, colours that everyone knew 'never went together'. She hoped it would prove popular but feared it wouldn't. It would do well enough to tie under her chin. And Hera was the Greek goddess of love and marriage so Minnie made up her mind almost at once. It would bring good luck.

Rosina suggested they had tea and cakes in the little restaurant, where they sat upon little spindly chairs designed by Charles Voysey, who had just designed H.G. Wells' house.

'I do so admire Mr Wells,' said Minnie. 'So young and so clever.'

'But he squeaks when he speaks,' complained Rosina, and pointed out that H.G. had been present at the d'Asti party and expressed surprise that Minnie had not been introduced.

'You mean the little man with the crowd of women around him? The one who upset Henry James by calling him a hippopotamus? Well, I suppose we must forgive him. He did write *The War of the Worlds,* after all. Such a diverting novel.'

'Diverting?' enquired Rosina. 'Hardly. Alarming, I should say. Wells points out that just as we overwhelm the poor Africans with our weapons and our scientific inventions, the same thing could very well happen to us.' Minnie observed that it was a great pleasure to find herself in a place where books were discussed and not just what a good hog could fetch in a competitive market. That too went down well with Rosina. They would be friends. Rosina's brow ceased to crease in such an alarming way. She was looking positively pretty. They ordered saffron tea. Rosina said it was good for the eyesight and for the complexion. It was made from crocuses which grew in Persia.

THE EARL MAKES A MISTAKE

3.30 p.m. Tuesday, 28th November 1899
Even as Minnie raised the cup of saffron tea to her lips and smelled its strange odour of damp pencils, so her Ladyship raised a cup of more familiar China tea to her lips in the House of Lords; she admired the view of the Thames, flowing slightly murkily, it was true, but certainly no longer stinking, as it had when she had visited London as a child. The London sewers had been finished and the city had much benefitted from the network, though it turned out that smell itself was not the culprit, but a polluted water supply. The Earl had invited his wife to listen to the third reading of some proposed legislation she might find interesting, since her charity At Homes were in support of St Joseph League for the Mother and Child. The Bill was to oblige all practising midwives to be licensed by the General Medical Council. The debate was fierce —

male obstetricians arguing that women should not be seen as professionals — even though the death rate from puerperal fever was rising and much of it due to simple lack of hygiene on the part of untrained midwives.

Private member's bill after private member's bill had been flung out, though after the pattern of these things, it would eventually become law. Not probably this year. Isobel had been delighted to come along. You never knew whom you might meet, and it was quite an event to meet her husband where he worked. He had slipped out of his own meeting with a sleeping Salisbury and various more alert and younger members of the War Office, to join his wife for a cup of tea. The cups were too delicate for their own good, small and too thin, with a pretty flowered pattern. Rather, his Lordship felt, like his wife herself, sitting like some delicate tea rose in this very solid stone male maze.

It seemed she had not been paying much attention to the debate. She had been brooding.

'This Flora of Arthur's,' she said, 'how do you come to know so much about her? That she has aspirations to being a courtesan, and dresses very agreeably, and you can recognize her at Pagani's? This common harlot?'

'Oh, that's all over,' he said, without thinking, 'a long time ago.'

She gave a little scream, and jumped to her feet, and stood, her arms across her chest, like some wronged stage heroine, her eyes wide and horrified. Fortunately the restaurant was almost empty. No wonder men went to such lengths to keep women out of male establishments. Women, even the best of them, made scenes.

'But what's the matter? I thought you knew.' Even as he said it, he feared his life with her would never be quite the same. Some things, once said, cannot be unsaid.

'Knew what?' Her voice was high and unnatural. What had he done? Had he done something so bad? Nothing worse than what most men of his age and class did. He'd kept a mistress, not for long, only months, some five years ago. He had not liked the secrecy involved, and had quickly brought the affair to an end. He loved his wife. Flora had been enchanting but it was dangerous. He could not expose Isobel to scandal. Come to think of it, he had given the girl up for Isobel's sake. He was to be congratulated, not chided. Perhaps it should not have happened in the first place, but marriage is long and sometimes relief is needed, however briefly. Women don't seem to realize this — how important it is and yet how little it means.

Flora had made a great fuss when he left her, he remembered, and claimed her heart was broken. Fortunately her tears just hardened his heart against her; she lost all remaining attraction for him when he was obliged to watch her weeping, her eyes so red, swollen and ugly, and her mouth so loose and out of control. She managed to seize the bank notes he held out to her, he had noticed.

He had not abandoned the girl: indeed, he had asked Reginald to organize his successor. Robert had not been pleased to discover the rogue had fixed the girl up with his own son, but there was nothing he could do about it, except be relieved that as these girls go she was healthy, clean and not too hysterical. There was no need to let Arthur know his own father was his predecessor in the girl's bed. The boy was fond of his mother. He'd assumed Arthur would quickly grow out of any attachment to the girl. But apparently he had not. The consequences of little choices you made which you assumed would just fade away and disappear could come swirling back through time to get you.

'It's all over, long ago,' he said to Isobel. 'It meant nothing.'

But her face was hardening into a mask of hostility and dislike. He shivered to see it. That was the last thing he should have said. When it came to women, as with politics, denial was the safest path.

'You can have your dinner party for the Prince,' she said. 'You can spend my money and your children's money on horses and cards, and whoring with your fat friend, whom even his own mother despises, but I choose my own guest list. Mrs Baum will only enter this house over my dead body.'

'But haven't the invitations gone off?'

'I held hers back, on seeing the postal district. I hadn't yet made up my mind. Now I have. I am my father's daughter.'

A thick yellow fog was beginning to curl up the river. It seemed a bad omen.

Robert could see that it might take time to win her round and he had none to spare. Affairs of State called. He kissed her politely goodbye, or would have, had she not jerked her cheek away from him; so he advised her to go home quickly to get out of the fog and made for the Cabinet Office, where the war meeting was under way and there were no women.

IN THE CABINET OFFICE

4.30 p.m. Tuesday, 28th November 1899
The latest dispatches were being discussed.
The news was mixed. The Queen had received one from Lord Methuen after the
Battle of Modder River to the effect that it
had been the bloodiest of the century; the
Boers had shelled from trenches with dreadful success before being charged by the British. Losses had been heavy. Nevertheless it
was a victory; the Boers had been driven
back. More detailed messages arrived. It
seemed that a force of over seven thousand
crack troops, including the Guards Brigade,
armed with bolt-action rifles and supported
by field artillery and four guns of the Naval
Brigade, with further reinforcements arriving by the railway, had been surprised and
pinned down by a larger force of Boers. The
latter had been cunningly concealed and
well dug in, armed with Mausers, several
field guns and a Maxim 'pom-pom' appar-

ently borrowed from the Orange Free State. It had taken ten hours to drive the enemy back just a couple of miles to Magersfontein. Some claimed the British had lost nearly five hundred men, the Boers only eighty.

Robert spoke into a stunned silence. 'A bloody victory indeed,' he said. He had found his courage. Having just faced Isobel, a room full of political dignitaries were as nothing. 'Some things become clear. We can no longer face this enemy armed only with inferior rifles. And where were the cavalry? If there were any not already laid low by fever, sea travel and the climate?'

Chamberlain said it seemed mounted troops were indeed involved and had reconnoitred, but had failed to notice the presence of an army eight-thousand strong. 'Then we can only conclude that the cavalry has no place in Africa. It is too busy avoiding ants' nests to pay attention to anything else.'

He was surprised at the strength of his own conviction.

'Young Winston feels very differently,' Salisbury woke up enough to murmur. 'He always believes cavalry is the answer. After his most theatrical escape from the Boers he's such a hero of the hour that I suppose we mustn't contradict his opinions.'

Robert replied that young Churchill saw horses as a living sacrifice to national pride. He himself rather liked them when they were alive. The Marquess of Lansdowne observed that Methuen's apparent abandonment of close formation tactics was dangerous and Robert told him that, on the contrary, had Methuen in this instance advanced in close formation, there would have been a massacre as the Boers mowed down not just one in sixteen, but one in eight.

'Well,' said Salisbury, opening one of his eyes quite wide, 'At least one of you seems to be awake.'

Balfour said what was done was done, and the immediate problem was how the news was to be presented to the public, who were becoming restless. Kimberley and Ladysmith were still besieged, and there was no getting away from that.

Robert saw himself and Isobel to be in the Battle of the River Thames. As with the Battle of the Modder River, the thing was to deny all, always show strength, and never admit weakness. She would forget, as the people of England would forget.

Robert said forcefully that the Battle of Modder River must be presented as a victory, a rout by brave British forces. After all, the Boers *had* been driven back.

Balfour agreed, glad to have the support he needed. Less than five hundred killed could be seen as a tribute to the courage of British fighting men rather than evidence of military stupidity. More care, he added, must in future be taken when dealing with the press. It was the way ahead.

Salisbury suggested that perhaps the Earl of Dilberne would care to join them for further discussions in the War Office.

TAKING TEA AT LIBERTY'S

5.05 p.m. Tuesday, 28th November 1899
As Isobel ran out distressed into the fog,
watched by the curious eyes of Palace of
Westminster officials, and his Lordship
advanced his political career, Minnie wrote
a cheque out for the bill for tea (which
seemed to her excessive). Rosina scraped
the last drop of cream from her éclair, and
finally came out with what she had to say to
Minnie. She found it more difficult than
she had thought.

First she advised Minnie that it would be
dangerous to motor down to Dilberne
Court with Arthur.

'Because of the Devil's Punchbowl?' asked
Minnie in all innocence. She had come to
like and trust Rosina. 'I know about that.
You must not worry. Arthur will be very
careful to make sure the boiler is not full at
the top of the hill. We won't pick up too
much speed.' She noticed she was crossing

her own fingers as she spoke.

But Rosina said it was nothing to do with the journey. It was to do with Arthur's character. Minnie should be aware that Arthur kept a mistress, paying for her flat in Half Moon Street, not ten minutes' walk from Liberty's, a very pretty little house which she, Rosina, would not be ashamed to live in herself. Perhaps Minnie would like to walk round there herself with Rosina and they could challenge her together.

The waitress had cleared the table and other customers wanted to sit down. Minnie was conscious of the great crush of expensive fabric bearing in on their table, heavy tweeds and cords, pliable velvets and satins all juxtaposed, in the jewel tones of the season, the imposing shoulder pads, the tiny waists, great puffed sleeves and plentiful gored skirts, high-frilled necks and bows and ribbons everywhere, and marvelled at how little wealthy women had to do but dress themselves. There was a heavy, uncomfortable smell of damp and sulphur mixed. Shoppers from all down Regent Street were crushing in here, Minnie realized, to get away from a drift of yellow fog. She could see its miasma begin to creep through tiny gaps in the sashed windows of the store. Really they should get up and go: their table was needed. But Rosina was not to be moved. She sat immobile and waiting for a response. What had Rosina said? Ah yes, Arthur's mistress. Walking round to visit her together?

'I don't think so, Rosina,' said Minnie. 'There's a nasty fog outside.'

Of course Arthur had a mistress. He was young and virile and hardly a virgin. Presumably he would give the girl up on marriage. Why would he need anyone else but her? She said as much to Rosina, who seemed disappointed.

'He can be prosecuted as a pimp,' said Rosina. Minnie caught an echo in her voice of the tone of delirium in Stanton's when accusing her of sleeping with his fellow painters. Poor Rosina. But she was glad the girl seemed to have friends. Like Stanton, she would have trouble finding them.

'He visits her with an equally caddish person, the brother of another good friend of mine, also affianced to another, while paying the whore's rent. The three of them go to it together. Can you imagine? There could be a dreadful scandal, which would drag down the Hedleigh name. You must save yourself, Minnie. Have no more to do with my brother. He has a very bad character, and is marrying you for your money.

He is not capable of proper feeling.'

Needled, Minnie told Rosina how she had lived in sin with a fellow artist for three happy months in the Burnt District of Chicago, in a pretty little house that had been spared the flames. She had kept house and got away from home and had been very happy. It had not been her doing that they had parted. Troilism was not unheard of between young and energetic people, she said. It was part of male nature to want to demonstrate its sexual prowess to others. In her case, her lover had become jealous of another man, an occasional visitor, invited in by her lover in the first place. He had come to suspect that she had more feeling for the new man than she did for him, and that she crept out to visit his rival behind his back.

Rosina was staring at her with startled, wide-open, slightly squinty eyes. The crush of fabrics beneath their elaborate roof of wide felt brims became oppressive. Minnie was jabbed in the arm by a succession of sharp-edged, beautifully packed parcels. Her eyes were smarting.

'Did you?' asked Rosina. 'Creep out behind his back?'

'Yes of course,' said Minnie. Though that was a lie. She had been most upset that

Stanton had insisted she shared him with his painter friend, embarrassed, humiliated and distressed. It had all been in the name of art though she could not remember his reasoning now. But as everyone said, Stanton was mad. One did not expect to make sense of it. She had perhaps been rash to trust Rosina with so much information. But at least now she could tell Arthur the truth. She was no more a virgin than he was. She could give up the pretence of purity.

Rosina walked her back to her hotel. They could see only a yard or so in front of them. The fog was thickest and at its most yellow and sulphurous at ground level. Rosina had an advantage, perhaps, being so tall. Height was at least good for something. Minnie refrained from saying so. Eyes watered and throats rasped. The streets were empty of traffic. Hearing was muffled. Even the horses could not make their way: automobile drivers were blinded.

As they groped their way forward together, hands splayed in front of them, something of fellow-feeling returned. Minnie remembered the stories about the Great Chicago Fire, the same mixture of companionship and dismay, excitement and dread, as the wooden city burned through a whole day and night, and home ceased to be home.

Drastic events reminded you of the basics of your existence, how fragile they were: how you just wanted to be able to breathe.

Rosina Goes to Vine Street

7 p.m. Tuesday, 28th November 1899

She's going to take no action whatsoever, thought Rosina. The girl has no morals and no shame. Arthur and she are as bad as one another. She braved more of the fog, though it made her cough and sneeze, and walked round to Vine Street Police Station, where she claimed to be a neighbour in Half Moon Street. Men and children were in and out of No. 5 at all hours. Heaven knew what went on there. An officer of the law wrote it all down assiduously, taking a long time about it. But at last someone was taking the matter seriously.

It occurred to Rosina on her way back home that Flora's little flat was being paid for by family funds and that she could see herself living there very comfortably indeed while she set about earning her own living. Whether that thought had already come to her before she went round to Vine Street she wasn't sure, but it wasn't the point. Rich men like Arthur should not seduce and ruin poor girls like Flora, let alone marry so callously for money.

IN THE SERVANTS' HALL

The first week of December 1899

Something had happened to sour the atmosphere at No. 17 Belgrave Square. The pea-souper had been nasty but cleared by the next morning. Her Ladyship put it about that she was indisposed, and either kept to her bed and wept or sat on its edge staring into space. If she did leave her room it was to rant around finding fault, inspecting the nails of the staff as if they weren't all perfectly clean in the first place, complaining of a burnt flavour to the breakfast porridge though no one else could detect it, and sending the bowl back to Cook, to her outrage.

'She has a nerve,' said Cook. 'Their very smartest friends all praise my cooking. If she's not careful I'll soon be off to Lady Fredericka. She's just as much a countess as her Ladyship is.'

Smithers and Elsie begged Cook not to

368

do any such thing, and pointed out that Lady Fredericka, in spite of her airs and graces, was wife to a mere foreign count, they were two a penny, and hardly counted as aristocracy at all. Cook allowed herself to be pacified.

'Poor thing,' she said. 'Her Ladyship's in such a mood. There's trouble between him and her, if you ask me, or it could just be *the change.*' She whispered the word so the men didn't hear.

Reginald said if matters got any worse he would leave service and get Master Arthur to start him up in a garage, though using internal combustion rather than steam to power his engines. There was a fortune to be made, even more than in brothels, which these days were coming more and more under police scrutiny. His Lordship slept in his dressing room, stalked off to the House of Lords every morning and went off to his club and stayed there until its doors closed at midnight. Elsie reported that the marital sheets did not need changing. Reginald reckoned this was her Ladyship's doing, not his Lordship's. He was eager enough to be let in, but she was badly offended and would have none of it. Reginald put forward the idea that it might have something to do with Flora. His Lordship had been her first protector, it was years back but the truth would out. Flora had turned up in the white mink stole at Pagani's the other night with Mr Robin from the Bank. That must have stirred things up somewhat. Supposing her Ladyship had found out?

Mr Neville observed that no one was safe from indiscretion when the gentry took it into their heads to keep company with the rougher elements in society, which these days they too often did. Wealthy men dined publicly with hopeful young actresses and girls of low repute, well-bred girls kept company with gangsters, good wives had themselves painted naked by artists. Pagani's itself hovered only just the right side of respectability. Trust the Americans to want to dine there of all places.

Her Ladyship in the meanwhile showed no signs of recovery: on the contrary.

It was while she was in one of her moods that she discovered little Lily in Rosina's room cleaning up after the parrot; she demanded to know who Lily was and what she was doing, and threw her out of the house.

The entire staff were summoned and accused of conspiring against her Ladyship.

'Everyone knew, nobody told me,' she complained, speaking as if the staff were her equals, which they resented, feeling she was taking advantage of them in some way. It wasn't their business to act as informers. Reginald concluded that she had indeed found out about his Lordship's relationship with Flora, and had been unbalanced by the news.

Cook, Mrs Neville, Smithers and Elsie all thought her Ladyship should stop making such a fuss and pull herself together. Reginald and Mr Neville were more censorious of his Lordship, insisting that he should have done more to keep the matter secret.

And how had she come to find out? That was the latest puzzle. Reginald denied any responsibility: he had not told Arthur of Flora's connection with his father when he first brought the pair together, and got an undertaking from her that she would not blab, but who was to say who had said what to whom, and under what provocation? Not that it had seemed to matter much. But now with the added complication of Mr Robin's visits to Flora — he being an acquaintance of Lady Rosina — Flora might have said something to him, he to Rosina, she to her mother? The leak could be anywhere. Be all that as it may, her Ladyship was upset, and taking her time about returning to normal. It was not good enough.

'Making a mountain out of a molehill,' Cook observed. 'And enjoying every minute of it, if you ask me. Poor little Lily.'

As it happened her Ladyship had quickly relented, at least where Lily was concerned, if not her husband, and had the waif brought back into the house — she had not got further than to huddle in the coal cellar when they went out into the streets to look. Lady Isobel, after a short interview, in which she found the child both fastidious and not unintelligent, decided to take Lily on as an apprentice lady's maid in Grace's absence. She was to have Grace's room to share. Mrs Neville was to look out a spare parlour maid's uniform for the girl, which was seen as an apology to the servants for her Ladyship's show of temper, and the latter was last seen teaching the child fine embroidery, which seemed to cheer both of them up. Reginald, who had hoped to make a few quid by taking the child round to act as Flora's maid, was piqued.

'A good little cleaner', he said. 'Pity. Now she'll have to spend a lifetime sewing instead of fucking,' and was roundly condemned by Mr Neville for use of language, and for days Cook banged his plate down in front of him so that the contents spilled, and Lily jumped with fright.

THE TRIP TO DILBERNE COURT

8.30 a.m. Sunday, 3rd December 1899

It was as beautiful as a December day could be when Arthur and Minnie set off, crossing Putney Bridge and taking the Portsmouth Road for Dilberne Court. A blue sky only mildly misted over: most trees bare of leaves and starkly handsome, a very few still riotous in shades of red, yellow and bronze, as nature properly settled in for the long hard run to spring. The weather, Minnie observed to Arthur, seemed to want to make up for the fog that had laid London low. She had often noticed that after some dire and dramatic natural event the climate seemed to want to make up for its unkindness by showing itself at its most beautiful and benign.

Yes, Arthur agreed, the weather wasn't too bad. Englishmen were not given to enthusiasm, Minnie had come to realize, but that did not mean they did not feel it. If they practiced an insouciance, a cynicism, a superiority, it was as a protective shield against damage to their emotions. It was not surprising that they needed protection. It was the custom here to send the boys away from home at the age of seven, for their mothers to keep vaguely in touch after the initial tears at the wrenching away, but not have them back until they were eighteen, and then send them as young adults straight to universities. The boys spent their lives amongst other men, as happened in savage tribes when boys were sent off very young to the men's huts; girls, only as they reached puberty, to the women's huts.

She had read about Professor Haddon's fascinating anthropological expedition to the Torres Straits in the *Oceanic*'s gloomy library, and discovered academic disciplines she had never heard of, in which it seemed members of the team of students who accompanied him specialized — who'd ever heard of 'ethnomusicology' or 'anthropogeography'? Haddon had even been to Borneo, and brought back photographs of the oddest primitive societies and their customs, but surely none were stranger than the way the upper classes of the British wealthy bought up their children, or rather failed to and delegated the task. She could see it suited the men. The mothers, deprived of their children, would have nothing better to do than concentrate on their husbands' welfare. All, men and women, were terrified that if they cosseted their sons they would turn out to be little Oscar Wildes.

Rosina, the daughter, instead of being glad to be spared, was actually envious of her brother because he had the benefit of this strange, unnatural and harrowing upbringing. Nor did she seem to love her mother as her brother did: on the contrary. Minnie could see that the less they saw of their mothers, the more sons would idealize them. The girls, on the other hand, seemed almost proud of the way they disliked their mothers.

Arthur had brought the Arnold Jehu round to Brown's in Dover Street to collect Minnie at eight in the morning. The automobile made a splendid sight, and staff had gathered on the steps to admire her as she glittered in the early sun on this brisk and beautiful day. Reginald had constructed a glass windscreen especially for the trip. The vehicle had been washed and polished for the occasion, red velvet seats soft and glowing, brass rails shiny, red wheels freshly painted, gently puffing and hissing steam, urging gently forward and back, anxious to be off. Grace was there to see her off; Tessa was still not out of bed. The latter had discovered Scottish oats for breakfast, to be eaten not with salt as at home, but with thick cream and sugar. Or perhaps she was being tactful, having realized the less she put in an appearance, the better were Minnie's chances of becoming wife to an English viscount.

Arthur was explaining the superiority of steam and the external combustion engine to the Brown's concierge, Mr Eddie.

'She's beautiful,' Minnie said to Arthur and meant it. Minnie had seen the Jehu already, but in the oily, cramped garage, and in bits. Arthur was, he said, designing and installing a condenser so as to reuse the water and reduce the amount, and so weight, that had to be carried. Now she could see the full wonder of the vehicle.

'So are you,' said Arthur, simply. And Minnie knew that it was true. The cloud that was Stanton was dissolving even as she stepped out into a bright new day and into the care of her new beau. They had had a silly, cynical, very English conversation when they first met. She remembered every line of it. He was to marry her for her money; she him for his title. They would pretend true love to save the feelings of others. But surely now the love was no longer pretence, but real. Had he been from Chicago she would simply straight out and ask him. But he was an Englishman and they thought differently from Americans. You never quite knew whether they would laugh or take offence. And you could only judge what they felt by what they did, not from what they said.

At least she knew that she was looking her best. She had made sure that she was. She was dressed perfectly for the occasion. She and Grace had worked from first principles to devise the suitable apparel for the lady motorist, there being few fashion plates or magazines to guide them.

Motoring was a dusty business, so she would have a silk coat, silk being a natural barrier to dust and dirt: it would have to be a heavy silk and lined with wool to keep out the November cold when the air raced by, Arthur claimed, at more than thirty miles an hour. She had chosen a rich dark blue corded silk, and a soft greyish blue in a fine wool for the lining, a William Morris pattern: two turtle doves with their heads turned away from each other. The contrast was most effective. She was a little worried about the way the doves were looking in opposite directions but Grace assured her she was being silly and superstitious.

Beneath the duster coat she wore a variant of Rosina's riding outfit, a close fitting tailored jacket in the same Morris pattern, a plain grey waistcoat, and a gored skirt, also in the Morris fabric, to allow freedom of movement and warmth, and on her head a strong plain straw hat with a wide brim, tied on with the thin, wide scarf — almost a veil — she had chosen with Rosina, the strong blue of the peacock's tails a softer version of the blue of the duster coat. She looked enchanting and knew it. England suited her. She bloomed in the soft damp air. If she was to be mistress of Dilberne she would be in the country and out of the way of the fog.

There was even a little applause as she and Arthur drove off. She thought she saw the head concierge take hold of Grace's hand as they left. But perhaps she was being too romantic, seeing love in the air where it was not.

Arthur was looking particularly handsome, she thought, his profile stern and unsmiling as he grappled with the Jehu's eccentricities, its occasional splutters of steam, and whenever the road went downhill, its unholy spurts of speed; she remarked on how quiet the engine was. His expression softened whenever he turned to her to explain the route as they bowled merrily along. Once he put his hand on her knee but she could not be sure whether this was by accident or design. She paid no attention to it. She could see that in courtship the problem was the same worldwide, probably even in Borneo, and throughout the ages. Did one assume a man was shy and encourage him, or risk rejection because he was not shy at all, just not interested?

There was very little horse traffic on the road and precious few automobiles. They managed to avoid, sometimes only just, such pedestrians who wandered into their path, unaware, as Arthur put it, that the roads no longer belonged to them. Once they fell into a race with a six-horsepower Daimler, and won easily, up hill and down; only to be mocked by the driver when he caught up, and racketed by in a cloud of smelly fumes, though this was only because they'd had to stop at the Bear Inn at Esher for Arthur to check the water reservoir and top it up. Then he asked her if it wouldn't be a good idea to have sandwiches and beer in the pub, which they did. Minnie was pleased that Arthur was the kind to stay for refreshments. Men on their travels were too often determined to get to their destinations fast, and begrudged all delay but Arthur seemed perfectly happy to do so. She could see a whole leisurely future stretching ahead, of adventurous outings punctuated by cream teas and the stretching of legs, and admiring of vistas. Her childhood had been dominated by Billy's impatience with any traffic ahead or behind, his anxiety to get home without delay.

A few miles on, Arthur pointed out a large country house across the fields which he told her looked very much like Dilberne Court.

'My heavens!' she said, seeing the scale of the place. She had imagined something cosier and more intimate, black-and-white-beamed, full of nooks and crannies, large, but set in a cottage garden. This house was imposing but without grace and somehow unloved, set in a rather grim landscape of muddy hillsides and bare oaks.

'Dilberne Court has taller chimneys,' he said. 'And is prettier. Dilberne was a wonderful place to grow up in as a child. Mind you, I was mostly at school.'

'Poor you,' she said.

'Oh no,' he said. 'It was my making. Any son of mine will go to Eton. It's a family tradition.'

He caught her eye and smiled. He means what he said in the first place, she thought. He means to marry me but no longer just for my money but because he loves me. Or else he wouldn't put up with my mother the way he does. He has seen her only once or twice, but he is so charming and courteous to her that already she adores him. I mean to marry him not in order to please my father by becoming the wife of an English earl but because I love him. I must love him or why do I feel so protective of him?

She talked a little then about her own home, a vast Gothic castle of a place, uglier even than the pile they'd just passed, crammed with art and antiquities bought by her mother through Duveen Brothers in New York. A renaissance throne here, a Da Vinci painting there, a bust of Augustus Caesar over there beneath the Gothic window.

'What about your father?' asked Arthur. 'Is he a good sort?'

'The best,' she replied.

The Jehu had reached the top of a long hill with a pretty view of a valley called the Devil's Punchbowl, and was starting the descent. She thought they must have reached fifty miles an hour before they reached the bottom and the vehicle slowed.

The speed was exhilarating and she did not care whether she lived or died, so long as she died with Arthur. She was a sorry case, she thought. They were to stay the night at Dilberne Court. The staff had been notified to meet them, so they would not be alone in the house, but there were always ways and means. She would be perfectly capable of abandoning all common sense and seeking out his bed. Why had she ever taken up with Stanton, who had left her with nothing but a shocking inclination towards sexual adventure?

But of course she would not seek out Arthur's bed. It would be most imprudent. A sin well in the past might be overlooked, but a bride-to-be should not show herself as predisposed to loose behaviour.

She wondered whether to tell him she was not her father's daughter but carried the blood of a well-respected member of the English artistic community, but decided against it. He might worry that her inheritance was in danger. He might marry for love and money but it was wishful thinking to suppose he would marry for love alone. Only the poor could afford such luxury.

'As well our house is so large,' she said, casually, 'to fit in all the art. I daresay at Dilberne you have heaps of family paintings?'

'That's so,' he said.

After they had survived the Devil's Punch-bowl she asked him who Flora was. He took his time before replying. She should not have brought the subject up but it was too late now.

'Ah,' he said. 'You have been talking to Rosina. I thought she might say more than she should have. It is quite true; I have been seeing a girl but not lately. When we are married I will of course give her up altogether.'

When we are married. She took him at his word, and did not enquire further. He took her gloved hand and held it, then delicately took off the glove so their bare hands met. He was hot-blooded. His hand should have been cold, unprotected as it was in the wind, but it was warm.

He slowed the Jehu down and steered it into an empty space of land beside the road and stopped. Then he kissed her. Stanton did not kiss but went straight to it. Arthur's speculative lips on hers surprised her and made her feel agreeably virginal, almost spiritual.

She quite hoped he would say he loved her but he didn't. He was an Englishman, and easily embarrassed. You had to tell what he felt by what he did. What he did say was that there was no real point in delaying the announcement of their engagement. It had been love at first sight. The sooner they were married the better. He would write to her father on their return to London asking for his consent to their marriage.

'There is something I must tell you,' she heard herself saying in her elation, even as she begged herself not to. 'I am a girl with a past. It would not be fair to hide it from you. You had your Flora. I had a man called Stanton, an artist. But it's all over now. It was not a happy experience.'

He did not reply, but stared fixedly ahead. A drop of rain appeared on the glass windscreen, and another and then another. They both stared fixedly at the runnels. His face, when she finally dared to look, seemed to have hardened. She saw the old man inside the young. She was up against something she did not quite understand. She saw Rosina in him.

'It's the kind of thing that happens these days,' she said, lightly.

'No. It is not,' he said. 'In America, perhaps. Not to me. Not to my family.'

He drove on to Hindhead in silence where he stopped to fill the boiler. They did not stay for a glass of beer and a sandwich. He had turned into the kind of man who never stopped on a journey if he could help it. At Hindhead he turned the car and they took the road back to London. She was not going to see Dilberne Court with its tall chimneys and pretty aspect where he had been happy as a child. She did not deserve to see it. He had set his face against her. She was a bad woman, fun, but not the marrying kind.

'Why should the rules be different for me than for you?' she enquired.

'Don't play the innocent,' was all he said.

The rain was heavy now. The wind whipped the scarf off her head and it danced around for a while and then vanished into the trees that lined the road. Her beautiful gauzy peacock tails, gone. Colour had drained from everything, all was black and white. She clung to her hat but the wind took that too, and it went after her scarf, flying through the air like some storm-tossed white owl. He took no notice, made no comment. It was getting dark. It was not called the Devil's Punchbowl for nothing. Ghosts and ghouls seemed to laugh at her from the trees. The wind got up and came from all directions so the trees tossed helplessly this way and that and lost their remaining leaves in great blustery clouds.

Some flew into her face and they were slimy. Piles of fallen leaves made the road slippery and the wheels lost their traction; the Jehu skidded and then slipped and slithered backwards and she hoped they would both die. Arthur regained control of the car, and up they went and up to the summit, and then down the other side with the horrid rigid silence between them. This time the descent was not so fast. Perhaps there was less water in the tank so the weight of the vehicle was not so great. Her hair was wet as rain blew in from the open sides. Her clothes were drenched. The duster coat might keep out dust but no one had mentioned rain. The silk had no defence against the wet. And after that, when they had reached level ground he remained silent, and she could think of nothing to say, and then they had to stop again to check the reservoir.

'I think the future lies in the internal combustion engine,' she said, and amazingly, he laughed, and looked young again.

A Household Upset

Saturday 2nd and Sunday 3rd December 1899
But all was not well yet upstairs. Her Ladyship's wrath had not subsided. She asked Reginald to deliver a letter to Mr Abbot at Pickford's in Maida Vale. Reginald reported below stairs that she seemed distracted and distressed when she called for him, that she was still in her wrap though it was eleven in the morning, and that it looked as if it needed a good wash; her face was puffy and her eyes were red. Lily said there had been another episode in the night between the Earl and the Countess. He had knocked at the bedroom door and she had screeched at him to go away, that she hated him, that she wished she were dead, she should never have married him. ('Just as if she were anyone,' as Smithers pointed out.)

'I will not have you in my room ever again,' her Ladyship had screamed. 'Nor will that woman get an invitation.'

Elsie reckoned she was referring to Mrs Baum, wife to the Mr Baum who had disturbed the household a month or so ago. Nothing had been quite the same since. He had been a bird of evil omen. A black crow bringing bad news with him.

Lily, who now slept in the side room opposite the master bedroom, for her Ladyship liked to have her near at night, had been woken by the racket and now reported it in detail. She had found her tongue. His Lordship had initially been calm and mumbled something about how she must pull herself together for the sake of the nation because 'this was affecting his judgement and was out of all proportion to his sin', and her Ladyship had reacted badly. He had, Elsie attested, tossed and turned all night in his dressing room, his bedclothes being so rumpled when she came to make the bed, and a pillow on the floor against the window, as if he had thrown it across the room. He walked to the House of Lords early and breakfasted there.

Mr Abbot was the man who normally handled the transport of family and staff to Belgrave Square. The expectation was that the move back to Dilberne Court would be made well after Christmas. A letter to Pickford's was obviously of interest to the staff, and Mr Neville decided it would be in order for Smithers to steam it open and for him to read its contents, inasmuch as her Ladyship was not herself and might need to be protected from her own actions. Mrs Neville thought this was wrong of him and had snatched the letter from him, and they had words. Trouble upstairs has its echo downstairs, as Grace observed; she had dropped by as she did every few days to pass on such news as she had gleaned at Brown's. The letter lay on the sideboard still unopened while they discussed the rights and wrongs of the situation.

Miss Minnie had gone off on an outing to inspect Dilberne Court with the young Viscount, and Reginald confirmed that the Jehu had been well polished for the occasion, and had 'scrubbed up nicely'. The general expectation was that an engagement would be announced on their return. Grace seemed to have quite come round to Miss Minnie, for reasons upon which did she not expand, but there was a general feeling of relief that if the O'Brien stockyard money came rather soon to the Dilberne estate it would be no bad thing.

Since Mr Baum's early arrival on the steps at the end of October there had been much talk of financial difficulty, and her Ladyship had certainly been rather cautious in her menus — twelve courses and only twenty-eight guests for a charity dinner which royalty was attending was unusually parsimonious — though Reginald attested that the spending on clothes was still lavish, especially in Mrs O'Brien's company.

But that was beside the point. Were they going to read the letter to Pickford's or not? All looked to Grace for a decision. She was moody and could be irrational but generally considered a deep thinker. She pondered for a while and then said, yes, the circumstances were exceptional and Mr Neville should go ahead. So Cook put on the kettle and the glue of the envelope was softened in the steam, Grace carefully and ceremoniously opened the letter and read the contents aloud.

It was a request to Mr Abbot to bring forward the date of the move to Hampshire from January 7th to December 4th. His Lordship and the Viscount would not be accompanying them.

'She can't do that,' said Mrs Welsh. 'The seventeenth is the royal dinner. She has to be here. The Prince is coming. I've got it all in my head, all twelve courses.'

'Oh thank goodness,' said Elsie. 'Alan will

need someone to keep him on the wagon over Christmas. I've been worrying so.'

'I've delivered all the invitations,' said Reginald. 'But it suits me.'

'It won't do,' said Grace. 'You can't uninvite royalty,' and went upstairs to see her Ladyship.

Reginald resealed the letter and took it round to Maida Vale and delivered it into the hands of Mr Abbot himself, who read it briefly and asked him to wait for a reply. It would take only a few minutes.

TESSA MAKES A VISIT

12.30 p.m. Sunday, December 3rd 1899

Tessa was surprised not to find Grace in attendance. She marvelled at how little time it took to become dependent on someone to do your thinking for you, how convenient to have your clothes chosen for you and to tell you how to conduct yourself in public. She must try and find someone like her when she went back to Chicago. If she went back to Chicago. Life here was so much more entertaining than it was back home. Even the newspapers were livelier. She had begun to read the *London Gazette* and follow the progress of the war England was fighting in South Africa. She had lost interest in the war in the Philippines. She no longer felt obliged to tell everyone how much better and bigger everything was in Illinois, from the cattle to the lakes. It was almost as if this was her own country, and she was here by right. She wondered what would have happened if she had met Eyre Crowe and had his baby before she'd met Billy, and moved back with him to London.

It had been a wild party that she and Eyre had gone to. There had been an incident with another of the artists whose name she couldn't even remember, but best not to dwell on that. Billy had been happy to acknowledge another's child as his and bring her up as his own. But to live all your life with a man you liked very much in an unconsummated marriage was surely not right. You could get the Pope to annul a marriage, if you wanted and could pay, which she could — she could pay anything these days, though Billy might try to stop her.

She could start afresh in a new marriage, in a new land where she could begin again. Billy, she assumed, but you never knew, would go on supporting her; and even if he didn't, Eyre probably had money enough for both of them. He was a well-established painter. His works hung in the Royal Academy. You did not stay poor if that happened to you. She had thought perhaps Eyre might be at the d'Asti party, but he hadn't been. She'd thought the guests were a rather mixed lot, and Grace had agreed. They were not all out of the top drawer.

Where was Grace? There could be no harm in just going round and seeing what Eyre looked like these days; you just didn't know after all these years. If he looked presentable she might just introduce herself to him. She knew he had not married. Perhaps he still thought of her, pined for her even? He lived (Mr Eddie had traced him through the Royal Academy, and Tessa hoped he was discreet) where Great Portland Street crossed New Cavendish Street. But she did not want to sit in a cab on her own, watching a front door like a jealous woman, with the cab driver sniggering away. Perhaps Mr Eddie would come with her? Grace was quite pally with Mr Eddie, she had noticed. On the ornery side Grace, but as a lady's maid, superb.

Which was why Tessa found herself sitting in a cab with Mr Eddie at half-past noon outside No. 88, as the door of the respectable town house opened and three respectable gentlemen came out, from the look of them going to lunch. One was Eyre Crowe, looking older and greyer than she remembered him. Well, of course she didn't suppose she herself she looked any younger, but Eyre had gone down the desiccated route while she had gone the fleshy way; he looked as if a mere breath of Billy's roaring laugh could sweep him quite away. He looked very different, now that she saw him in the flesh, from the man in the Whistler painting, much more like the man she remembered. One man she recognized as the curator from the Royal Academy, the other she did not know, but he was like one of those kind of guys you met in the corridors of the Art Institute back home, thoughtful peering creatures who knew everything there was to know about everything arty or philosophical, except how to get a woman to bed or enjoy a good dinner.

She opened the side window and listened. They paused just by her cab; the conversation absorbed them, and they did not even notice her. Mr Eddie sat still and listened too. He had been a pleasant escort, pointing out sights of interest on the journey, and asking no impertinent questions.

'It was Hallam's argument,' one was saying, 'that scepticism in philosophy, atheism in religion and democracy in politics, is the only way to achieve truth.'

'All very well,' Eyre was saying. 'But where does that leave Art?'

Tessa thought she had heard all she needed to hear, seen all she needed to see. Let them get on with it. Anyway she loved Billy: a cuddle was better than many women got at her age, and it was only on a bad day that she thought he was so busy making money he wouldn't notice if she was there or wasn't. Of course he would be hurt and upset if she left. She closed the window gently — not that there was much danger these brainy old men would notice what was going on around them — and said to Mr Eddie:

'That's enough. Let's go home.' And as the driver whipped up his horse, she added: 'Little does he know what a narrow escape he had.'

Mr Eddie took note of the remark. He would pass it on to Grace and he knew she would be relieved that Lord Master Arthur's father-in-law would not suddenly change. Such things could happen.

THE BEAR AT ESHER

6.30 p.m. Sunday, 3rd December 1899
The Arnold Jehu puffed up to the entrance porch of the Bear Inn and Arthur escorted Minnie inside. He asked the landlady to see to her wet clothes. Minnie returned in half an hour or so, comparatively dry and dressed in a simple blue skirt and white shirt and woollen wrap which the hotel, he supposed, was used to providing these days for drenched lady motorists. He himself had been protected from the worst of the downpour by his long leather coat, and a rub down with a towel sufficed. He ordered a simple meal of steak and kidney pie and a bottle of wine between them.

He apologized when she reappeared.

'I apologize,' he said. 'My behaviour was not excusable. But you must acknowledge it was something of a shock. I was surprised that you did not tell me from the beginning, but *autres pays, autres moeurs.*'

Minnie responded by demanding a whisky and soda. When it came she complained that it tasted differently from the whisky she had back home.

He said no doubt she knew. No doubt her past life was full of whisky and sodas of one kind or another. She glared at him and drank it down and asked for another. She was looking very pretty, and they ate by candlelight.

He told her all about Flora and how he kept her in a house in Half Moon Street, and how, pressured by his parents he had panicked and even asked the girl to marry him, then, having met Minnie, changed his mind. He did not mention bloody Redbreast; that seemed unnecessary. He told her he'd realized he was unwilling to give Flora up — 'What a pretty name!' said Minnie — even after marriage, so perhaps the answer was not to get married at all. He certainly did not want to embark on a marriage knowing there was a third person in it, even though marriage was for procreation, and pleasure taken outside it merely human and excusable. He was not as low as that. His parents would have to solve their financial problems leaving him out of it.

She pushed away her plate of steak and kidney pie, saying she did not like meat —

her father ate little else, though he sometimes tempered it with corn or hominy grits.

'I thought the Irish lived on potatoes,' he said. 'At least you don't inherit that particular tendency.' She looked at him oddly.

'You must see,' he said, 'that a man from a family like mine, whose son will eventually be an earl, must be very careful. The wife must be above reproach. The line has to breed true.'

'I am not a bitch,' she said, and ordered some sole and then when it arrived complained that the lemon was dry and had no juice in it and demanded another. She lacked the *savoir faire* of his mother, who would have thought it beneath her to complain about a dry lemon. In her own household, of course, yes, standards had to be kept up at all costs, but outside it, no. His mother had been of comparatively humble, though wealthy, stock, on her father's side, but knew how to behave. This girl tried, but couldn't quite. *Not a bitch.* He'd never heard a girl say the word like that. She had the instincts of an Irish peasant, a background in the Chicago stockyards. All the same, with her hair falling lavishly about her face as it lost the last of its dampness, she was very attractive. He would not have been sorry to marry her.

He wished she had not made it impossible. Flora could have faded somehow into the background, but Minnie had to bring it up. He would have it out with Rosina when he got back. Confounded Rosina could be a terrible mischief-maker. Because she was not happy she wished everyone else to be unhappy.

'For a bitch not to breed true,' Minnie said, 'she needs to have had pups. I've had no children.'

'People try to argue that on this side of the Atlantic too,' Arthur said, 'but it is not the case. With mares and bitches, all they have to do is get out once and they're never the same again.'

'The hog that a sow happens to get out with first,' she said, 'makes no difference whatsoever to the litter she produces when properly mated. How can it? I am a child of the stockyards. We breed scientifically. You English are just romantics.'

And she, talking like this, was most certainly not a romantic. Minnie of the stockyards! He could hear his friends laughing.

'There is no reason we cannot remain friends,' he said. 'In fact I hope we do.'

He knew she liked him. He could tell from the way she inclined her body towards him. She would be easy. A girl who does it with one man will do it with another. Girls quickly get a taste for sin, learn to compare one man with another, enter the realm of the animal where Flora dwelt, comparing 'doodles' one to another, and go on looking for perfection until the end of their days, never satisfied.

'I've asked them to light a fire in the bedroom upstairs,' he said. 'It's very pleasant up there. Shall we go up for a nightcap?'

She didn't jump to her feet and scream or stab him with the knife with which she was cutting her cheese, though the expression on her face suggested she might — but just stiffened and enquired coldly,

'Are you out of your mind?'

And then, in a gesture worthy of the Chicago stockyards, she slapped his face.

Arthur went out to see that the Jehu was safely tucked away for the night, and when he went back inside she was nowhere to be seen.

ROSINA CHALLENGES HER MOTHER

11 a.m. Sunday, 3rd December 1899

Her Ladyship looked askance at her daughter. The girl had abandoned her customary unconventional yet tasteful garments for a motley gathering together of clothes which looked as if they had been chosen by a child. A pair of striped black and white pantaloons, like a clown's, a white smocked shirt like a baby's, and a man's waistcoat beaded with the kind of glitter a magpie would steal.

She seemed to be in fancy dress, and, her mother thought, looked almost insane. 'You look very peculiar, Rosina,' she said. 'Perhaps we should call a doctor.'

'It is not I, but you who are behaving oddly, Mama. You cannot uninvite a Prince. It will cause comment. And you have seen fit to fetch that poor waif upstairs and try to train her up as a lady's maid. She is irremediably incompetent. These garments are Lily's choice: they are what she picked out for me. I wear them only to prove a point. She has put a silk shirt of mine in with the laundry wash, and allows *you* to go around looking like a madwoman in a soiled wrap and with your hair undone. Grace would never have permitted such a thing. Please bring Grace back. Mother, I need her. You neglect me. And all your concern goes to perfect strangers, and American ones at that. Why? Because you want their money? It is disgraceful.'

Lady Isobel, who had been feeling much better now she had made the decision to spend Christmas in Hampshire, so that she could order her life again, feared she might well be flung back into despair and confusion by her daughter's nagging.

'My early return to the country has nothing to do with the Prince,' she said, 'though I daresay he is much to blame in all this. I don't mean to remain a day longer than I have to under this roof. Your grandfather was right. I should not have married your father. He was only an Honourable when I met him, and a second son at that. I never expected to have to live like this.'

'Be reasonable, Mama,' said Rosina. 'Father only did what men do,' and she launched into a tirade, which amounted to a validation of her decision not to marry, and made her mother regret that she had trusted Rosina with the cause of her distress. All Rosina could do, Isobel said, was think about herself. It was almost as if other people had no reality.

Rosina repeated that she saw no point in trusting her feelings to someone who was bound to hurt them with the passage of time. She did not intend to be a wife.

'A wife grows old, so the husband looks elsewhere,' she said. 'A wife is obliged to have children, and likely as not dies horribly in childbirth, and is told as she dies she has done her duty to her husband. No, if one can afford not to, no woman should marry. It is a form of slavery. In return for a wedding gown and a declaration of love, a woman offers her sexual and domestic services in exchange for her keep for the rest of her life. Obliged to do things she doesn't want to, like inviting the heir to the throne to dinner.'

'Mr Shaw again,' said her mother. 'You'd have never turned up for the Prince's dinner in any case. You'd have found a meeting to go to, one that seemed more important to you than any service you could possibly offer me, your mother.'

'The Prince finds my *décolletage*

irresistible,' said Rosina. 'He likes to stare at it, finger it, and if I am sat next to him, to brush his hand against it as he manages to lower his hand to my knee and give it a good pinch.'

'But Rosina,' said her mother, 'when have you ever even met the prince? All talk of him but few see him.'

'On occasion, Mama,' said Rosina, 'he is to be found at the d'Asti salon. He likes to keep up with the thinkers and artists of the day, the ones you so studiously avoid. Where but there is he to meet so many actresses?'

'This is fantasy, my poor Rosina,' said her mother.

'If only it were, Mama. Combine a good *décolletage* with a good intellect and a good pinch and our Prince turns into a slavering idiot. His pleasure is in finding a woman who thinks, and then depriving her of the capacity to do so. He squeezes it out of her. He is very big and very heavy, but also very good at what he does. Flora reports that Father is also very good at what he does, which I am sure you know, and why you are in such a state now. You must be more like the Princess, Mama, and be nice to your husband's mistresses.'

Isobel stared open-mouthed at her daughter.

'You are astonished, Mother, that the Prince should like me in this way. You think I'm so plain no man will look at me. Of course, he seldom gets to see me standing up. When I am seated I suppose my height is not so noticeable. When I am seated my bosom is at eye level. I expect that is what he likes.'

'My dear, you are perfectly capable of attracting any man you want, if only you would not stoop, and stand tall and look them in the eye, and not scowl and thrust your chin out at the same time. It is a bad habit. I had no idea that this went on. My poor girl!'

'You think I am mad,' said Rosina, sniffling a little. Isobel was always nervous of sympathizing with her daughter. At the first 'you poor little thing' Rosina would burst into tears. Perhaps she was at fault in the way she had reared her daughter? Been hard when she could have been soft, unkind when she should have been kind? Told her daughter how pretty she was instead of pointing out her faults?

'My dear, you are a lovely girl,' Isobel said, 'and have a noticeably graceful body,' and even as she said it saw Rosina's face relax and the scowl disappear. Really, was it so easy? But Rosina had not finished with her mother yet.

'Why do you think the Prince keeps Father so close? The Prince is after me. Father is not so great a wit, though I daresay good enough for a drunken evening on the tiles when the Prince is short of a friend brave enough to go gambling with him. I inherited my mind not from Papa, thank God, but from you and my grandfather Silas. Inasmuch as I am responsible for his death, and I know it suits people to say so, I am truly sorry I killed him, if I did, and of course I did not mean to. I think you should stay quietly here until you feel better and give your dinner as planned. I will come and face the Prince out, and if he fingers my bosom, simper like all the other young women round your table hoping for his favours.'

Isobel thought her daughter had lost all touch with reality. Why would the Prince be bothered with a girl like Rosina? She was no beauty. It was true that the girl had a quick mind and was well-informed, which the Prince seemed to appreciate in a woman. Rosina's was a nicely shaped bosom which many admired; that could not be denied. But to attribute her father's friendship with the Prince to herself — that way madness lay. Rosina was unhinged. Her father Robert's abominable behaviour —

which somehow the girl must have come to know — had triggered off some kind of manic episode. And on top of everything else what had the girl said? *'I think you should stay quietly here until you feel better?'* How dare she offer her mother advice! The mother she had cruelly orphaned, and ought to honour the more. Rage mounted.

'I wish you had never been born,' Isobel almost said to her daughter, but managed to stop herself. There was no escape from duty. Once one was a wife and mother one's own personal life was at an end. To give in to rage and sorrow was to weaken the props that kept the entire structure of family and household going. She had a vision of the Modder Kloof mine, awash with murky water, ironwork eaten through by rust, the wooden props already rotting and failing, and saw it as a metaphor for her own life. If she was not careful everything would fall in upon itself.

'Oh please go away,' she said and Rosina did.

Rosina Sets Pappagallo Free

11.30 p.m. Sunday, 3rd December 1899
Rosina gave a little skip and a jump as she went to her room. She felt happy. She had made all that up about the Prince, and her mother had believed her, and even told her she had a graceful body. She had been waiting years for her mother to say she was pretty. Now she could be. She was not ugly and plain and impossibly tall. She was, come to think of it, just the kind of intelligent girl the Prince did seem to favour. Lily Langtry was no dullard. Princess Alexandra was tall and everyone loved and admired her. She, Rosina, should stand up straight and be more like the Princess, and not spend her time stooping and looking at her toes and trying to be little and small. She must practise not scowling.

She took off her silly clothes in front of the mirror and tried standing tall, and liked the way her small breasts seemed to perk

409

up, and the nipples stand out. Of course the Prince admired them; everyone did.

It was chilly in the room, in spite of the fire. Her limbs were long and thin and shapely, much longer than Minnie's. If she relaxed her brow, her mother was right; her chin seemed to sink back and be no more protuberant than anyone else's. She might try changing to clothes that fitted more tightly and didn't hide her shape in flowing velvets and velours; she would think less about comfort and more about the impression she was making on others. Next time she was at a meeting she would stand up and speak her mind. She had seen advertisements for classes in public speaking for women and she would investigate them. She wouldn't just think about the possibility: she would actually do it.

She went to her wardrobe and looked through her clothes. Why had she felt it so impossible to choose her own, but that she must instead rely on someone else to do it? Perhaps because thus she had been making Grace responsible for her very looks? It was an absurd way to behave. She would be proud and daring — continue to be as she had at the d'Astis' salon, in the blue dress and the rakish hat with the leopard-skin band. Boldly she picked out the narrowest skirt she owned, in a plain blue wool, and a white shirt with no frills, and buckled it tightly round her waist. She found her leopard-skin hat, looked at herself in the mirror, and lo, it was what she had made, like God, and like God she saw that what she had made was good.

Rosina wondered how Arthur had got on with the American heiress and hoped the stupid girl had sent him packing in disgust. She said 'stupid' advisedly. Only someone really stupid would dismiss so tragic and profound a work as *The War of the Worlds* as 'diverting'. If, in pursuit of the title she craved, Minnie had managed to 'forgive' Arthur, she, Rosina, could always tell Arthur that his future wife was illegitimate, a bastard, conceived out of wedlock. That would soon put paid to his knavish tricks. Even Arthur would not let the house of Hedleigh fall so low, and the Earldom go to the son of a bastard wife.

Pappagallo squawked and flew across the room and landed on her shoulder, startling her. Its wings had grown; they needed clipping. It was unfair to keep this pretty creature trapped in a stuffy room. Its nature was to fly free. She went over to the window and flung it open. The bird launched itself on the instant into space. Immediately she was anxious. How would it survive? Where would it find the fruit and nuts it needed? Winter was coming. It might freeze to death. Perhaps parrots had enemies who flew about the skies? Hawks? Buzzards? It occurred to her that she knew so much about everything yet so little about the real world. The parrot fluttered and faltered but made it back to the windowsill and then jumped back upon her shoulder. They were both saved.

She remembered she had called in at Vine Street Police Station and regretted it. But it would probably be all right. Just another mad woman, stumbling in from the fog, making a mean complaint. Getting others into trouble. They would probably forget it.

HER LADYSHIP FACES THE TRUTH

Monday, 4th and Tuesday, 5th December 1899
Her Ladyship decided rage and loathing must have a stop. That she simply did not have the strength to see a move to the country through without Robert's help and support. Cancelling the royal dinner would be far more tiresome than giving it. And, of course, Freddie would crow and make mischief and spread gossip.

Lily was nowhere to be found, so Isobel saw to her toilette herself, taking her time. She could see that it was hopeless to try to punish Robert. He simply would not understand what he had done, how he had turned her whole married life into a lie, how cruelly and suddenly destroyed the illusion of the love between them for which she had thanked God on her knees, and thought herself so blessed, that singular good fortune, that 'specialness' from which she had for thirty years construed her very existence, and borne her children too. She had been a fool, and had to face it. Hers was not the only body Robert had enjoyed, or could enjoy. But that was what it was like for women. One man all your life, the purpose of sex procreation, forget pleasure. Men were allowed more liberty, the force of their animal instincts forgiven by Church and State and increasingly, society. She must acknowledge that, once fired up, men could not help themselves.

Fredericka even permitted male guests declared the guilty party in a divorce case to sit at her dinner table. Times were changing, a new century nearly here. Next time Robert came knocking at her door she would do her duty, try to forget that these limbs had once entwined with another woman than herself, allow him to penetrate her as he had another, and show no disgust.

She had no choice but to face reality, forgive Robert, bring her daughter to her senses and her son back to face his responsibilities. The royal dinner would go ahead. But she would not invite Mrs Baum. She would not humiliate herself that far.

Even as she decided this, Mr Neville came in with a letter. It was a reply from Mr Abbot at Pickford's. They had replied with exemplary speed. When she opened it she realized why. The firm thanked her for her instructions but could not oblige until they had been paid the amount owing for the last five moves over four years. Their account totalling one hundred and thirty pounds had been presented five times but they had so far received no response. As soon as the matter was settled, of course they would be only too happy to oblige his Lordship and family.

She kept her face unmoved for Mr Neville's benefit, but her blood ran cold. This was unheard of. People like her did not receive letters like this. It was outrageous.

'Will that be all, ma'am?' She thought there was a new tone in his voice, one she did not quite understand. She glanced as if casually at the envelope. It was hard to tell, because the back of the envelope was torn, but the paper along the seal did look a little damp, wrinkled and stretched. It was not beyond the bounds of possibility that the envelope had been steamed open, the contents read, and it then resealed. But no one on her staff would surely do anything so petty and dishonourable.

'Will you ask Cook to come and see me?' she asked. 'I think we will have an extra course after all on the seventeenth. We could have roast beef and Yorkshire pudding before the sorbet. The Prince is very fond of it, I hear.'

When Mr Neville had gone she tried to get hold of Robert at the House and failed. She telephoned Mr Baum instead and asked him to call on her. Then she went to Robert's study and started opening and collating all the unopened envelopes, so many of them brown, that she could find.

Arthur Goes to
Half Moon Street

2 a.m. Monday, 4th December 1899

It was two in the morning before Arthur got to Half Moon Street. Minnie had allowed him to take her back to Brown's since she was left with no other way of getting home. He had found her stamping around in the lobby of the Bear Inn trying to hire a cab when it was obviously impossible to do so.

The pair had driven back in silence, she in clothes still not properly dried, too proud to complain and too angry to speak, though he did do his best to be pleasant. It would have been much easier for everyone if she had been prepared to stay the night in Esher — she could have taken her own room, but nothing would do but that she went home immediately. She even talked about her reputation, which in the circumstances was fairly absurd. When they finally got to Brown's he had had to rouse the concierge to gain admittance. He had

417

thought surely such a place would have a watchman on duty through the night. But no.

It was unfortunate that just as he ran the bell on the reception desk, Grace appeared out of nowhere to cluck over her young lady and fuss about her welfare. There would be extra explaining to his mother now. She was upset enough as it was. He himself had been fairly upset when she told him about his father's misbehaviour. Her grief had probably contributed to his realization a man could not honourably marry a wife when he had a mistress in tow. Well, others could; no doubt someone like Redbreast could, he having the nerve of the devil, which he, Viscount Hedleigh, did not.

One way and another it had been a devil of a day and he deserved time with Flora. He parked the Arnold Jehu outside the house. She was rather muddy but he looked forward to showing her off to Flora in the morning. Bother what the neighbours said. At least an Arnold Jehu was quiet, being a steam car, and didn't wake the street with the clackety noise of an internal combustion engine. The little house was in darkness, which was a relief. The memory of seeing Redbreast and Flora entwined and silhouetted behind a lighted window blind had engraved itself on his memory. He wished he could have Flora to himself. He supposed it was not possible that he loved Flora? That he had given up his fiancée — well, almost — rather than lose his mistress, when it came to it? He might even be using Minnie's past — which to some people would not seem so terrible — as an excuse to get out of the marriage. Of course the poor girl had been upset. She was a nice, bright, attractive girl, and virtuous too, as her immediate response to his suggestion had proved. He would have to apologize. Life, which had once been so simple, with right and wrong so obvious, was getting very complicated.

He knocked again upon the door; and again. There was no reply. He called softly up at the window but had the impression there was no one there to hear. Something was amiss. He could see in the murky light from the streetlight that the aspidistra plant was not standing in its normal place on the windowsill. He found his key and used it, though she did not like him doing this, preferring him always to knock. But there was something wrong.

When he went upstairs the rooms were empty, cleared of furniture, plants, orna-ments. There were a few discarded clothes in the wardrobe, the odd crushed hat, the odd fashion plate, a couple of rugs left behind. An overflowing waste paper basket lying on its side. There had been no robbery, but a swift packing, a complete but untidy removal of all belongings, a faint whiff of Flora's cheap scent hanging in the air, and a ghostly trill of laughter but it might have been the water in the pipes. He found a note. It was from Flora and addressed to him.

'Dear Arthur,' it said, in Flora's careful hand, blue ink on flower-decorated pink paper. *'Forgive me, but I have gone to Robin. He loves me very much and looks after me. Remember me with affection as I do you, your loving Flora.'*

He went out onto the landing, and sat on the stairs because there was nowhere else to sit. He felt very sleepy so he took a dusty old rug and put it in the bath and pulled another one over him and lay cramped and shivering until he fell asleep.

Early in the morning there was a tremendous knocking on the door, which made the floor shake. He clambered out of the bath in a hurry, aware of an evident emergency. He looked out of the window and a helmeted policeman with brass buttons and a small neat moustache was walking round

420

the Jehu, making notes. Somebody else seemed to be hurling themselves against the front door trying to break it open. Arthur hurried down the stairs and opened the door just as two more policemen fell inside, these two both wore tremendous moustaches. One was very tall and fat and the other one quite small and weedy, and wearing thick-lensed spectacles. He couldn't help feeling that for some reason they wanted to make him laugh, so he did.

They did not laugh in return but, grim-faced, pushed past him in their eagerness to get upstairs and catch whoever it was they were after. He went after them. He was very stiff from sleeping in so uncomfortable a place as a bath.

'Your bird has flown,' he said, as they stopped, surprised. Because there was nowhere for anyone to hide. They looked under the rugs in the bath but there was no one there either.

He found himself laughing again, and the little one said, 'It's no laughing matter, sir, as you will find out.' They showed him badges which claimed to be from Vine Street Police Station and one of them bent and picked up a discarded pink camisole from the floor, inspected it, and said, 'Be so good as to adjust your dress, sir.'

He asked them what they were doing and the talkative one said, 'Making the area safe for respectable folk, sir.' Arthur said he was perfectly respectable folk and a man can sleep in a bath if he wants to, and when they asked for his name and address, he gave it as Viscount Hedleigh and No. 17, Belgrave Square.

One of them asked if that was where the Earl lived. Arthur said, 'Well, obviously.'

They looked at one another and murmured something inaudible. He wanted badly to sit down but there was nowhere to sit. He opened the window and sat upon the sill and swung his legs. This seemed to annoy them: they ran to where he sat and swung his legs back on the floor. He was not accustomed to being manhandled and said so, and adding that if anyone owed anyone respects it was they to him, not he to them: they were surely the servant of the tax-payer not the other way round. He hoped he was right about this. If Minnie had been around she could have told him. He said they had no business breaking into the property of honest citizens.

Everything quietened down. He thought perhaps he had hit one of them: there was some muttering about 'in the course of their duty'. They asked after a Miss Flora Evans and Arthur said he did not know her whereabouts. She had lived here once but had recently moved out. They asked him how long, and where, and he said he had no idea, and they suggested that cooperation would be to his advantage. He said he was more than anxious to cooperate, which by now was true.

They asked for the name of the occupant of the flat and asked him who paid the rent, and he said he paid the rent. He remembered Reginald once saying something about the new vagrancy laws but could not remember exactly what, and surely they were meant for the lower classes not people like him. Arthur was sensible enough not to say this. No, there was no other occupant. They said the neighbours said otherwise. No, he did not live in the premises. They asked him in that case why had he been there in the morning after obviously staying overnight and leaving his automobile parked outside. He had no answer. They said he was under suspicion for aiding and abetting in the keeping of a disorderly house or brothel. They would not detain him at present, but they would be in touch with him in the near future. He asked them who their informant was and they would not say. They asked for the name of his solicitor and he gave them Mr Baum's. Arthur drove away in the Jehu. For the first time he engaged the new condenser. It seemed more important than anything that the steam pressure did not suddenly fall. As it was, water levels must be very low, for distracted as he had been, he had foolishly failed to top up the boiler when they were at Brown's and had had the opportunity. He had installed the condenser in time for the trip to Hampshire but when it came to it had not engaged it, inasmuch as there had been one or two minor explosions when first it had been tried it out. Fortunately the Jehu, his faithful servant, now roared off into Park Lane and home with no embarrassing loss of power.

He wasn't sure why he was laughing, save that one bad dream seemed to be easing into another. He had left Minnie. Flora was gone. He had slept in a bath. The police were after him. Heaven knew what would happen when he got home. But home he'd got, and in style.

He parked in the Mews and went in the house through the servants' entrance. He ate what was on the sideboard in the morning room. It was too early for breakfast, but thick soft warm new rolls, a big slab of butter and Cheddar cheese had already been laid out. There was no sign of any staff. He made plump cheese sandwiches and bit into them and for some reason this made him think of Flora, something about the contrast of softness and hardness between his teeth. How would he live without her? Then he thought of Minnie, and somehow it was the coldness of the butter as it melted in the warmth of his mouth that had made him think of her. What had he done?

He took a long hot bath to get the stiffness out of his limbs, got into bed and went back to sleep. It was just as well because it was going to be a busy day.

Minnie Weeps All Day

Monday, 4th December 1899

Minnie spent most of the next day crying. She wept on her mother, she wept on Grace. She wept for every trouble she had had in her life, every undeserved snub, insult and rejection she had ever received — because when she was five her best friend Louise stopped speaking to her, and never explained why: because when she was six, and a little boy she didn't know pushed her over and she grazed her perfect knee, and how then her nurse Emmylou had tried to pick the gravel out with a pin so it hurt, instead of foaming it out with peroxide. She wept for the loss of a toy and the death of pets, and for the failure of Stanton to love her properly and understand the remarkable gift that the use of her body was. What worse humiliation and grief for a young woman was there ever than to be pushed aside by the man she loved?

Tessa cried in sympathy, and explained to her daughter that she was weeping not only because she had lost Arthur, but for the sum of all those sorrows past as well. Sometimes everything got together and came up and hit you. But Minnie wasn't listening.

Tessa used every approach she could think of. Arthur was variously a vile seducer who had tried to take advantage, a silly young Englishman who had been sent away from his mother too young — and she had half a mind to give his mother what for — and couldn't Minnie try being angry for a change, instead of falling into self pity? There were more fish in the sea, they would go to Italy next week, he was not so great a catch as a duke and she had heard there were one or two of those available — Mr Eddie had told her the Duke of Alvechurch was a widower and looking — Grace interjected that he was far too old, and just a pity the young Duke of Pentridge was no longer available. Tessa observed that some women were perfectly happy just cuddling, what was Grace talking about, and Minnie stopped snuffling to say she wasn't the cuddling type and Tessa said she could see that might be the case. Minnie started howling again.

Minnie said she didn't give a hot hoot

about titles any more; she just wanted to be settled and happy. And she had been so nearly settled and happy. If only she hadn't blurted out the truth, if only, if only, if only . . . sob, sob, sob.

Now it was Grace's turn to comfort her. There was bad blood in the Dilberne family: Miss Minnie was well out of it; the father had kept a mistress, the same one as the son's — a startled 'What?' from both Tessa and her mother — everyone had known about it except the poor Countess herself. It would only have happened to Minnie in the end. Bad blood would out.

Minnie said she didn't darn well care, a few years of happiness was worth a lifetime of misery.

'You didn't say that when Stanton left,' said her mother, and Minnie howled.

Minnie was such a pretty girl, Grace said, so spirited and brave, and any decent man would be glad to have her, only it wasn't wise to take the whalebones out of bodices, and perhaps next time she shouldn't show herself to be so well-read and certainly be a little more discreet about her past, though times were changing and soon virginity might cease to be a prize and experience more valued.

Minnie wept on. There would never be a

next time. She would never risk heartbreak again. Grace rang down for some strong coffee and black cherry gâteau and Minnie stopped crying and wolfed the latter — it was so delicious.

Minnie said she had so looked forward to being mistress of Dilberne Court: she wanted like anything to be the lady of a stately English house, and Grace said as lady of the house she'd have to forget leisure, she'd have had her work cut out taking soup to the tenants and overseeing the gardeners. Minnie had had a close shave, if you asked Grace, and she should thank her lucky stars she was saved. Just as well she'd had the spirit to slap the Viscount's face. Otherwise her reputation would be ruined on both sides of the Atlantic.

What do I care, said Minnie and she just loved Arthur and that was that, and she wanted to have children who would be half-her and half-him and that way they could never be parted. If only she'd gone upstairs with him when he asked her everything would be different.

'It sure as hell's bells would have been, Minnie,' said her mother. 'He'd have left you this morning instead of you leaving him last night. Nine months' time and you'd know all about "different"!' But at least,

Tessa said, now they could get back home where people spoke how you could understand them. Billy would be over his pique and they could all be happy again. Home was home to her so long as it had Minnie in it. Grace was to go and ask Mr Eddie for tickets back home on the next liner out of Southampton, so long as it wasn't the *Oceanic.*

Minnie, touched, flung her arms round her mother, and said, 'I love you, Ma.' Then she asked, 'Can we take Grace with us?'

Tessa looked at Grace and asked, 'How about it?'

'I would like that very much,' said Grace, after only a second or two's thought.

'Well whadd'ya know, whadd'ya know!' said Tessa. 'Poor Mr Eddie!'

Minnie finally dried her tears: they'd stopped running: she'd used them all up. She was finished with men for ever.

A BUSY DAY AT THE BAUM'S

8 a.m. Tuesday, 5th December 1899
Over in Golders Green the Baums were
beside themselves. Eric had not yet managed to get to work. The children were playing up: it was not surprising; both had
dreadful coughs and colds. Their little noses
were inflamed and their nostrils red-
rimmed. Eric felt their ill health was his
fault: some of the windows had not been
fitted properly, and they were waiting to be
replaced. Fog had curled in through cracks
like a kind of poison gas. People did not
seem to realize just how dangerous this new
kind of sulphur fog was. One of the reasons
he had bought land up here was that it
would be out of the reach of miasma. He
hated to be wrong. Worse, there were financial implications for the state of the coal
industry; the domestic coal fire was the
bedrock of its profitability, and now there
was even talk of their being banned in

London altogether — nothing seemed to be going right for him. Worse, the excavating of the Golders Green Tube Line had been cancelled again, yet another construction company having gone bust, and it might be a whole ten years before the system was up and running, and his journey to and from the office made easier. He looked back on their earlier days in Islington as a golden age when he could walk to work and he and Naomi were happy together and she was always in a good mood, and receptive and generous in bed.

He could not wish the children out of existence, but this morning they were playing up to such an extent that he almost did; the little girl refusing to dress and whining, and the little boy darting around and pinching his sister: both so noisy he could hardly think, and annoying their mother to such an extent that over breakfast the normally patient Naomi had slapped little Jonathan on his leg and little Barbara on her arm, and then burst into tears herself. He, who once had been so good with the children, now seemed almost unable to cope with them.

The postman had been and there was still no invitation to the Dilberne's royal dinner though he had reminded his Lordship several times. It was such a small thing to ask, just a simple social invitation in return for the work he had done on his Lordship's behalf: setting up a loan, finding enthusiasts for what was still a speculative project, establishing a new syndicate of reliable investors. It was all work, not magic out of thin air, as Dilberne seemed to suppose. He, Baum, could still pull the plug on the family any time, but he was reluctant to do it. Cassel wouldn't like it one bit. Dilberne had increasingly powerful and influential friends. It would certainly not do Naomi's social ambitions any good.

It was a shame that a clever woman like Naomi — who had a real scientific bent and a good mind, and had done so well in her exams — though of course she could never graduate — should be confined to household duties, but there it was. She had been born to marry and have children, and there was nothing for it for the rest of her life, but she must wipe the noses of small children and believe her position in the world depended upon meeting a rascal like the Prince of Wales. It was shocking that a person like the Countess of Dilberne — who had not even been born into the aristocracy but into trade — was able to dictate his wife's happiness.

He had not put himself out to get to work this morning because his office had rung through on the newly installed telephone line and told him that the Countess of Dilberne had summoned him to attend her. And he didn't see why the blazes he should.

And then Naomi stopped crying and flung his arms around him and said she was sorry, she loved him, and all that mattered was that they were happy together. He felt a great surge of love for her and the children, and a great surge of anger towards the Countess of Dilberne. He would certainly go and visit her. He would get an invitation out of her if it killed him.

Before he left for the muddy walk to Hampstead Heath and the long journey down to the City on the 210 bus, the telephone bell rang again. Vine Street Police Station had been in touch with the office and wanted to know details of the Dilberne rental of Half Moon Street. Should the clerk tell them it was now shared with the Hon. Anthony Robin, or stay mum? Stay mum, said Eric, if in doubt stay mum, he would deal with the matter when he got there. This could be interesting. He had another lever to pull.

A Busy Day Below Stairs

Tuesday, 5th December 1899

Down in the kitchens the relief was general. The royal dinner was on. There was to be no sudden departure for Hampshire. Only Elsie was disappointed. Her Ladyship had seemed quite herself again when she had sent for Cook.

The latter was worried by the prospect of serving a Yorkshire pudding for royalty. Such batter-based foods could be tricky; if they were to rise the oven had to be just so and the pudding placed beneath the joint to catch the drippings. Oven space would be at a premium, what with the patties — though they could be cooked earlier — the grouse, the ducklings, the lamb and now the beef as well — a lot of juggling would be required between hot, medium and resting ovens. Cooks got good incomes but early deaths, she observed, bitterly.

Mrs Neville had snatched the letter from

Pickfords from Mr Neville's hand even as he held it in steam from the kettle, and refused to let him read it. The contents of the reply remained a mystery. Enough to know that the royal dinner was back on.

The Viscount had crept in before dawn and eaten all the bread and cheese. No one could quite make head or tail of that. He was meant to be down in the country. Reginald said the Jehu had had a soaking which had done no favours to the upholstery but at least his Lordship had finally tried out the new condenser and it had worked.

'What's a condenser when it's at home?' Smithers asked.

'Only what I've been devoting my genius to for the last three months,' Reginald said, blessing her with a smile. Good cheer seemed to have returned to the household.

Her Ladyship had made herself look presentable and had settled into his Lordship's office and was now sorting through his papers. Just as well, the staff decided, that someone was at last doing so; the task had been postponed for far too long. Mind you, it was understandable. His Lordship had been very busy both at the House and re-stabling the horse with the funny foreign name, Agripin, on the Roseberry estate. Mr Neville spelled it out for both Elsie and Lily, who was getting on nicely with her reading, and told them it meant 'wild horse' in Russian.

All felt slightly shamefaced at having steamed open a private letter — it smacked of a real disloyalty — but were grateful that Mrs Neville had saved them from the further disgrace of having read it.

A Busy Day Above Stairs

2.30 p.m. Tuesday, 5th December 1899
In the early afternoon the Countess summoned her son to her side. He found her in surprisingly fine form: composed and efficient, surrounded by papers and in his father's office, apparently recovered from her fit of pique. There were no menus or fashion plates to hand.

She told him briskly that he must expedite his wedding to Minnie. There was no choice in the matter. The news of the engagement would be announced at the royal dinner: the wedding would be in June. She had added up his father's debts and found they were indebted to the tune of some seventy-two thousand pounds to persons and companies, racing stables, book-keepers and gaming houses. Some of the letters she opened had not been very civil; a few threatened violence. The bank had declined more credit.

Arthur looked at his mother with wide eyes. It was all very well urging him to expedite his wedding, but how? What wedding? All was over between him and Minnie. He had called by Brown's, and she had refused to see him. He had slipped the concierge a guinea and it made no difference, only that he now owned a piece of paper with the single world written upon it: *Hypocrite!* He could hardly deny the accusation, especially now it seemed he was to be up on a charge of keeping a brothel.

Isobel was now telling him that his father had been concentrating on political matters and new mining concerns in Africa, further north and out of reach of the war, which was why he had left financial matters unattended to. She did not doubt that matters could be cleared up very quickly, but in the absence of the Earl — she had been trying to contact him for a couple of days, but had failed — she had asked Mr Baum to call upon them.

In the absence of his father? What could she mean? Where was he? And cleared up quickly? It seemed unlikely. And why Mr Baum? What was going on?

'Mr Baum? I didn't think you liked him very much,' said her son. 'Or is it that you think he can be useful to you?'

'I very much hope he will be,' said Isobel. 'Indeed, we are lost if he is not.'

'Then I hope you sent off the invitation to Mrs Baum,' Arthur remarked, remembering something Rosina had told him about the lawyer's wife.

'I did not,' said his mother, 'and I will not.'

Like mother, like daughter, thought Arthur. Both could be completely unreasonable. Perhaps it was Rosina's doing that the police had turned up in Half Moon Street? It was possible, but would she have done that to her own brother? Surely not. But she was the kind to know about the new Vagrancy Act, and she did not think it proper for him to marry Minnie; she had made that clear, and this would be a good way of stopping him. Once the female descendants of Silas Batey took a moral stance they would abide by it even though it destroyed everything around. Rosina had all but killed her own grandfather by accident for the sake of a principle. But how could she have known Flora's address? Wormed it out of Reginald, perhaps, in which case Reginald was a snake in the grass and would be lucky to keep his job.

'I have not invited Mrs Baum,' said his mother, 'because I will not have guests at my dinner table simply because they are useful. It is such bad form. It is how Freddie chooses her guests, that, or because they are famous or infamous, she does not care which. Break down the normal social barriers and where will it all end? Eating at the same table with the servants?'

'But supposing you have no table, because it has been sold off?'

'I hardly think it will come to that,' she replied. 'Where can Mr Baum be? He is late. Where can Robert be, come to that?'

Like son, like father. Arthur thought for a mad moment that perhaps the Earl was even now in Flora's arms, and the letter saying she had gone to Redbreast was a lie to put him off the scent? Or perhaps the Earl had taken his own life in despair at his debts and even now his lifeless body was swinging from some tree deep in some forest somewhere? In which case he, Arthur was the new Earl, and could move his mother and Rosina into the Dower House and live in Dilberne Court by himself and somehow get Minnie back and build a racing circuit and pay off all the family debts. The future lay in entertainment. But suicide did not somehow seem in his father's nature; he was more likely to be trying to restore the family fortune at the races.

'Where is my father?' he asked. But his

mother declined to reply to that or further questioning, and merely suggested he call upon Minnie as soon as possible.

ROSINA THE BEAUTIFUL

4 p.m. Tuesday, 5th December 1899

Arthur went down the corridor to Rosina's room and found her feeding Pappagallo, her parrot. His sister was looking uncommonly beautiful, something which it had never occurred to him that she could be. She was dressed rather as Minnie had been on the night of the storm, enchanting in a plain outfit provided by a pub's landlady because her own clothes were wet. The simplicity of dress suited his sister as it had suited Minnie, and he said as much. Rosina actually blushed and looked pleased. Perhaps one day some rich man would seek his sister's hand in marriage; and that way he would be let off the hook, and could live life as a bachelor.

Except, Arthur realized, he did not particularly want to be off the hook. The idea of marrying Minnie seemed increasingly attractive. He should by rights be lamenting the loss of Flora, yet he was not. One should keep company only where one liked and admired, and he had never really liked Flora and and he no longer admired Redbreast. Minnie, however, he liked, respected and admired. But it was too late. How could he face her now, make it up? Soon he was to be a convicted criminal. Billy O'Brien would hardly come up with the money even if his daughter forgave and forgot.

Arthur told Rosina the family's financial plight seemed to have risen once more to danger level, and she shrugged and said that was hardly news. More interesting surely was the whereabouts of their father. According to Lily, her new little maid, his Lordship had left home, gone away for good, driven into another's arms by her Ladyship's refusal to let his Lordship into her bed. All men were like that, according to Lily. They couldn't help themselves. Would Arthur say that was true?

Arthur, enraged, told Rosina she was a fool to believe servants' gossip, he had his own problems, and gave an account of the morning's police raid. Rosina's only re-action was to say, 'Well, they took their time. I told them ages ago.'

He had surmised it, but could hardly believe it. She was his sister. He asked her why on earth she had done it — and found his voice was coming out quavery, as it had when he was her little brother and trying not to cry at her unkindness, because his mother said boys didn't cry, especially if they were a Peer of the Realm. Indignation took over the from self-pity. His voice steadied, deepened. Did Rosina really hate him so much, he demanded? What was her grievance? That he had gone to Eton and she not? That she was three years older than he, yet he inherited everything? Because he was to be a Dilberne and she would stay a mere Hedleigh? These were things that had never been aired between them. It was time they were.

'Good heavens,' she said. 'Nothing like that!' She had done it for the greater good, and for his sake, she said, to save him from the threat of Minnie despoiling the Hedleigh name. Imagine having Tessa to family dinner, and heaven forfend, Billy O'Brien, meat baron and gangster. And the law was the law anyway and he had broken it. 'And we must be able to universalize our actions, as Mr Mills said, and if all men married for money where would it end?'

'With a lot of rich men,' he said. Rosina was standing straight for once and topped him by two inches. He felt sorry for her, as well as angry. It was not her fault that she had grown so tall, and with every extra inch the more wronged and miserable.

Because of what she had done, he told her, his life was ruined. Minnie could hardly put up with a convicted pimp, nor did he expect her to, and she would go back to the States, and the Hedleighs be disgraced by a bankruptcy. And it wasn't just about the money. He loved Minnie. He did not want to live without her. Even as Arthur said it he knew it was true.

Rosina just said he shouldn't worry; she didn't think Vine Street had taken her seriously. They had just thought she was loopy. He said in that case then they were right, and left the room.

MR BAUM MAKES HIS MOVE

6 p.m. Tuesday, 5th December 1899

Evening had fallen by the time Eric Baum came up the steps of No. 17. He was made no more welcome than he had been at the end of October. The servants kept him waiting at the door, forgot to take his coat, and in general behaved as if he should by rights have gone round to the servant's entrance. Well, they would learn. He could, and might well, one day quite soon, buy the lot of them three times over.

Her Ladyship, when he was finally shown in to her presence, made no bones about her requirements. She wanted to borrow money, but when he asked what security she had to offer she looked vague, and offended, and said her good name, of course. Given time, she would of course pay him back — there was land, property; he surely knew their circumstances well enough — plus the disgraceful rate of interest he no

447

doubt required.

Eric said he would prefer to discuss matters such as this with her husband the Earl, but she said the bills were a matter of urgency and he said bills always were, in his experience. Her husband, alas, it seemed, had not been quite frank with him and his colleague Mr Courtney about the scale of the sums his Lordship owed, but now they had been brought to his attention by her Ladyship, a new and unfortunate light was shone upon existing arrangements. He feared several ongoing projects could be put in jeopardy.

'In other words,' she said, 'you're thinking of calling in our existing debt?'

'I have thought about it,' he said, then adding 'there are, however, some other considerations — an invitation for my wife, perhaps, to the dinner at which the Prince of Wales will be present.'

He could hardly be more direct. She raised her perfect eyebrows in amused and somehow insolent surprise.

'No,' she said firmly. 'No. That is out of the question. In my world invitations are offered, not demanded.'

It occurred to Eric that if he demanded that her Ladyship spent the night with him, she might object to that less than she would a coerced invitation to her dinner table. Any normal woman, he thought, in the kind of dire circumstances in which Lady Isobel now found herself, with a feckless husband, a wasted inheritance, faced by shame, social disgrace and actual bankruptcy, and wholly in his power, would be hopelessly distraught, quite likely throwing herself upon him, even offering him favours in return for his protection. It had happened to him before, but, thank God, he had resisted the immoral temptation. He played his next card.

He said, 'I have been asked by the police at Vine Street for details of the property rented by the Viscount in Mayfair. I have fended them off so far. But it could become quite awkward for the boy. The last thing we want is a scandal, and your son convicted for keeping a bawdyhouse.'

That got a response. Her nostrils quivered and dilated, and her fingers tightened slightly on the desk. She was a very handsome woman. Supposing he asked? Supposing she said yes?

'Are you trying to blackmail me, Mr Baum? I suspect you have a very persistent little wife tucked away there somewhere on the hills of North London. The answer is still no.'

He could scarcely believe it. It was mad but it was magnificent. She would pull the whole temple down upon herself, her husband, her children, like a female Samson, rather than change her mind. Did that make him Delilah? The thought was amusing, but he couldn't bring himself to laugh.

'Believe me, it is not personal,' she said kindly. 'It is simply a matter of principle. Good day, Mr Baum. Please don't let me detain you.' She went back to her papers and Mr Baum had no option but to leave.

THE RETURN OF HIS LORDSHIP

6.30 p.m. Tuesday, 5th December 1899

Dismissed, he was already through the front door, held open grudgingly for him by Mr Neville, only to meet his Lordship loping towards him up the wide steps. He was carrying a leather suitcase. The Earl was exuberant, his face exuded delight. Mr Neville took the suitcase. The Earl seized Eric's hand and pumped it vigorously up and down. It was out of character. What was the matter with the man?

'Oh . . . Baum,' his Lordship cried. 'Have you been visiting my wife?'

'We talked of business in your absence, my Lord,' said Mr Baum. He felt the need to explain himself in case his Lordship could read his thoughts. What, Eric Baum from Golders Green in bed with Lady Isobel, Countess of Dilberne, she of the perfect eyebrows? How could he even have dreamt of it?

'Excellent, excellent,' said his Lordship. 'Come back in, won't you old chap, and we'll share a toddy.'

Mr Baum, mesmerized, followed him meekly. How did you deflate so much confidence? But he would. He would have a word with Sir Ernest and it would be done. The bankruptcy courts loomed for the Earl. It had all gone too far. Dilberne might go to law later as he found others benefitting from the one simple, great idea he had handed over to Baum and Courtney for a plethora of unromantic metal ore mines across Southern Africa, making secure the rare ones that glittered. But the Earl would have the devil of a job proving it.

'Where have you been?' her Ladyship asked crossly when Robert bounced into the room followed by Mr Neville with the suitcase, and a hesitant Mr Baum behind. She was like any wife, half-anxious, half-annoyed, thought Mr Baum, just as Mrs Baum would be when her husband finally got home safe, but late, after some minor misbehaviour. She added 'my dearest' as if to soften the question. His Lordship pecked her on her cheek in what seemed to add up to an apology on his part and forgiveness on hers.

'Big day at Newbury. Steeplechase. Didn't

tell you I was going? Sorry about that. Spoke to Agripin's trainer; the beast had bone, he reckoned, they were bringing him on as a jumper. Didn't have much of a chance, he said, only four weeks in training but you never knew. But I knew, in my water. That was the St Anthony's Cup, the last race. I had my Yankee, didn't I? Started with two hundred quid and ended up with this lot. Most exciting day of my life. Open it up, Mr Neville.'

Mr Neville found a side table and opened the suitcase in front of Isobel to disclose pile upon pile of large crisp white banknotes. Ten, twenty thousand? More? Mr Neville, eyes slightly goggling, bowed and left.

'I had to go to the bank with the bookie. I cleared the poor man out.' His Lordship closed the case and pushed it away with a careless foot. Then he turned to Mr Baum.

'You well, Mr Baum? How's the wife? Looking forward to the royal dinner?'

He did not wait for an answer and Mr Baum gave none. The more exhilarated his Lordship showed himself to be, the more despondent Mr Baum became. No matter how good his cards were, how well he played them, Mr Baum could see he would never win. Nobody won on an accumulator like that. So many horses to get in the right order. These people had luck on their side, and against luck there was no defence. Their gold mine could be flooded but everything would turn out all right. The Israelites might be God's chosen people but God was clearly an Englishman.

'What's all this nonsense here?' the Earl asked, nodding at Lady Isobel's folders and jotted figures. 'Why are you worrying your head with all this? I deal with money matters, not you. Your purpose in life is to be beautiful.'

Her Ladyship raised her perfect eyebrows a fraction, smiled sweetly and began to tidy away the documents.

'Let's have that whisky, Baum,' said the Earl, beaming.

'I have to get back to help Mrs Baum, sir', said Eric. 'The children aren't well.'

'Sorry to hear that, Baum,' said his Lordship amiably, but didn't argue. Her Ladyship for her part simply nodded towards the door for Baum to leave. So she would have nodded at a servant. He marvelled at how, once again, and without saying a word, she made it clear she no longer needed him, and never really had.

'Only money, Baum, only money,' said his Lordship to Baum as he left.

Only money! It had been said to aggravate

454

him and had succeeded. It was too bad. Some people worked hard, tried hard, made money, saved money: others romped through life, and somehow got away with it. Everything came so easily to those who had everything already. He had lost all will to be revenged. Better to just go along with it. The mine would strike a seam of, say, copper: all would profit, no one would lose, but heaven knew what he would tell Naomi.

On the way out he passed the young Viscount, who was looking remarkably down in the mouth. The lad was right to be worried; he had been playing with fire. Eric had no reason whatsoever to be nice to him, on the contrary; there had been jibes about Shylock, and so forth, and Eric would not forget them, but some sense of a male brotherhood moved him to put the boy out of his misery.

'By the way,' he said, 'the police were on to me this morning about your Mayfair place. But you're in the clear. Only yesterday the Honourable Mr Robin cancelled his cheque towards the rent. No way they can get you now.'

The lad had inherited his father's good looks and his luck too. There was no justice. Why people bothered looking for it in this life he could not imagine.

'Good-oh,' said the boy. And then, 'Thank you for your help, Mr Baum.'

Then when Mr Baum was almost at the foot of the steps Elsie came running after him with a large square envelope. He opened it. Inside was a truly handsome invitation for Mr and Mrs Eric Baum. Their presence was requested for dinner on December 17th, in the presence of his Royal Highness the Prince of Wales.

'Her Ladyship asked me to give you this,' the maid said, 'and she looks forward to seeing you on the seventeenth.' She smiled respectfully. Mr Baum supposed he could now be accepted in Belgrave Square as a guest and not a servant. The question was whether he wanted to be. On the envelope was scrawled *So sorry this was late. An oversight!* and the initials, 'ID'. Isobel Dilberne. Naomi would smile again. But he, Eric Baum, would never understand the English upper classes.

A ROYAL DINNER

EXTRACT FROM 'FASHION NEWS' IN *THE TIMES,* MONDAY, 18TH DECEMBER 1899

A newcomer on the scene at 17, Belgrave Square last Saturday night was Mrs Eric (Naomi) Baum, who wore a delightful dress in a heavy red silk, its topskirt looped away to show a rose embroidered underskirt, the bodice embellished with antique lace. Her perfect décolletage appeared to advantage, set off by a very pleasing diamond necklace given to her for the occasion by her husband, Mr Eric Baum the financier. She was seated next to the Prince, who was seen to be most taken by her. They were overheard discussing this year's excellent production of the play *David Garrick* at the opulent new Wyndham's Theatre in Charing Cross Road. Both were seen to laugh.

Our most gracious hostess, Isobel, Countess of Dilberne, wore a simple white satin gown with the new drooped sleeves, and was later seen in animated conversation with Mrs Baum. Mrs Tessa O'Brien wore a flowered pink ensemble with a ruby necklace and earrings, a gift from her husband Mr Billy O'Brien the philanthropist, sent over on a liner of the White Star Line for the occasion of this very special dinner. Miss Melinda O'Brien was as ever a delight to the eye in rustling pale green taffeta, well set off by a splendid antique emerald engagement ring on her left hand. Lady Rosina was not present, being indisposed. The Prince expressed his sympathy and disappointment.

Dinner was a great success and the Prince announced himself particularly taken by the crab patties, the pastry being, as he observed, pleasingly crisp and light.

The excitement of the evening was when the Earl stood to announce the engagement of his son Arthur, Viscount Hedleigh to Miss Melinda O'Brien, to take place at St Martin-in-the-Fields in June, 1900, in the presence of the Prince of Wales. We wish them very well in their future life together.

ABOUT THE AUTHOR

One of the most successful advertising copywriters of her generation, **Fay Weldon**'s credits as a writer of fiction include classic novels like *The Life and Loves of a She Devil* and *Growing Rich,* as well as the pilot episode of the original TV series "Upstairs Downstairs." In 2001 she was awarded a CBE for services to literature. She has seven sons and stepsons and one stepdaughter, and lives on a hill in the West of England.

The employees of Thorndike Press hope you have enjoyed this Large Print book. All our Thorndike, Wheeler, and Kennebec Large Print titles are designed for easy reading, and all our books are made to last. Other Thorndike Press Large Print books are available at your library, through selected bookstores, or directly from us.

For information about titles, please call:
  (800) 223-1244

or visit our Web site at:
  http://gale.cengage.com/thorndike

To share your comments, please write:
  Publisher
  Thorndike Press
  10 Water St., Suite 310
  Waterville, ME 04901